LEO

Mr. Boss

THE TWELVE SIGNS OF LOVE

(The Zodiac Lovers Series)

Written by Tiana Laveen
Edited by Natalie Owens
Cover by Travis Pennington

Aries
mar 21-apr 20

Adventurous and energetic
Pioneering and courageous
Enthusiastic and confident
Dynamic and quick-witted

Selfish and quick-tempered
Impulsive and impatient
Foolhardy and daredevil

Taurus
apr 21-may 21

Patient and reliable
Warmhearted and loving
Persistent and determined
Placid and security loving

Jealous and possessive
Resentful and inflexible
Self-indulgent and greedy

Gemini
may 22-june 21

Adaptable and versatile
Communicative and witty
Intellectual and eloquent
Youthful and lively

Nervous and tense
Superficial and inconsistent
Cunning and inquisitive

Cancer
june 22-july 22

Emotional and loving
Intuitive and imaginative
Shrewd and cautious
Protective and sympathetic

Changeable and moody
Overemotional and touchy
Clinging and unable to let go

Leo
july 23-aug 21

Generous and warmhearted
Creative and enthusiastic
Broad-minded and expansive
Faithful and loving

Pompous and patronizing
Bossy and interfering
Dogmatic and intolerant

Virgo
aug 22-sep 23

Modest and shy
Meticulous and reliable
Practical and diligent
Intelligent and analytical

Fussy and a worrier
Overcritical and harsh
Perfectionist and conservative

Libra
sep 24-oct 23

Diplomatic and urbane
Romantic and charming
Easygoing and sociable
Idealistic and peaceable

Indecisive and changeable
Gullible and easily influenced
Flirtatious and self-indulgent

Scorpio
oct 24-nov 22

Determined and forceful
Emotional and intuitive
Powerful and passionate
Exciting and magnetic

Jealous and resentful
Compulsive and obsessive
Secretive and obstinate

Sagittarius
nov 23-dec 22

Optimistic and freedom-loving
Jovial and good-humored
Honest and straightforward
Intellectual and philosophical

Blindly optimistic and careless
Irresponsible and superficial
Tactless and restless

Capricorn
dec 23-jan 20

Practical and prudent
Ambitious and disciplined
Patient and careful
Humorous and reserved

Pessimistic and fatalistic
Miserly and grudging

Aquarius
jan 21-feb 19

Friendly and humanitarian
Honest and loyal
Original and inventive
Independent and intellectual

Intractable and contrary
Perverse and unpredictable
Unemotional and detached

Pisces
feb 20-mar 20

Imaginative and sensitive
Compassionate and kind
Selfless and unworldly
Intuitive and sympathetic

Escapist and idealistic
Secretive and vague
Weak-willed and easily led

Welcome to the "Zodiac Lovers Series" — The 12 Signs of Love.

This is a series which features a hunky hero for each zodiac sign of the year!

This series is stand-alone, so whether you wish to only purchase one or two books of this astrological romance series, or all 12, you can do so without missing a beat. Each Hero embodies typical characteristics of their zodiac sign, but please bear in mind, this is simply for fun — and not to state emphatically that any sign mentioned will act as described. Each tale chronicles the life of the hero and heroine's quest to love and romance, and each story is unique.

Some of the heroes are serious and brooding, others capricious and fun loving. Some of the tales will feel like a modern-day fairytale while others take a more serious tone. Some tales may lie somewhere in between. This series is written from the heart.

Enjoy!

COPYRIGHT

WARNING!

DON'T STEAL OR ILLEGALLY SHARE AUTHORS' WORK!

BLURB

Lazarist Zander is the wrong man to cross…

He is passionate about business, family, and money, and he always plays to win. As the owner of 'Fallen Angel', one of the most popular, eclectic clubs in Brooklyn, he strives to work hard and play harder. He has all a man could ever want—success, women, luxury—or so he thinks, until he meets Sky…

For Sky Jordan, teaching dance and doing choreography is her life, and she works hard at being the best at what she does. After all, the competition in the Big Apple is fierce. Growing up, she was sheltered from the cruel world by an overprotective and loving father. Now, she knows what it's going to take for her to succeed and protect herself. A messy, complicated relationship isn't in her plans, but after a chance meeting with Lazarist, she realizes the man is deaf to rejection, treating it as a foreign language he refuses to learn. The last thing Sky has time for is another arrogant, pompous, pretty boy professing to offer her the world on a platter, then delivering zilch.

However, Lazarist is persistent and addicted to

the chase.

And the little pussy cat named Sky is smack dab in the middle of his radar.

What begins as a game of cat and mouse turns into an all-out, passionate love affair that neither anticipated.

The heat at times is too hot to handle...

Can Lazarist put his ego and pride aside and truly love a woman with all of his being?

Can Sky ever trust again after dealing with the cruelty of past love, and so much more?

Read "Leo – Mr. Boss" to find out!

HEADS UP!

Please bear in mind that each book in this series is adult in nature and includes:

Profanity – (sometimes gratuitous depending on the characters/specific book in the series)

Explicit intimate encounters – (this is consistent in all 12 novels of this series.)

Adult topics and situations – (This could be anything from drug abuse to mental illness, violence, incurable disease, etc.)

If you are offended or triggered by any of the abovementioned, please consider this before moving forward.

Thank You.

DEDICATION

This book is dedicated to the Kings and Queens of the jungle, the almighty, royal Leos. You are fearless, loyal, clever, stubborn, bossy and prideful. You are generous, demanding, and at times overly sensitive and charismatic, too. There's good cause for thinking why you make such good friends but often find yourself wondering why people aren't as good to you as you are to them. Loyalty is extremely important to you, and when your trust is broken, you take it to heart. Remember, self-care is crucial.

You must also be a friend to yourself. You can't control anyone but *you*, so stop trying to co-pilot other people's lives. Please remember that being a boss is not always about being in control – it's about leadership, strength, understanding, compassion, and dedication. You don't mean any harm, Leo, but bragging is a sign of insecurity, so be mindful of that, too. Take it from one Leo to another (Yes, crazy ass Tiana Laveen is a Leo) – your heart is big and beautiful; let your kindness, humor, and wisdom lead you and help you change the world.

When you know what you're doing and who you are,
there is no need to declare it.
Your actions will show for themselves.
…And usually they do.
Roar!
I hear you, baby!
It's your time to shine!
XOXOXO

TABLE OF CONTENTS

LETTER TO THE READER

To my Laveen Queens and Kings, welcome. If you've been rocking with me for a while now, then there are no words to express my gratitude. To any new readers who happen upon this book—welcome, and thank you for going on this journey with me. All right, so as to the question that many will ask: Why did you create this series, Tiana? Since a very early age, I have nurtured an interest in the field of astrology. It wasn't something I relied upon necessarily, but I was intrigued by it, especially if a specific forecast rang true. Regardless of anyone's personal beliefs, astrology can at least be considered an interesting study. Some believe it to be total nonsense. Others believe there may be some credibility, but it is still rather farfetched. Yet others believe that the entire subject is evil while some tend to take it quite seriously and consider it no laughing matter. Whatever your beliefs, please suspend them for the reading of this romance series.

None of the books in this series are about conjecturing, prophecy, predictions, etc. They are merely avenues, or tools, if you will, to view the astrological sign as a gateway into a particular character. This is used to highlight a few key characteristics, be they good, bad, or indifferent, about all 12 zodiac signs from a male perspective.

I am an author who writes lengthy books by default. You would be hard-pressed to find over 10% of my portfolio that does not hit the 100k+ word mark. With that being said, I wanted this series to be full-bodied, but not overwhelming. I wanted to write love stories that unfold in a timely manner, something a reader could knock out in a day or two, but not be explored so fleetingly that the reader misses my signature character and story development. I prefer to write extensive novels because I am practically addicted to the human mind - the psychology behind a character. Why did he say that? Why did she do that? How did this happen? Who were their parents? And so on and so forth.

This kind of in-depth exploration takes time, which equals a longer page count. Longer does not always equate to better, however, and in my personal writing journey this series has been inside my mind for quite some time and needed to come out. I wanted the series to be standalone, meaning if a reader only wished to read Pisces, Cancer, and Libra, they could do so without missing key components. In fact, my "Raven Maxim" series is similar - no book is contingent upon the other, though the stories take place in the same town. That series is ongoing and may never end, because I have given myself permission, as an author, to fully explore the characters, the city, etc., and not worry about readers waiting a long time for a conclusion due to a succession of cliffhangers. Series are mostly either loved or hated, but standalone books in a series, to me, merge the best of both worlds. In the Zodiac series, the link that binds the books is that you, the reader, are looking at the hero's astrological sign. But there is so much more to these men, these exciting heroes, than this.

These guys are all different, from all walks of life. They tell their tale in the manner that they see fit. Some are entertaining, others inspiring.

In this 12-part series, you will meet 12 men and their love interests.

12 signs…

12 different minds…

12 lifetimes…

You will sit back and watch the magic unfold.

Please get comfortable, grab your favorite beverage, and enjoy the, "Zodiac Lover Series – The Twelve Signs of Love."

It is a gift from me to you…

Tiana Laveen

LEO ♌

Here's the thing about me: I always put my best foot forward. I am a genuine person, through and through. I'm pretty honest, perhaps too much so. I'm often mistaken for an asshole... Maybe it's not a mistake, but whatever. I pretty much act the same way behind closed doors as I do in public.

I do like my alone time, and in my line of work it's crucial. People seem to either love or hate me, but they'll never forget me. I'm loud, wise, silly, caring, controlling, bossy, and many times, quite self-aware, despite the fact that I rarely admit when I'm wrong and I wouldn't be caught dead cowering down to another bastard on my worst day. I hate being wrong, so I have to really fuck up big time to let it be known that I take full responsibility for the shit storm that has followed from whatever error I've made or stupid crap I've uttered. I'm one of those people who believes that if you want something done right, do it yourself.

I find it really hard to trust people as an adult, because as a child I tended to open up to just about everyone. Big mistake. People are users and liars in general, and I really have no respect for either quality.

My friends have told me I can be patronizing and sarcastic. Yup. I sure can. It's a superpower. I'm extremely ambitious but also encouraging, and I tend to move on from heartbreak rather quickly, although the scars tend to remain. I'm rather quick tempered – people in general get on my fucking nerves. And at times I can be vain, too. Hey! It's not my fault I'm so fuckin' sexy! God made me this way... take it up with Him! Speaking of the man upstairs, he made some of the most beautiful creatures to walk the planet: Women.

Damn, I love women! I appreciate all kinds, heights, shapes and sizes, but I do tend to have a type. Usually the eyes are the first thing I look at. I love big, pretty eyes on a woman; this gets me every time. I love feminine and confident women. Women who like to laugh and have fun, just like me. The woman who will own my heart has to make me feel like a king and I will do everything in my power to make her feel like a queen. One of my problems in love, though, is that I tend to romanticize it. I like falling in love. I truly do. That whole process is magical to me but then reality hits and I see what a bitch she is, and how she's stopped cooking for me, comes to bed with a big T-shirt on and pajama pants that are two sizes too big, and won't do the same shit she used to do.

I can't have that; I'll lose interest. I'll either break it off or cheat, for I just can't deal with someone who doesn't deliver the same way she did in the beginning. I am generous to a fault. Anything my woman wants, she gets; all she has to do is meet me half way and keep her end of the bargain. I love to spoil a woman and once I'm in love, I'm a mess... it's like a drug to me. Want to know how to turn me off and get me to leave you alone forever? Talk down to me or give me good reason to believe you're cheating. That's a sure way to get me to give you your walking papers and never look back.

I don't take criticism well unless I'm in a good mood. I'll admit it, I'm prideful as fuck. I take friendships and loyalty seriously so if you double cross me, I *will* get revenge. Period. Point blank. I can be rather petty when my feelings are hurt, but I tend to get over some things rather quickly. I am pretty easy to please – all a woman has to do is follow these simple rules:

1. Keep yourself up – You don't have to look like you just stepped off a runway, but comb your hair, stay clean, wear something pretty for Christ's sake, and take your vitamins.

2. Stay consistent – If you started off greeting me with a kiss every morning, then I expect that to continue. If I give you roses once a month, you can expect that to keep happening, too. Consistency is *very* important to me, as well as people who are reliable. If you break an important promise to me, I will never look at you the same way again.

3. Suck my dick and let me do freaky shit to you in bed – I refuse to have a boring sex life. Those who say sex is overrated are doing it wrong.

5. Understand that there's only one head of the household, and that's me – I'm the boss but don't fret, I'll let you take control of some aspects. My lady will always ride shotgun.

I don't need a submissive woman I need an attentive and intelligent woman who has some traditional values but is open-minded, with a bit of a freak in her. I can't stand stupid chicks, so I don't expect a lady to play daft and dumb with me, thinking that will turn me on and keep my attention. If we don't argue at least a few times a year, I know she's faking the funk. I get on my own nerves every now and again, so certainly I'd get on the nerves of the woman I love, too. Just tell me. I may take it well, I may not, but trust, if I love you, I will care enough to do everything in my power to try and make it right.

Women tend to like me fairly early on, and I love that because I am a sucker for a sincere compliment, affection, and adoration. If you *really* want to catch my attention, let me be the aggressor. I like to take control of everything from the boardroom to the bedroom. I enjoy frequent romps in the sack, and I am romantic by nature. I can be cruel, and I can be kind. The way I feel about you will determine which behavior you get from me.

If I want you, you'll know it, baby.

I'm a lion. We see. We stalk. We hunt. We pounce.

The one thing that I am not is shy. I'm sure of myself, I'm assertive, and I love to love you, baby. You'll not find a greater provider, lover, and protector.

I am your Leo lover…

LEO

CHAPTER ONE

Wicked Women and Whitetail Whiskey

I T WAS COMEDY night in the Rum Rapture Room of Club Fallen Angel, a thriving, hip, eclectic bar, restaurant, and dance club in Brooklyn, New York on 6th Street in Prospect Heights. Dressed in a black suit jacket, dark red tie, black slacks and Gucci sneakers, Lazarist made his typical rounds, ensuring his customers were smiling, paying, smiling, then paying some more.

"Everything okay here?" He smiled wide as he leisurely leaned into a table surrounded by half-intoxicated women who looked fresh out of college.

"Yeah…" one of them slurred as she eyed him like a free rum and coke.

"Good. I'm the owner, Lazarist Zander. I just wanted to ensure that you received everything you needed from the wait staff and that you're having a good time." He stood to his full height of six foot five, smoothed out his tie, and crossed his arms over his chest.

"Actually," one piped up, reminding him of a big-eyed mouse as she tucked her blond, blunt cut hair behind one ear. "It's, uh, a little cold in here." She looked around as if searching for a vent, something that could be the culprit that brought on an unpleasant draft. She wrapped her lavender jacket a bit snugger around her shoulders as she eyed him, waiting for him to no doubt alleviate the issue, to come and save the day.

"Well, the last thing I want is for you to catch a cold and be uncomfortable." He winked in her direction and was pleased to see the shy smile that fast creased her face. "I'll turn it up a degree or two."

"Thanks."

"You're more than welcome, sweetheart."

Like fuckin' hell I am. It'll turn into Hell in here. I'm not turnin' the goddamn air conditioning off. You shouldn't 've worn a dress that was so fuckin' sheer, I can practically see the color of your damn nipples! Do you have any fuckin' idea, lady, what hot vomit in the heat smells like from some fucker who came in here and couldn't hold their fuckin' liquor? Nah, not gonna happen…

He stood there smiling at the women, making small talk, and pretending to give two shits about their desires before moving on to the next table. Suddenly, the host was back on the stage, announcing a new comedian to take the spotlight—Flan Perkins. Lazarist hadn't seen him in a while and decided to camp out behind the bar to listen for a while, and then continue his parade around the tables to discuss customer satisfaction.

"Give it up for Flaaaaaaan Perkins!" the host exclaimed before the skinny Black guy approached the stage dressed in white. Music blasted out of the speakers as he made his way to the microphone. "Hard in Da Paint" by Waka Flocka Flame got the crowd amped.

"Yeah, yeah, yeah!" The man chortled, dismissing the crowd, causing a burst of laughter. "Lookin' good tonight, people! Got some good lookin' women out in the audience I see, too. Damn!" The man bopped his head in approval. "I will answer the burning question all of you wanna know... yes." He dramatically rolled his eyes. "My sexy ass is single again."

This caused a few chuckles. Flan grabbed the microphone stand a bit tighter.

"See, the datin' world is too complicated now. I'm old school, you know? I ain't in a rush to have the latest gadgets 'nd shit. Why replace somethin' if it still works? Some of y'all are so addicted to technology – all of these new-fangled VCRs, cassette tapes, cars with V-6 engines and beepers! Ya think you're big ballers now!" Pockets of laughter filled the place. "Oh, 'scuse me... bought some bad weed and it made me believe I was in a time machine. Well, since I'm back here I'm going to reeeevvve it back even farther to 1945 and give Trump's father a vasectomy with a pair of chicken cuttin' sheers..." The crowd lost it then and broke into applause and raunchy cheers. "Make sure there's no chance of that shit growin' back!" He grinned. "Ahhhh, lay down, Mr. Trump senior... This'll hurt just a little bit, but your bleedin' will make sure my favorite Mexican restaurant doesn't go outta business in 2019." The crowd chortled loudly. "Extra salsa…"

"Wouldn't wanna risk it… Speakin' of love affairs we'd like to erase from history and bustin' unfortunate nuts, I went out with this one chick the other night and things was all right at first, right? I pull up to her apartment, she comes out. She looks nice, I suppose. She gets closer and stops walking. I ask her, 'What's wrong?' She lookin' at my car and says, 'What tha fuck is this?' Maaaan, I said it's a classic!

"A 1982 Corolla… in mint condition! She says to me, 'Why it got a boot on it?'" She obviously had no idea that you can drive with a boot on! The ride is slower, but hey, that just gives you time to take in the scenery! It's no big thing. Just leave the house a little earlier so, as you go ten miles per hour, you will eventually reach your destination."

Giggles rolled through the crowd. "So, I look her up and down and see she's into all that designer shit. I tell her, 'cause it's fashionable… let's go get the otha one so it becomes a pair."

"She tells me she what about the other two then, since I have four wheels? Bitch, I'll do a willie on two tires! Askin' me stupid ass questions! Get yo' ass in the car!'" The crowd burst out laughin'. "These boots were made for walkin'… but I defied the rules and refused to stay in the parked lane… that just proves I'm a rebel … a rebel without a caaaaar."

Lazarist chuckled at that. Fixing himself a whiskey,

he leaned against the bar counter to watch a little more of the show.

"Went out with another lady a couple of weeks ago. She was sooo materialistic. I can't hang wit' you ladies! See, I'm from Milwaukee, Wisconsin, originally." A few people clapped at that. "Yeah! Where my cheese heads at?! You New Yorkers are tough and the women so hard they walk around wearin' Prada and razor blades under their damn tongues. Ain't did a day in prison, but always got a shank… wanna fight a mothafucka and then call him 'son' after threatenin' his life. 'Yo! You mad weak, son!' Then they get to wavin' that weapon around, tryna cut a mothafucka until you promise to take 'em shoppin'…" More laughter erupted. "Anyway, the date… I got sidetracked by Razorblade Rachelle…

"So, she and I, you know, we meet up at this bar and after we're there for a while, havin' a pretty good conversation, my phone rings, right? I pull it out and she screams! I'm talkin' like at the top of her lungs like she's seen a monster! Now, I'm used to that happenin' when I whip my dick out, you know, but we weren't at that point yet…"

Flan grinned wide as the crowd burst into cheers and wolf whistles. "I say to the woman, 'What's wrong?' She grabs her jacket and purse, hops off the bar stool, and says she gotta go! She says, 'I know you don't have any money, 'cause mothafucka, you got a flip phone!'" The crowd laughed even harder. 'She was lookin' at me like I told 'er I just ate bath salts or some shit and planned to eat every part of her *but* her pussy! Maaaan!"

Lazarist laughed as he sipped on his drink.

"Ol' materialistic ass!" He paced the stage nice and slow. "I can't fuck wit' you women out here… You're too much for me. My ex-girlfriend and I had been together though for six years… six damn years, man! She said I was never committed. What kinda shit is that?" The comedian threw up his hands. "That's a lifetime, right? She said I wasn't loyal, that I was a dog. That's an oxymoron." The crowd chuckled. "And if six years ain't committed, I don't know what is… that's a lifetime in dog years…"

The place went nuts and Flan had to stop until the cheers died down. The show went on but Lazarist emerged back into the audience, weaving in and out, offering a few complimentary drinks, praising several attractive women, and slapping some hands of male patrons who were loyal customers. An hour or so later, he exited the Rum Rapture Room and headed to the restaurant portion of his club.

Things were far more relaxed and chill here. The music was contemporary jazz at a low volume, though muted sounds from the Rum Rapture Room could be heard. Candlelight, quality menus, and a five-star chef created the perfect ambiance and dishes.

He went into the kitchen and talked to the employees, making sure they didn't have customers waiting for extended periods of time, and urged them to keep pushing the dessert purchases. He needed room for fresh inventory and the cream for the crepes was expiring soon. Vacating the restaurant, he headed to the dance club portion, which was located on the upper level. He passed one of his bouncers on the bottom floor, gave him a head nod, and made his way up the steps until he was greeted by the thumping techno music.

Dark red curtains obscured a steel door.

"'Sup, boss," Heathen said, the man standing six foot seven and big as a linebacker.

"How's everything tonight?" Lazarist shoved his hand in his pocket and rolled back on his heels.

"Good... full house."

"I don't want any bullshit like last Saturday. Are there two bouncers inside, is the bar stocked, and the cop I hired... did he ever arrive?"

"All systems check. Got a new DJ this week, too."

"I can tell... the music is better from what I can hear." Heathen got ready to open the door and let him inside. "No need for that tonight. I don't have much time. Just make sure the bartenders cut off people by 2:15 A.M. Last call for alcohol up here. It's cut off at 2:30 A.M. in the Rum Room so if need be, have anyone still wanting something to go in there."

"Will do."

"Good. Ya doin' good. Here's a little bonus." Lazarist dug into his pocket and pulled out a bankroll. He slipped off a hundred dollar bill and handed it to Heathen.

"Thanks, Boss."

"You're welcome." He patted his shoulder. "It's hard to get good help nowadays. People I can trust..."

Lazarist's eyes narrowed on the man, then he turned and walked away. Minutes later he was in his office, tucked away on the premises. He immediately turned on his electric fireplace, fired up his MacBook, and snatched his tie off, tossing it onto the desk. He sat there for several minutes scrolling through a maze of purchases for his club, looking at the talent scheduled to come in and perform in the Rum Room for the remainder of the summer, and checking to see if all deposits for people renting various rooms in his club for their parties and get togethers had been paid.

After about an hour of sending out emails such as contacting the company he'd hired to take care of the payroll about some missing hours for two employees, he resolved that it was time to go home. Moments later, he was saying his farewells to several staff members and vacating the premises. He walked up to his candy apple red '67 Mustang Shelby Cobra, started it up, and headed towards his home in the Colombia Street Waterfront district, on Rapeleye Street.

"Just want to get in here and go to bed," he mumbled to himself as he parked in his small garage. Grabbing his briefcase, he headed inside his property. After removing his dark brown leather jacket and hanging it up, he made a beeline towards his chef's kitchen.

The building had originally featured several rental loft-style apartments, which he'd turned into a single family unit that afforded him access to three floors. The property now boasted six bedrooms and five bathrooms, including a private balcony and outside eating area. The white oak herringbone and concrete floors gave it a clean and streamlined appearance. His galley, though he rarely made any time to cook, was one of his favorite spots in the entire place. It featured a Caesarstone island, Liebherr French door refrigerator, and wine icebox.

"Alexa, play 'Killing Strangers' by Marilyn Manson." The song began as he opened his kitchen cabinet door, removed a glass, and poured himself some Scotch. Soon, he was clenching his teeth and rubbing his forehead. The migraines had been getting worse as of late. Just then, his phone buzzed. He reached into his pocket and plucked the vibrating iPhone out of it, then placed it on the kitchen counter. He noticed a couple of missed calls, then landed on the text message from his ex-wife, Mimi:

> **Mimi:** *Yesterday was total bullshit and you know it. Taking you back to court.*
>
> **Lazarist:** 🌑 *The judge ruled in my favor yesterday. No increase in alimony. I'm not giving you another dime. You are already sucking me dry and at the end of this year, you will be totally cut off once and for all. Three years was plenty of time for you to get yourself together.*
>
> **Mimi:** *I wish I had never met you.*
>
> **Lazarist:** *That makes two of us. Don't you have something else to do? Like fall into another sucker's lap? Go deep-throat your way to another dollar.*
>
> **Mimi:** *Fuck you. ARROGANT ASSHOLE. Nobody likes you!*
>
> **Lazarist:** *You did. Go suck your neighbor's dick.* 🍆 *Maybe he can spare some change, whore. It's obvious you're drunk again, too. You need help.*

Mimi: *That's funny coming from the guy who slept around so much, your last name should be Serta. At least I was a professional.*

Lazarist: *A whore I am not. A lover of fine pussy I am and at least I can afford everything that I have and don't have to depend on a person I was married to for only 10 months to foot the bill. You don't want to fuck for funds anymore, so now you do it for free? How stupid is that? Get off your back and get a job like the rest of us, Mimi. A REAL job.*

Mimi: *Drop dead.*

Lazarist: *Almost did when I was still married to you. Thank God I woke up and filed for divorce before it was too late. The gravy train is approaching its last stop. Here's where you get off.*

He abruptly turned off his phone, ceased the music, poured himself another Scotch, then a Whiskey and headed up the steps to his master suite on the third floor. Polishing off his drink, he set the glass down on the white mirrored dresser, and turned on his flat screen television that drifted from the ceiling, awaiting his command. He didn't turn it on because he was particularly interested in the day's events, catching up on his sports scores, or even to fall prey to some documentary about England's violent medieval past, which he rather enjoyed. He simply wanted the background noise. He undressed himself, letting the clothing hit the floor whichever way it went. Looking towards his bedroom window, he took note of the tops of the high buildings, and could hear the occasional honking.

His neighborhood was fairly quiet, and yet bits and

pieces of the city still managed to reach out with their long, sparkly fingers covered in lights, flickering bits of falling money, fresh piss, and tap him on the shoulder. Lazarist slumped down on the bed and took a look at himself in the mirrored closet doors. He smiled sadly at his reflection, feeling some pity for himself.

I'm about to be forty-fuckin' years old… feel like I've lived a hundred lifetimes. Jesus…

His tall, muscular body was etched with various tattoos, a few he regretted, fueling his spiral down the never-ending tunnel of sorrowful thoughts.

I need to get a cover up job on that one ASAP…

He ran his finger over Mimi's name, hating her all the more as he read it across his left arm in thick, bold font. It had been a whirlwind romance… perhaps he'd been too hasty. He'd tricked himself into believing *that* time it would be different. But it wasn't. Now with two marriages under his belt, he avoided the notion of settling down again like the plague. His first marriage had been to his high school sweetheart, and they'd simply grown apart. He wished her well and he imagined she wished the same for him. This last time, he conceded, however, had been a boneheaded move—that move being primarily driven by his dick.

Mimi was a gorgeous woman, the kind that needed little makeup or fuss. She woke up looking naturally as if she'd been airbrushed. The shit was uncanny. Though he'd viewed her from a superficial lens, things became clear quite early on that not only were they not compatible, but he disliked her personality to the utmost. He couldn't trust her; shit from her past kept rearing its ugly head and her temper, paired with his, only caused fiery arguments that led to explosive sex. But after a while, that got old, too. He needed someone who could help him unwind, not make him want to slit his own throat.

They'd been divorced for two and a half years, and yet Mimi managed to keep wiggling herself into his world. They had no children together, not even shared custody of a dog, cat, hell, even a goldfish. He couldn't fathom why they were like magnets, pulling and drawing from one another, a battle royale to the finish. They had crazy chemistry, and it had seemed as if she would stick with him and give her heart completely to him. He believed that she also wished for them to reconcile, despite her vicious insults and so much more. Lazarist sat on his bed, wracking his brain about the failed marriage. Why? He wasn't completely certain... It had happened so long ago, but the questions and answers to it all haunted him. He loved her at the time... he truly loved her, and that's what hurt the most.

And it was her body... that fucking body...especially before all the plastic surgery...

He rubbed his chin with the palm of his hand as he deliberated over the matter. She was a tall, shapely Latina who'd made her mark in the adult entertainment industry, retired from the industry when they met and boy could she fuck. That was Lazarist's downfall—a pretty, feminine chick who could work her mouth, pussy, and ass on him just right, laugh at his jokes—even the ones that weren't that funny—and make him feel like a king. That was sometimes all it took. The women who warmed his bed were just placeholders. He hadn't been in love since Mimi, and he preferred it that way. Love was too taxing, exhausting, and debilitating. It made him feel weak and feeble; it stole his zest for life. No doubt he was better off forever single... just him and his business, his friends, trips around the world, and women as fuckbuddies were all he required at that point. He still got laid often, and the empty sex, though fleeting, gave him temporary reprieve from the devastation of something he wanted, but just wasn't cut out for. Love.

"Ouch."

He winced for his head throbbed harder now, the headache not slowing down or letting up. He crawled into his bed, reached into his nightstand, and pulled out a bottle of Aleve. He popped two of them, though the dosage specified just one. After pulling the sheets a bit further up his waist, he rested there, looking aimlessly at the television. He surfed somewhere between exhausted and horny.

Horny lost out, for his lids became heavy and before he'd even been given a warning, he saw nothing more than a curtain of soft darkness...

LEO

♌

CHAPTER TWO

Bitch, I'm Sorry...

...Two Weeks Later

DOJA CAT'S "SUCKER Punch" blasted through the speakers in the three-tier club, "Fallen Angel." Sky Jordan was blowing off some much-needed steam, sitting at a VIP table with a bucket of wine, five of her no-good friends, her hookah, and her sexiest black dress that barely covered her ass. Crossing her long, deep caramel legs, she tapped one foot, rocking her favorite four-inch black heels. A dog collar with studs was wrapped around her neck, completing the edgy outfit. Bobbing her head to the music, she watched all of the people dancing around to the infectious beat of the music.

"Sky!" her friend Toi yelled out as if she were standing fifty miles away, with her drunk ass. "Come to the bathroom with me. I gotta piss..." Toi wiggled out of the booth, not waiting for an answer. Sky leisurely placed her hookah pen down on the table and grabbed her purse. "Save my seat," she said to her friend Candace, who was sitting right next to her.

When Toi stood, her green skirt had ridden to the top of her ass and exposed two big butt cheeks that were chewing up a G-string like the crack of her behind was named Jaws. Sky screamed her friend's name, but the lady didn't hear her. She wrapped her hands around her mouth for extra amplification, but that didn't help either. All their other friends did was point, gawk, and laugh as Toi wobbled away, her bright red weave swaying back and forth like Ariel's, the little mermaid.

"Toi! Hey, Toi! Slow down! Fix your dress!" But Toi kept on moving, staggering back and forth like a bobblehead. "Bitch! Ya ass is showing!" Several men paused and smirked, some a little too long for her comfort, their faces like hungry vipers and rattle snakes out on the prowl for prey.

"What are you lookin' at, bum?!" Sky screamed, not liking the greasy grins on their faces.

"Don't get mad at us, shortie!" a stout one yelled over the booming music. "She's the one with that thang hangin' out! Yo! Look at that ass! I wonder if she got room for one more. Heeeeey, baby! Lemme eat the booty like groceries!" All of his friends bust out laughing.

Sky turned away, suddenly realizing that the gap be-tween her and Toi was even greater now due to the idiots she'd wasted time with. She huffed and chased after the woman, who was moving about in a zig zag fashion amongst a rowdy, thick crowd of intoxicated fools. The place was packed practically wall to wall—the spot was particularly popular. This bar inside Club Fallen Angel had some of the best drinks for the prices, and there was a restaurant on the premises, as well as an area where they did live shows and comedy. It was the place to be. She finally caught up with the woman and yanked her arm.

"Finally!" Sky blustered. "I never would've thought your drunk ass could move so fast!" Sky huffed, a bit out of breath.

"Wha…? Why are you jerking me around like that?!" Toi said with an attitude, her hand on her hip.

"Did you not feel the breeze, Toi? Ya ass is hangin' out!"

Sky reached for the hem of the dress and tugged it down like a window blind, with both hands. The woman pursed her lips, then burst out laughing.

"Ohhhh, girl! I ain't even know."

Sky rolled her eyes, wrapped her arm around Toi's, and headed towards the john. She hissed in annoyance once she saw there was a rather lengthy line. Still, they stood, waiting their turn.

"Mmmm, giiiirl," Toi slurred as she held her stomach, her face tight like she smelled a bucket of shit. "I don't feel so good…"

"Awwww, hell!" Sky ran her hand up and down her friend's back. "Just hold tight… COME ON! If anybody is in here just reading on their damn phone while sittin' on the toilet, get up and mooove! Got a sick girl, here!"

Minutes later, Sky was standing in the stall with the woman, holding that red weave in one hand and staring up at the ceiling, silently asking herself, 'Why me?' as Toi vomited her entire life away.

"It must've been the Long Island!" she said between choking and coughing.

"It must've been all ten of them, then… I told you that you were drinking too much. Do you feel better now?" Toi nodded, then moaned. "Come on, get on your feet. Let's get you cleaned up and out of here."

Helping Toi to the bathroom sink, she practically dunked the woman's face in the rushing, cold water. With one hand, Sky dug around in her purse, found a ponytail holder at the bottom of her red Coach bag, and looped it through the cherry colored tresses.

"Oh, God…" Toi sat up, gripping the sink with both hands and looking downright pathetic. The woman stared at her in the mirror, latching on to her reflection with sad, sullen eyes. "You're such a goooood friend, Sky. Thank you, bitch… thank you so fuckin' much. You good people, yo…"

"Mmmm hmmm." Sky rolled her eyes. Hooking her arm around her friend's waist, she helped her out of the restroom. "Let's get you back to the table, then home."

A few minutes later, Sky reached the VIP area she'd recently vacated, only to see that most of her friends, with the exception of Scarlet, were gone.

"They're dancing," Scarlet explained between sips of her wine. "They probably won't be back for a minute because they're not trying to leave tonight without promises of a hookup."

Scarlet set her wine glass down and looked like a boss bitch if Sky had ever seen one. The woman sat there holding a hookah in one hand and rubbing her bald head with the other. Large gold earrings hung from her lobes and she looked completely disenchanted, as if her mind were somewhere else.

Sky helped Toi sit down for a spell and planned her exit strategy.

"Scarlet, I am not about to chase them all around. tell them I said bye." She pointed to the dancefloor. Her friends were lost in the swarming crowd. "I am going to call a Lyft and get Toi to her place, then go home my damn self. Are you coming?" Scarlet blew smoke from her hookah and shook her head. Khia's 'Next Caller' came on, causing a ruckus on the dancefloor.

"Mmmm mmm, baby. You all go on. I'm tryna get me a sugar daddy, secure a bag."

Sky burst out laughing. "Girl, what are you talking about?"

"See, I'm out here making moves, Sky." The woman's eyes grew dark as she smirked. "The owner is about to make an appearance and I heard he likes *our* type…" She winked and rubbed her index finger across the back of her hand. "This is a big ballin', White mothafucka. He's a bachelor, easy on the eye, no fuckin' kids, and he tosses money like it ain't nothin' but a thing!" The lady cackled. After a brief glance at her cellphone, she shot her a mischievous grin, then crossed her long, shapely legs.

Sky shook her head. "You are a trip! I've been here a half a dozen times and never met him. Who told you he is coming?"

"Brittany. She said every Saturday night he stops by the front door area of the club, but most times, he comes in and talks to a few of the patrons, kind of like checking in. When he does that, he always comes over to the VIP tables. Why do you think I paid extra and got us this shit tonight? Oh yaaasss, bitch. It's about to be on and poppin'. His name is Lazarist Zander. Is that sexy or what? I've never seen him in person, but he's tall they say... and a freak... and his ex-wife was some famous porn star."

Sky wrinkled up her nose at that.

"Girl, that man probably got a disease that nobody has even heard of! Fucking a porn star? Next!"

"Baby, please!" Scarlett waved her off. "Porn stars are some of the most tested people in the world. We're the dirty mothafuckas." The woman rolled her eyes as if she were personally insulted. "Anyway, this is about the time they say he arrives." Scarlet perked up, reached in her purse, and pulled out her lipstick."

"All right then, well, I'm going to get Toi home." She glanced over at her friend who was now sitting only half way up, her eyes closed and her complexion ashen, turning green. With a sigh, she turned towards the front door of the club, where rolls of red and white smoke filled the area.

What the hell is going on?

People began to hop up and down as Cardi B's 'I

Like It' blasted through the club speakers. A small light from the front of the place caught her eye. The door had opened and someone walked in, making the entire club fill with a crazy energy just from his presence. A tall, broad-shouldered White man was twirling a sparkling white cane. He was dressed in an expensive gray suit with a navy tie, and donning one hell of a swaggerlicious smirk as he began to stroll about. He moved slow and easy, like a big ass lion on the prowl. The man removed a hat from his head and out tumbled a mass of dark locks. People began to walk towards him, surrounding him like long lost loved ones, their faces painted with grand smiles and looks of admiration.

Shiiiit… I bet that's him.

As if in slow motion, Scarlet turned around to see where Sky's eyes had landed. Her friend rested her peepers on the man in question and a shit-eating smile split her face. Just as Scarlett predicted, the man made his rounds, and they both watched, for different reasons of course. Sky found this display downright intriguing. Human behavior had always been a source of interest for her, especially when the mob mentality was playing out right before her eyes. People fawned over him like he was some celebrity, and perhaps in his own way, he was. He seemed to feed off the energy, overdosing on it, maybe even needing it. Sky tilted her head to the side and admitted to herself that he was spellbinding…

There was just something in the way he moved, the way he smiled, and the way he interacted that made him a source of curiosity.

"Girl… here your friend comes. Secure the bag," Sky teased as she shook her head and tried to break the transfixing spell the man had on her.

Laughing, Scarlet stood to her feet, holding a glass of red wine and waiting her turn. She pulled at the top of her dress, forcing it down to reveal more of her ample cleavage. Oh yes, the bitch was ready. Sky glanced at Toi who was now sound asleep, her forehead planted on the table. Grimacing, she turned away and watched Scarlet prepare to work this shit to death.

"Hello, ladies!" the man shouted over the music. His rich, musky cologne floated past her, awakening her senses. "My name is Lazarist Zander, owner of the Fallen Angel Nightclub and restaurant. Are you having a good time?"

He stood with his legs rather far apart, jammed his cane beneath his armpit, and stood there reeking of charm. Scarlet moved so close to the guy, he probably had little room to breathe.

"We most certainly are."

The guy grinned in a tight sort of fashion as she pushed up closer to him and then, that smile slowly faded when he turned towards the table and caught a glimpse of Toi.

"Hmmm, not all of you it seems are having a good time… is she okay? Should we call for help?"

He pointed at Toi, who looked deceased. The slight rise and fall of her back gave her away, though.

"She's asleep… a bit too much to drink," Sky spoke up, trying to usher the conversation in the right direction. "But, uh, Scarlett here, my friend, has been dancing all night at your club and having a great time! Haven't you, Scarlet?"

"I sure have…" Her friend licked her upper lip in a slow, seductive way. "In fact, I was just going to—"

"That's wonderful," the man abruptly cut her off. He looked at Scarlet almost dismissively, but took her hand and kissed it, then turned back in Sky's direction. "How about you though… Have you been having a good time?"

He let Scarlet's hand slip away and moved closer to her, holding his cane now at both ends as his piercing light blue eyes stared daggers into her. Sky swallowed and glanced up at the towering man, able to see him much better now.

His hair was dark brown and cropped at the sides. A low cut beard and mustache complimented his keen features and his lower lip was plush and suckable. He moved his leg a bit as if readjusting himself and she could see his damn dick imprint…

Huge.

Taking her hand, he kissed it, too. She could feel Scarlet's eyes on her; in some way perhaps she felt betrayed, but what could she do?!

"I, uh, yes… definitely having a good time. I need to get my friend home though. Going to call a Lyft, you know, and make sure she gets in safe."

The man glanced back towards the table with a look of concern.

"Yes, I can see that's an issue. I tell ya what." He

clapped his hands one time as if coming up with a novel idea. "I will take care of it. I will have one of my employees, whom I trust, ensure she gets home. He'll drive her himself. But, uh, you though…" He looked her up and down and pointed his finger in her direction as if it were some gun. "You look *awfully* familiar. I never forget a face. What's your name, baby?"

"Sky…"

"Sky *what?*" He sounded authoritative, like some principal who dared her to not give him the information he so desired.

"Sky Jordan."

"Hmmm, I see. Do you come here often?" His eyes narrowed on her during his inquisition.

"No… only on occasion." Scarlet cleared her throat. Loudly.

"But Scarlet here is a loyal patron! You see, she—"

"Thank you, Scarlet. I appreciate that. I'll get you a free drink." He nodded to her friend, but then turned away before Scarlet could respond. It was brutal to witness…

"I want to thank you for coming out tonight, Sky. What an absolute pleasure. Here, take my card." The man slipped his hand in his pocket and removed a glossy business card. He placed it in her palm and closed her fingers over it, never once taking his eyes off her. "You're beautiful, you know? I saw you as soon as I walked in…"

"Oh. Well, uh, thank you." She offered a watered down smile, but inside, her heart was thumping a mile a minute.

"I want to talk to you privately when you have time… one on one." He slowly released her hand and took several steps back, twirling that cane like a baton. "I want you to call me, okay? Promise me you will…" His black, thick brows dipped.

"Oh… we'll see," She shot Scarlet a glance and caught the woman staring daggers at her. "I have a boyfriend, but Scarlet is single… and ready to mingle." She laughed nervously.

"Boyfriend?" The man rolled his eyes dismissively. "Well, if that's your thing, that's fine, but I'm not a boy, Sky… there's no comparison. I don't play games and plastic trains aren't my thing. When you want to talk to a man, you call me, all right? I look forward to hearing from you. Good night."

He then turned and walked away, disappearing into the smoke and the crowd.

Whew, Lord… all right… okay… that was intense!

Sky dared to look over at Scarlet. The woman was sitting back down in the booth, holding her hookah and shaking her head.

"Girl! I am so sorry! I wasn't flirting with him or anything. I just—"

"Oh, shut up, Sky." The woman cackled. "I know… shit," she said, shrugging her shoulders. "He chose you, point blank, period. It wasn't your fault."

Less than ten seconds later, a man came over dressed in a dark suit.

"Is there a Toi here?"

"Yes, uh, she's the one knocked out at the table. Are you the driver, I mean, employee he mentioned? We actually don't need one anymore now. I'm not staying. I'm going to go ahead and—"

"No, Mr. Zander gave strict instructions that I am to escort both of you home, free of charge. Is there a Scarlett here as well?"

"Yes." Her friend perked up a bit.

"Great. All of your drinks are on the house this evening. The bill is wiped clean. Mr. Zander sends his regards. Oh, and he wanted me to remind you, Sky, to call his number on the card to make sure you and your friend got home safely. He said he didn't care how late it was. Please, just do so."

Scarlet's smile quickly faded.

"Okay, uh, let me get her up." Scarlet seemed to quickly recover and push her pride aside, for she jumped in and helped to get Toi on her feet, then slumped back down into her seat. "Scarlet, I'll call you tonight as soon as I get home, okay?"

"You better. I want to make sure you're safe, too." She winked in her direction and blew her a kiss.

Sky felt a bit better that it appeared Scarlet wasn't devastated by the blow. After all, her friend was a gorgeous woman who got attention wherever she went. The night hadn't gone remotely close to planned for any of them, Sky imagined. Moments later, she and the driver were walking Toi away towards the exit. As she neared the door, she caught a glimpse of Mr. Zander out the corner of her eye.

"Sweet dreams, beautiful!" he yelled out.

When she turned completely in the direction of the voice to respond, there was no one there.

What a strange turn of events...

LEO

CHAPTER THREE

I Don't Know Karate,
But I Know Ka-raaaazy!

L AZARIST GRIPPED THE cold steel bar and bent at the waist. Sweat tickled his flesh, dripped off his form, and soaked into the white fabric of his karategi, some onto the light oak wooden planks of the floor. Lazarist took pride in his eighth-degree black belt status in the art of karate. He was striving for his ninth, but with his schedule as of late, he wasn't certain how realistic it was to keep up such rigid training.

I'll try anyway… Gotta do this. I want it.

"Thanks… I'll see you all later." Standing straight, he waved goodbye at the others, exhaustion taking over.

He turned away from the room filled with fellow students and the sensei, their lesson still not over with a few minutes to spare, and grabbed his gym bag. He cursed under his breath when he recalled he had to take Miller to Tae Kwon Do practice. Miller was the son of his best friend, Tobias French, who was preparing to go out of the country on business that evening for several days. Tobias and Miller's mother were no longer together; besides, it was Tobias' week for custody, so someone had to step in and assist. The nanny could only be expected to do so much.

He headed towards the bathroom to splash his face with some much-needed cool water, sip from his stainless steel water bottle, and simply breathe. Things had been happening in record speed—changing. He hated surprises, but it seemed every other day, there was some emergency or issue he had to address in the trenches. He'd made a lot of damn money over the years, and he had important connections, his network now like a finely tuned web. Yet, the little free time he possessed was shrinking more and more. At times he daydreamed of surrendering to his natural laziness—something he'd never admit to anyone but himself. He'd take a two week vacation to do absolutely nothing but sleep in all day, enjoy the nightlife, and fuck until the sun rose.

But, when Lazarist was passionate about something, he'd work himself to the bone and become fixated to the point of obsession. Everyone on his team knew this too.

He was very particular about who he aligned himself with. Trust came at a premium. He'd been backstabbed more than once in different ways, but each time he learned quickly from his errors. He kept this close to his soul, but he wasn't above acts of revenge... In fact, there'd been times in his life when his heart was so broken, he saw no other recourse. Someone had to make the wrongs right, and he was just the motherfucker to do it. Now, everyone was regarded with suspicion until they proved their worth. Ex-wives, ex-girlfriends, business associates, friends who lied and schemed… he'd had a fucking 'nough. Regardless of his cynicism though, he was known as a generous and fair boss, but he didn't get the 'Slave Driver' nickname for nothing.

At times he hated when some of his staff would teasingly call him such, but he recognized it as true, and knowing the real deal was half the battle. Truth be told, his behavior wasn't completely selfish; when he pushed that way, it meant that he cared, and he wanted the best out of the people around him, for them to bring their A game. He didn't expect perfection, but he did ask for loyalty, reliability, no attempts to be played for a fool, and compassion for one another, along with understanding, mutual respect, and appreciation. When he saw talent and effort in the people he worked with, he connected with them in a way he was certain they'd never understand, because that was Lazarist's greatest frailty. He loved hard, but he covered it well.

Besides, he preferred to show with his actions what he had in his heart, and if he said so himself, what a very big heart he possessed indeed. He was loyal to a fault and would take whoever helped him rise up to the bright blue sky right along with him.

Life to Lazarist wasn't a road to be travelled lightly. It was a daily adventure, a winding trail with falls and dips, sudden stops along a cliff and dives into the ocean below. He wanted to hear the music at full volume, feel his skin gliding against a beauty of the female persuasion, taste the sweet valley between her legs, savor it… smell the fresh money being deposited into his bank account, then tear his competition apart with his bare teeth. All of these thoughts consumed him—responsibilities, ambition, a need for rest, projects in motion.

I need to get home and get back out… so much work to do. Shit.

After letting the water cool him down, he sat down on a bench and waited for his heartrate to return to normal from the intense karate session. Digging into his gym bag, he pulled out his cellphone and checked for important emails, voicemails, social media posts about his club, and any other pertinent information he might have missed.

He had four missed calls, one of which came from a number he didn't recognize.

With a yawn, he crossed his legs and played back the voicemails. The third one struck his curiosity the most…

"Um, hi, Mr. Zander. This is Sky… Sky Jordan. We met at your club, Fallen Angel, this past Saturday. I know that you said to call Saturday night, but my friend Toi had gotten sick and my mind was a blur. I had an early morning rehearsal yesterday, too, so yeah," she chuckled, "I work on Sundays, and I was just exhausted… It completely slipped my mind. Toi is fine now, and so am I. Thank you for, uh… the ride. That was really considerate of you. And thanks also for paying for our drinks. Well, I guess that's it. It was nice meeting you. Take care."

He took another gulp of his water and ended the playback. Minutes later, he was dressed in a loose black jogging suit and sneakers and planted in his car. He turned on his car stereo and out poured 'Fell in Love with a Girl' by The White Stripes. His first stop was to get his ass home. He could already feel the water from a nice, long shower.

I need to head over to the club, ASAP.

He had a brief meeting scheduled with the head chef of his restaurant and a wedding coordinator to ensure that a wedding rehearsal dinner party paid the rest of their due amount and that everything happened as planned.

Moving like lightning, he finally made it home. As soon as he hit the door, the word 'rehearsal' rang in his head. His brain got to working overtime again. It seemed to be the theme of the day. He tossed down his car keys on a small white marble table he had in the foyer.

She said she had a rehearsal on a Sunday morning. Today is Monday. That means she probably has a job in the arts or it's church related, since she said she was there for work. I know I've seen her somewhere before. Sky Jordan... Sky Jordan... hmmm...

He marched up to his bedroom, stripped down, and rushed into a hot shower. As he shampooed his hair and conditioned it, he continued to wrack his brain, but nothing came to mind. Sooner than he wished, he was stepping out of the shower, snatching a thick, white towel from the rack, and drying off. He wished he could've stayed in there all day, but there was so much to take care of and do. He began to resent himself…

"Alexa, play 'Panic Station' by Muse." He bopped his head to the music as he raked his comb through his wet hair, detangling his dark, rich mane just right. He brushed it back away from his face, and his widow's peak was now as prominent as ever. Looking at himself from various angles, he ran his hand across his low cut beard and deliberated on touching it up.

It can wait another day…

Turning off the bathroom light, he headed to his massive walk in closet and selected a pair of khaki pants, a button down white shirt, and Christian Louboutin shoes. From the chest of drawers in his bedroom, he pulled out a fresh pair of socks and some dark gray boxer briefs. As he dressed, he wished for a bit of quiet…

"Alexa… turn off music." The song faded until it went silent. Snatching his cellphone from the middle of the bed where'd he'd tossed it, he scanned his phone log and found the number he desired in the Missed Call log. A woman answered on the fourth ring.

"Hello?" she stated breathlessly.

Is she fucking? If so, why wasn't I invited?

"Hey, is this Sky Jordan?"

There was a brief pause on the other end of the line.

"Yes…"

He smiled at her hesitation…

Cautious little minx…

"This is Lazarist. I doubt at this point saying my last name will be needed… In any case, thank you for eventually getting back to me, though due to your lack of follow up, I had already ensured you'd arrived safely once I didn't hear back." He could actually hear the woman swallow. "I spoke to the young man I had drive you home. He provided the information you neglected to pass on."

"Oh… ohhhhkay, well again, sorry about that."

"No problem. It's over now. That's not the reason for this call, though. Are you busy? You sound busy?" He made his way to his bedroom window and looked out. People watching was a pleasure he didn't often have the luxury of indulging in much anymore, but he found it rather relaxing when he could sneak it in every now and again.

"Well, yes. I'm in rehearsal and—"

"Rehearsal for *what*?"

"I'm a dancer and choreographer."

"Word of professional advice, Sky, when you are asked what you do for a living, state that you are a dance choreographer and leave it at that. If you answer dancer first, or even last, you are placing less significance on your actual job title… one that I'm certain you've worked hard to earn. Additionally, in this day 'nd age, saying you're a dancer can conjure up thoughts of poles and silicon filled titties jiggling all over the fuckin' place for cash. Nothin' wrong with being a stripper…" He shrugged. "But that's *not* what you are, so leave it out of your response from now on. Got it?"

"Uh, okay… you're something else."

"What else am *I*?" His brows dipped. "Never mind.

I'm just fuckin' with ya... I know it was just a figure of speech."

The woman laughed nervously on the other end.

"Well, thank you for calling. I really have to—"

"No, you don't have to go right now. You're just choosing to. I am making you uncomfortable because of an underlying situation."

"And what situation would that be?"

"You've been avoiding me because you're loyal to your friend, Sharice... Apparently, she either has a crush on me or believes I'm a bank that she can withdraw from, perhaps both. The crush is fine, but I don't pay for pussy... at least not in the sense she's looking for. I know a lion out on the prowl when I see one... because *I am* one. Same shit, different day."

"Scarlet. Her name is Scarlet."

"Thank you for verifying what I wasn't one hundred percent certain about but now you've filled in the blanks and confirmed it. I appreciate that." He chuckled, and it sounded as if she had, too, before perhaps she caught herself. "I knew her name, by the way... Anyway," He glanced down at his watch. "She's quite attractive but not really my type... *you* are. So what are you going to do about that?"

"Do about *what*?!"

"I tell you what. How about we have dinner this evening?"

At this, the woman burst out laughing.

"Mr. Zander, I have *never* encountered anyone like you in my life, and though it is entertaining, like watching a skit gone wrong, I'm going to stop beating around the bush." *I was hoping to slide deep into yours...* "I really don't think it's a good idea for us to meet up or go out, okay? I'm flattered... I think. But anyway, despite the fact that you're not really feelin' my friend, it wouldn't be a good move on my part. I think that would be really awkward."

"As awkward as you telling me about a fictitious boyfriend, finding me attractive, and being, at the very least, a tad bit curious as to how a date with me would go?"

He was met with another brief moment of silence, then another eruption of laughter.

"Did you just become like this or is this your behavior twenty-four-seven from birth? There's such a thing as too much confidence, Mr. Zander."

"No such thing. Lack of confidence and belief in oneself makes a man weak. Back to the topic though, your friend and I were never dating. I don't even know the woman. There is no betrayal... you have nothing to concern yourself about. Besides, can you blame her? Who wouldn't want to spend some time with me? I'm attractive, I'm fun, I'm rich, and so much more."

"I can't with you."

She cackled, but he knew he was warming her up... bending her to his desires.

"I'm arrogant, I'll be the first to admit it—but I can back it up." He drummed his hand on the windowpane and smiled. "Look, at the end of the day, I'm just a poor kid from Brooklyn who grew up to become a successful businessman. I know what I like and don't like, and I'd like to get to know you better, Sky. Period. I will have someone pick you up tonight at 6:45 P.M. No, better yet, I will come get you myself. Clear your schedule."

"I'm busy."

"Make yourself un-busy. If I can blow off a few important executives, you can ditch your responsibilities for an evening. I promise it'll be worth your time." He disconnected the call and made his way down the steps. Grabbing his keys, he tossed them in the air before exiting out the front door...

LEO

"5,6,7, 8! COME on, Tyson! Lift those legs!"

Sky looked at her phone in disbelief. The man had hung up, and all she could do was stand there with her mouth hanging open.

"See... these motherfuckers from Brooklyn... so sick of them! And his White ass is obviously no better! He acts like he has swag falling out the ass."

...In fact, he did.

Fucker.

She mouthed a string of cuss words under her breath as she left the dance studio's coat closet where she'd been hiding to take the call, and returned to the floor. Adrianne, her colleague, was working with their new pupils, five of them. This was a class of seasoned adult actors who had a few dance numbers to learn for a major Broadway show that was set to begin in a few months, and she had been selected out of hundreds to instruct them. Snatching a towel from a nearby dance bar, she dabbed her forehead and stood in the middle of the room.

"Turn on 'Lose Control' by Missy Elliott, please." She dropped her head and waited for the beat to drop. "All right, listen up! This is not the song you all are using for the scene where the robots come out, but it has the exact same rhythm. You need to be able to perform this dance to *any* song with a similar rhythm. Now watch me…"

The music became louder as she moved about the floor, popping and locking, her limbs flowing to the beat. The students began to whistle and clap as she went through the routine, her hair swinging wildly to and fro. She was dancing with all of her might, burning off steam, bringing in the day. She smiled. Here, in the zone, she felt safe. Each fluid motion was like an extension of her very soul.

Every part of her temple was involved in the edification of dance. She praised it; it was her personal Goddess. Adrianne wolf whistled a couple of times, but soon enough, Sky could neither hear nor see anyone. She was just sliding, gliding and moving, swaying to the beat within her heart, and fast becoming a happy, sweaty mess. Pulling at the high waist band of her leggings, she snapped it against her flat stomach and ran her hand along her ribcage. Her black crop top was stuck to her skin and her body was practically on fire, but she didn't mind...

Dance was life. Life was dance.

The students clapped and applauded her.

"We're not going to be able to do that," one of them said, his tone worried. "How long have you been dancing, Sky?"

"Since the age of four. I've been dancing profession-ally since age eight. I've always loved it... knew it was what I wanted to do. Look, everybody." She clasped her hands together and began to pace in front of them. "I don't expect you to be an expert or even great, but you can be good—impressive, actually. Usually, I train other dancers. You all are not, but for me, that just adds to the fun. You're a challenge, and I have no problems stepping up to it. You're actors. You have a good command of the stage, so that is a plus. Just follow my lead... I got you, I promise..."

LEO

♌

CHAPTER FOUR

Quick Change of Plans...

Later that evening...

U MI SUSHI LEFTOVERS were always delicious...
Sky lounged about on her favorite, broken in raspberry red couch in her most comfy bra and panties, enjoying her downtime in her apartment in Queens. Soy sauce packets lay strewn on the coffee table, along with a warm bottle of diet Coke and the television tuned to reruns of 'True Blood.' It had been a long day. The ride on the subway was particularly hot, and worst of all, it was far from peaceful.

She'd ended up next to the idiot that wanted to sing vintage 70's tunes at the top of his lungs all while wearing no shirt, smelling like sautéed onions and donning booty shorts with rainbow striped roller skates on his feet. Her thoughts drifted back to the dance studio. She'd earned every dollar and then some. What a crowd.

Damn these actors... it's all good though...

Newbies were energy suckers. Some were rather uncoordinated, others moved well but didn't seem to have the oomph to follow through and recall their steps. It was amazing how some award-winning actors could memorize an entire movie script but forget a simple two step. She yawned and stretched, her limbs slightly sore and her world filled with clouds as the desire to nap grew fangs and sank in deep. Her eyelids fluttered and before she knew it, she was seduced by the lazy lover of sleep. However, someone had other plans…

BANG! BANG! BANG!

She suddenly shot up like a bullet blasted out of a gun as she heard a pounding on her door. Rubbing her eye, she flung the quilt off her body and tried to get her bearings. She deliberated on asking who it was, but just in case she wanted to pretend to not be at home, as she often did with uninvited guests, she thought better of it. Tiptoeing towards the door, she looked through the peephole and her heart thumped like a sledgehammer. There, on the other side of the door, stood a tall, debonair man wearing a V-neck money green sweater and loose jeans, holding a bouquet of purple ombre flowers in a clear plastic wrapper, crunched in his grip.

Lazarist…

Resting her hands against the door, she continued to peer out, now standing a bit on her tippy toes. The man cocked his head to the side, smiled, then winked.

With a gasp, she quickly turned away, her back pressed against the wood. After a couple of heart pounding seconds, his deep voice broke the silence.

"So... you're just going to leave me standing out here, huh? That's the plan?"

She quickly spun around and looked back out the peephole. His smile was replaced with a smirk.

"What are you doing here?"

Now that was a dumb question! The man said he was picking me up... but I didn't think he was serious!

As if reading her mind, he repeated her thoughts. "What do you mean what am I doin' here? I said we were going out and that I'd pick you up at 6:45 P.M."

"I, uh, had to work late, and I'm tired."

"So am I... I tell you what, Sky. I'm going to go back out to my car and sit in it. I am going to give you fifteen minutes to join me. If you don't, you'll never hear from me or see me again. That'll be *your* loss." He slowly bent down, placed the flowers at her door, and walked away, taking easy steps towards the elevator until he was out of eyeshot.

"Oh my God!" She raced to her small living room where she'd been perched. Snatching up her phone, she dialed Toi... then hung up. "Toi wouldn't know what to do! I'll call Candace." She called her friend and got her voicemail. "Damn it!"

Slamming down the phone, she paced for a moment or two, chewing on her nails. A part of her wanted to find out what this persistent bastard was all about. There was something exciting about a man like Lazarist, a fellow who seemed to have the world in his hands. And that man was coming after her—full steam ahead. She'd never been in such a predicament. Sure, she'd been pursued by attractive men, but this was different. She couldn't figure this fucker out to save her life. Who would know what to do?

Scarlet...

She took a deep breath and deliberated over the dilemma as she retrieved the flowers from the front door, sniffed them, then set them down on the coffee table.

Scarlet wanted him though. What kind of person would I be to call up one of my best friends and ask her advice about a guy that dissed her and came for me instead?!

But she told me it was cool, and he had a point earlier today on the phone. He doesn't even know her. It's not like they were dating or anything...

But her saying she was fine with it may have been total bullshit. We say that kind of crap all the time, knowing damn well we feel some kinda way...

But Scarlet is well versed in these sorts of things...

Sky paced her floor in a panicked state, so much so that she wondered why she didn't burn a hole in it. Phone back in hand, she peered out her window to see if she could catch a glimpse of him. Almost out of view sat a shiny red and white vintage car, looking to be a Mustang. It had never been there before...

She swallowed.

Just do it.

She dialed Scarlet, a part of her hoping and pleading within that the woman didn't answer.

"Heeey, bitch." Sky smiled into the phone, so happy to hear that voice. Or was she? The jury was still out. This could be a murder trial.

"Hey, Scarlet, please don't be mad at me, but I need your advice."

"If it's about using name brand lube for anal sex versus that cheap 99 cent shit, the answer is still yes. That's not something you want to cheap out on, Sky. A mothafucka will have your ass feelin' like it's been lit with kerosene if you don't take the proper precautions."

"Stop it." Sky laughed, a bit relaxed at the woman's jabs. "I'm serious."

"Do I need to roll a blunt for this? What's happened?"

"Shit. Scarlet, I don't really know how to say this, but uh… that man, Mr. Zander, has asked me out. I blew him off, I've been so tired and busy, and then of course… I cared about your feelings as well. On top of that, I also honestly didn't think he was really serious. Well… I was wrong. He is waiting for me outside in his car!"

After a few moments of hairsplitting silence, Scarlet cleared her throat. Sky could hear what sounded like a lighter being struck, then smoke being exhaled.

"Mmm hmmm, you know I'm pissed about this, right?" The woman chuckled. "But it is what it is. Now, putting that aside and sliding on my real woman panties, I'm ready to lend a hand. Like I told you that night, he chose *you*. I could see by how he was looking at you before he even reached our table that he was digging you, but you didn't even seem to notice. Before I do my friendly duty though, I only have one question."

"What?"

"Why didn't you keep yo' ass at home that night?! You fucked up my whole get rich scheme, Egyptian pyramid, gold diggin' in the Nile arrangement up! I coulda been set up for life! You don't *ever* go nowhere with us any other time!"

Scarlet burst out laughing, and so did she, but she knew the woman was half-serious.

"Girl, I don't know, but I *do* know that I have about seven minutes to throw on some clothes, lipstick, run a brush through this mess on my head, and act as if I couldn't care less about him stopping by. Should I go out with him or not show up? He can't take a hint."

"Alright, Bambi, with your innocent, naïve self. First, I want you to put me on speaker phone as you go on and get ready. We need to lay out some ground rules."

"So go out with him? All right, I'm on it."

Sky made a beeline to her bedroom and began the grooming process. Her underwear was discarded on the floor and replaced by a prettier set. As an outfit, she selected a button-down copper colored tunic top and a pair of chocolate leggings to go with it. She finally sat on her bed to lace up her mocha heels.

"First things first. He is going to try to fuck you. Don't do it, bitch. I'm warning you ... and this isn't the jealousy or Hennessey talking. It will be enticing, trust me, but you have to resist. No matter how tempting it is, with men like this guy, they want to chase your ass. Make him work for it. If you give it up too fast, they'll see you like all the others. Think about it. Women throw themselves at men like him."

"Like you did?"

"Bitch, I will hang up this mothafuckin' phone faster than your twenty-two-inch Brazilian body wave weave can spin and leave your Golden Girls, Rose Nylun behavin' ass in the lurch." Sky burst out laughing. Scarlet was the only person who could insult her this way and get away with it. She knew it all came from a place of love. "Now be quiet and listen. Back to the sex... if you drag it out way too long, they'll lose interest. You have to find a happy medium."

"I do that anyway with most guys I date. You know me." Sky shrugged as she got to her feet, grabbed her brush off her vanity, and made haste to comb her hair in a decent style.

"Nuh uh, no way, sweetie. You got it wrong. You think this is going to be a cakewalk, but it's not. I'm telling you, I've dealt with these sorts of men before, okay? Everything is a test to them... a game. He needs to know that you want him; that will get him on the hook and right before he thinks he has the deal sealed, you have to pull the plug... make him leave there frustrated and wanting you. See, men like Lazarist Zander can have just about anything and anyone they want. Now, here's a bit more about his history. He didn't have shit growing up, so he's not one of these mothafuckas walkin' around here who's not in the land of reality, that silver spoon shit. This man climbed his way to the top."

"Like King Kong on the Empire State Building... Yes, he mentioned very briefly that he was just a poor kid from Brooklyn."

"Right. So, that's good, but remember, keep it sassy with a dash of trashy. In other words, swallow the innocent act and let your freak flag fly, but only at half-mast. He is looking for excitement but not too much, because as a hunter, he is in the market to find his next main squeeze. This man has been officially single for a while now. I imagine it's by choice or he hasn't found what he's looking for. If you want to secure the bag, baby, leave him panting."

"So, seduce him… Girl, I got the game of seduction on lock!" Sky chortled. "I got this. Thanks for your help."

"Awww, you're sweet and trusting, Sky… good Lord." Sky wrinkled her nose at her friend's words. "Bitch, ain't a damn thing you can do or say that he hasn't seen, heard, or done before. You just have to do it *better…*"

"Do it better… all right." Sky grabbed a pair of small gold stud earrings and placed them in her ears.

"One more thing… I heard he is a *major* freak in bed, Sky… I mean, he is on some *other* shit. That white cane he walks around with at the club ain't just for show, if you catch my drift. If you're only used to that mission-ary, patty cake bullshit, you better read up or something because this mothafucka is going to want it *all…* everything on the menu and frequently… and he's intense. His ex-wife was in the adult film industry like I told you, and word on the curb is that many of his ex-girlfriends were models and the like – so be warned. He is used to a certain level of, shall we say, experience."

"And how do you know I'm *not* experienced?" Sky put her hand on her hip. "You don't know what I do behind closed doors, Scarlet."

"I know that Scarlet rhymes with harlot, and Sky rhymes with shy. 'Nuff said. But you don't need to worry about that right now anyway. You're just doing the seduction. But when the time comes, if he's into threesomes, call me, bitch."

"Girl, bye!" Sky burst out laughing and disconnected the call before spritzing herself with a bit of perfume. She exited her bedroom and looked out the window one last time. The red and white car was pulling away from the curb. Her heart beat a mile a minute as she dashed towards her front door, grabbed her purse from a stool sitting right next to it, and called his number.

"Hello, Sky…" he responded. "I almost didn't answer. It's been seventeen minutes. I've left. What is it that you want?"

She could not believe this motherfucker!

Okay… just play it cool…

"I got dressed to go. I am actually at the elevator on my way down."

After a brief silence, the man loudly sighed in what sounded like extreme annoyance.

"All right. I'm circling around the block. Stand outside and I'll pick you up."

"Okay."

And then he hung up. Moments later, she was outside her apartment building, looking for the red and white vintage car. Soon, he pulled up as promised. She walked up to the car, but the man promptly got out and opened her door.

Wow… chivalry isn't dead after all.

"Thank you." As soon as she got situated in the car, he returned to the driver's side.

The interior looked practically brand new. *He takes good care of his toys…*

When he sat down, she took note of how far his seat went back, but for good reason. The man had incredibly long legs. In fact, he appeared to have a basketball player's build, with a bit more meat on his bones.

"You look very nice," he stated as he took hold of his steering wheel and entered the stream of traffic. "But of course, I'd expect nothing less. It's not too hard to polish up perfection," he complimented, a slight smile on his face. He kept his eye on the road.

"Thank you. So uh, where are we going?"

"It's truly up to you. I had something planned but I have no idea what you like and don't like. That's why I'm here, so I can eventually answer those questions." He chuckled, causing her to smile. "So, if you're hungry, I can make some suggestions. If you'd prefer to just have a coffee or drink, we can do that, too."

"Actually, I already ate, but a drink somewhere sounds good. I like a bookshop with a café that isn't too far from here."

"So, you like to read?" His brow rose as he ran his finger along his chin.

"Yeah, I enjoy it when I have the time. The

bookstore is called, 'Topos Bookstore Café.' It's on Woodward Avenue. I figure we can browse, get some drinks and talk there."

Soon, the man was speaking to his phone, asking for directions. She found it rather interesting that he simply didn't ask her where it was...

More odd human behavior for her studies. People were incredibly strange indeed. As she mulled that tiny tidbit around, she surveyed him from head to toe. Her stomach somersaulted. The damn thing was having a physiological response to his entire aura...

No wonder women flock to him. He's the perfect balance of sexy, aloof, warm and cool. I should have been a psychologist. Or a forensic profiler. Damn, I'm good. She grinned to herself as she crossed her arms and looked out the front window.

"What is making you smile?" he questioned as he approached a red light.

"You're a little unusual."

"Unusual? You don't know me yet. What makes you say that?"

"My brief interactions with you thus far have been highly unusual, Lazarist. You're demanding, conceited... yet there's something about you that comes across as approachable and kind, too. I like examining people. You're an interesting study." She shrugged.

"An interesting study..." he repeated and bobbed his head, as if mulling it over.

"Let me ask you something, Lazarist."

"Yes?"

"Now, don't get defensive." At this, he burst out

laughing but didn't comment at her disclaimer. "Why do you believe that your time is more valuable than mine? Why didn't you ask me for the directions to the bookshop? And what makes you think it's all right to come to someone's house without calling first?"

"Okay. First of all, I don't think my time is more valuable than yours. I distinctly told you that I'm busy, too. That was not negating your needs, just stating a fact."

"No, but you said—"

"Hold up. Let me finish!" He put up his finger, his voice slightly raised. "I told you that if I could blow off some executives, which I did, you could ditch some responsibilities, too. When I arrived at your place, I could smell the Asian food and hear the television. You weren't doing anything so—"

"Yes, but you didn't know that!"

"I *did* know that, because like you, I study people too! It doesn't make sense! Number one, Sky Jordan, if you are a dance choreographer and you are at work by 7:00 A.M. and not finished until 5:00 P.M., you are going to be pooped. Nobody makes plans after a day like that unless it is waaaay later that night, after they've rested. You are using your body for hours at a time and before you ask how do I know your work hours, I looked you up and saw that you run a dance studio and those are your hours of operation. Furthermore, what the fuck does it matter if you were in your apartment writing a goddamn thesis on how to end world hunger or jerking yourself off to monster elf porn? Fact of the matter is that I *did* tell you I was coming by… on the phone, earlier today.

"I didn't just pop up on you like some jack in the box. So that answers your third question even though you stated originally that you wanted to ask me something but it was actually *three* questions. Now, in reference to your second fuckin' question, doll…"

She could now hear the Brooklyn accent pouring into the bastard's words, now thick and heavy. Up until now, he'd been speaking rather professionally. The mask was off. And oh, how quickly it fell…

"I don't ask people for directions because everyone's mind works differently. I prefer maps and verbal directions from a navigation device. It's just a preference, nothin' personal. We're here."

Sure enough, she'd been so involved in giving it to him, a perfectly constructed rebuttal, that she hadn't even noticed they'd reached their destination.

She reached for the door handle, but the man was out of the car and on his feet faster than she could move. He swung her door open, looped his arm around hers, and helped her out of the car.

"You're an asshole," she said coolly as he took her hand and walked towards the shop.

He opened the front door on her behalf, allowing her to move in front of him. The scent of freshly brewed coffee soothed her, taking her to her happy place. And then she felt his hand along her lower back.

Leaning low, he whispered in her ear, "I like you, Sky… I imagine you probably called your friends and told them we were going out. If they gave you any advice, asked for or unsolicited, ditch it. I don't come with instructions…no one can figure me out so don't even try. Any books you may have read about human behavior is also out the window and I'm not one of your pupils… this *isn't* a rehearsal…this is real life…"

LEO

CHAPTER FIVE

I Can Read Between the Panty Lines...

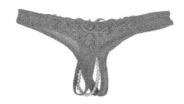

THE SMELL OF old and new books permeated the air. Lazarist watched from a distance as his prey ... er ... his date perused the narrow aisleways of Topos Bookstore and Café. It was a small place, but not claustrophobic. It was quaint, likeable. He'd never been before and told her as much as she went about her way, removing a book from a shelf here and there, flipping through the pages of various novels that caught her eye. He cocked his head to the side as he watched her flip her hair over her shoulder and slowly finger the pages of a hardback with a velvety green cover. Curiosity drove him further. He wondered what interested her, what her favorite genre was, and he hoped and prayed it was erotica.

She loitered in the Historical Fiction section for quite some time, much to his dismay. In fact, he was surprised, assuming she'd be more into romance or something like '50 Shades of Grey.' After all, when he'd first seen her, she'd had on a black leather studded dog collar around her neck. All kinds of dirty fantasies had invaded his mind at such a sight.

She placed the book slowly back on the shelf, then shifted her attention towards another display. Her face wrinkled in surprise and her beautiful eyes widened. He heard a slight gasp of excitement escape her lips as she plucked a purple colored paperback from a lower ledge. He closed in on her, brushing his chest ever so slightly against her shoulder. Her perfume called to his cock, making it twitch in the confines of his briefs. He hooked on the image of her lips and imagined the delicate skin surrounding his dick sliding in and out of her mouth, against the soft pallet of her wet, pink tongue, until he was balls deep, his sack resting against her chin as she gagged and swallowed his cum. As if sensing his gaze on her, she peered up at him with those almond shaped dark brown eyes, thick black lashes a mile long.

I wonder if she cries when she orgasms... I bet she's a scream-er, too...

"Did you find anything of interest?" He casually leaned against the case and crossed his ankles.

"Yeah, this is 'Island of the Mad', by Laurie R. King. I've been wanting to read this for a few weeks now... I'm lucky it's in here, actually."

"What's it about?" She paused for a spell, as if challenging his invitation to a discussion about such things. Then, her facial expression relaxed, replaced with a smile.

"Sherlock Holmes re-invented. Takes place in Sussex in 1925. A wealthy woman comes up missing. From my understanding, this is a really good one. It's been highly anticipated. It delves into all sorts of things, like Mussolini."

"Mussolini?" He leaned closer to her, peering down at the open page. "You're talkin' my language now. I may have to check that out." He ran the side of his thumb along the edge of the book. Her eyes focused on the slowly moving digit, then she looked him in the eye.

"Well, you can't just jump right in. You need the backstory. It's part of a series... I've been reading it on and off."

I can't just jump right in... you need foreplay... I need to get to know you first, huh? You going to play with me on and off... make this hard. I can read between the lines of your novel of life, Ms. Jordan.

"So." He clasped his hands together. "I'm going to look over here..." He pointed in another direction of the store. "I'll get a book or two and then hopefully we can secure a table soon and sit down and talk. Sound good?"

"Yup." She grinned hard at him then turned back towards her book, as if it were more intriguing than him... more exciting... more inviting. It couldn't be. *Nothing* was more exciting than him...

Why isn't she fawning over me?

He stared at her, wanting to snatch the damn thing out of her hands, rip the pages out, chuck it to the ground, break the binding, then stomp it with his foot.

I'm jealous of a fucking book.

This is an all-time low for you, Lazarist. It's not like it's the Bible or anything. It's a fuckin' fictional historical mystery novel, for Pete's sake. She's going to be trouble. She's pretending... playing games.

His cock twitched once again at the realization. Turning away, he journeyed to the Self Help section. Perhaps he could play on her sympathy. Yes, he could gather up a few books, keep them pressed close to his chest, then let them tumble in front of her... exposing his quasi-broken heart for the world to see... portray himself as in need of self-discovery, of healing of a wounded soul... one who wished to delve deep within and rid himself of his demons ... a man in desperate need of love and understanding that only the mighty Sky could administer...

Poor, helpless Lazarist. Whatever shall he do?!

THOSE. FUCKIN'. PANTIES. ARE. COMING. DOWN!

Minutes later, they'd reunited at a small table for two by the window. People sat all around, indulging in banana nut bread slices, coffees, and Italian sodas. He observed her side-eyeing his collection of, 'How to Win Friends and Influence People', 'You Can Heal Your Life', and last but not least, 'The Seven Principles for Making Marriage Work.'

That's right, baby. I'm all about being fuckin' sensitive to your needs 'nd shit... I'm loving and marriage minded. Never mind that my feet will never walk down the aisle again and I couldn't care less about all of this relationship business... but I can see you're not as naïve as I suspected, Sky... what a fuckin' pity. You talk too fuckin' much for one, ask too many questions. You look at me suspiciously so now I have to bring out the big dogs. Heart strings on pull in 3, 2, 1... showtime!

"You know," he began as he clasped his hands together, making sure to look immersed in thought. "With all the work I do on any given day..." He shook his head, his expression glum. "It doesn't give a lot of time for, say, getting to know *me* anymore. I don't spend enough alone time with myself. I want to grow and expand, you know? I'm interested in human study, too. Introspection."

"Really? That's wonderful! We have a lot to discuss, then." Her lips curled at the ends and her eyes widened with what he could only describe as a look of complete and utter conviction.

I've got you now, bitch... operation legs open has commenced!

"So, what have you been thinking about lately, you know, in regard to your own self-improvement?"

Plunging deep inside your hot pussy with my fingers then cock and making you scream. That would be a BIG improvement!

"Uh, well." He flipped through one of the books, pretending he needed to think on it... put his words together just right. "Life and work balance, actually." She nodded in understanding. "I tend to see my life through my work. It defines my existence to some extent." And that was true...

"So, how do you think you can make that better?"

He shrugged. "Not so sure... I'm not always convinced it's a problem, and that could be part of the problem, too." Again... he gave her another nugget of honesty. "I've tried and haven't always been successful. I love what I do too much, Sky." He tossed up his hands and smiled. "See, owning a club like Fallen Angel has been a dream of mine since I was in my early twenties. I used to wish there was a place I could go to, where I could shoot pool, eat a fancy meal, and dance my ass off all under the same roof. I didn't wanna have to hop on the train, catch a cab, or get a ride from a friend just to have one solid Saturday night. I wanted something all inclusive. Now sure, those places exist, but not like mine..."

"I'd have to agree with you there. It is definitely unique. That was creative on your part, and you filled a need in the city, too."

I can fill your needs as well, Sky...

"Thank you. Fallen Angel is in a league of its own. I've never once been in the red, my employees are top notch, and I don't hesitate to cut someone who isn't pulling their weight. I make sure the food is good and fresh, that I have highly trained chefs. I guarantee that my comedians and entertainment acts have a good resume. I never want to bring in someone that's lacklus-ter. I ensure people get good drinks, none of that watered-down shit and I charge a fair price, too. The music for the club needs to be to the liking of the crowd, the place clean... bathrooms spotless. I take my custom-ers seriously. Most days."

They both chuckled at that. "The VIP sections are

just that … for very important people. Red leather half circle booths with a drink and appetizer menu catered just for them. I want people to have a good time. Come out and blow off some steam… unwind after a long work week. When you come to Fallen Angel, it's party time. No ifs, ands, or buts about it."

"Why did you choose to open a club versus, say, a retail shop, bar, or something like that?"

"People laughing and having fun is a passion of mine. I am a born entertainer, but I'd rather do it behind the scenes and vicariously through others… kind of like these books." He pointed to her small stack. "My words are in my feats; my characters or the employees and the work I put in—they do my bidding and I am pulling the strings. I don't need to be in the limelight all the time… I much prefer that the chefs and comedians and the DJ get the accolades. That's kinda a misconception about me. All I need is to be acknowledged. That's *really* where my heart lies, and I'm cool with that. I'm a people pleaser too… but within reason."

He winked at her. Picking up his lemon flavor Italian soda, he took a sip and set it down.

"You speak with such passion about work! I really like that."

She leaned back in her seat and pressed her arms against her body, inadvertently drawing attention to her lovely tits. His eyes rested on that cleavage for a spell, his mind entertaining visions of him slicking his tongue all over them and tasting her nipples.

Too soon, he snapped out of it and looked back into

her eyes.

"Yeah, it's my passion. I don't have any family, 'cept my mother and sister, my friends—they're like brothers to me. I don't have children, nothing like that, so essentially, my work is my wife, my kids, my car, my home, my heart... my God."

"That's tragic."

His smile slowly faded. He couldn't even fake his disappointment in her inability to simply go with the flow, not make this hard. The prey was acting up...

"How so?" He turned his plate to and fro and sank his fork into the thick slice of banana nut bread. He hated banana nut bread, but she insisted he try it. In an effort to get her ass naked before the end of the night, he complied.

"Because you just went through an entire spiel about how you want to help yourself, stop the life – work balance from being so one sided. Hey," she said with emphasis. "I get it. If I could dance for eighteen hours a day, I would, but I know that's not healthy. Not only that, I used to do just that it seemed. It practically killed me. My father had had enough and made me relax. I've been in your shoes. You have to stop the grind and look at the world around you, boo." She smiled sadly. "At least every now and again."

"You're so right... see?" He shot her a grin. "I'm trying... but it's hard, baby. I think I probably need someone around who can remind me of that, you know? Someone in my corner... Perhaps I need a special person who would make the slow down worth it? After all, what's the point in reducing progress if there is no motivation to do so?"

"No motivation? You and your mental health should be motivation enough, Lazarist."

"My mental health is contingent upon my bills being paid, my mother being taken care of, my friends and associates who work for me getting their checks on time, and my dream constantly being fed, Sky."

He pressed his finger into the table and could feel the crease in his forehead growing with aggravation. He hated that she was getting on his fucking nerves. Why couldn't she just nod and agree? Why did she have to be so fucking difficult?

Here I am, telling her what she wants and it STILL isn't good enough! When I said I needed motivation, this bitch was supposed to say, 'I can try to be that motivation.' That's what happens nine times out of ten. These broads usually want to fuck me so they can get close to me, get licked by the lion, win my trust, and then go on fuckin' shoppin' sprees on my dime. I don't mind that — we're doing favors for one another essentially, but this woman really wants to help… she really wants me to live my best life. What kinda cockamamie bullshit is this?!

He smiled hard as he remembered he was in the line of fire, then shoved a piece of the banana bread in his mouth.

"Good, right?" She grinned.

He rolled his eyes, feigning ecstasy.

"Ohhh, is it ever!" he said with his mouth full. "This is *amazing!*"

This dry ass, flavorless shit tastes like the bottom of a fuckin'

dumpster behind Lin Lui's Kitchen on a hot ass summer day!
Jesus Holy Trinity, what the hell have I eaten as I Walk Through
the Valley of the Shadow of Taste Bud Death! Christ! It tastes
like crackers from 1975! I'm dyin' here!

He swallowed roughly, grabbed the Italian soda to
help shove the shit down, almost gagging along the way.
The woman's brow rose as she watched him gulp down
the remainder of his beverage to chase the brick that was
caught in his throat then hop out of his seat to go
purchase another.

"Would you like anything else?" He pointed to the
counter up ahead that featured the pastries, beverages,
and candies.

"No, thank you." She smiled then opened one of her
books as he sauntered away.

Something odd was happening. He felt exposed, as if
all of his private inner workings, the rusty gears and all,
were in full view. As he stood in the short line to wash
away the rest of the horrid flavor from his mouth, he
wondered why suddenly he felt that she could do what *he*
could do so well, too? See through people's bullshit with
a mere glance. But he usually played along... never
letting the liar, thief, or backstabber in his midst know
that he was on to them until it was too late.

I've been played...

He'd thought he had her pegged...

Sky had come across as a bit silly, airheaded, and
young at the club and during their first phone conversation. She had a kind of caretaker persona, too—the way
she doted over her drunk ass friend and kept shoving

him towards the attractive bald chick with the spinning green dollar bills in her eyes. What a kind-hearted, gullible soul. An easy target.

But... she was beautiful, too, which only added to the prize. He saw her as soon as she'd arrived that night. He was in his office and had just checked his cameras to see her piling inside, getting carded and her hand stamped, along with her band of friends. He'd leaned in closer to the camera, then hit zoom. After magnifying her face and body on the screen, he literally salivated.

I want her...

There'd been no denying it that night, and certainly not now. When he'd discovered later that she was a dancer, his dick saluted. He was one lucky son of a bitch.

Dancers were limber...

But now, things were uncertain.

She's on to me...

She hadn't said as much. Perhaps she was being polite, but typically he found it rather easy to roll over on a woman, make her believe in white maned unicorns, glittery rainbows, princes riding in on said unicorns under those goddamn rainbows... and all of the stupid shit that was required just so he could knock her pussy walls clear out the frame and never fucking call the broad again. After all, women were excessively emotional creatures; playing on that was as easy as 1, 2, 3.

And though he wasn't convinced she wasn't in that category – either way he sliced it, she had a mean poker face. The woman was rather hard to read at times, and that only added to his intrigue and irritation over the entire ordeal. He stood there feeling some sort of way… a mixture of frustration and admiration. Before long, he had another drink and was sitting back down, only to see that her face was planted firmly in a book.

She isn't messing with her cellphone… she's just into the book. ~~*Interesting. I need to ask how old she is. Maybe she is older than*~~ *she looks. She acts it.*

"So." he opened the beverage and chugged it. "Tell me about how you became a dance choreographer."

"Well, it just so happens that I've always loved to dance." She slowly closed her book and crossed her arms along the table. "My father was instrumental in support-ing me and my dreams, and he got me into dance classes when I was very young. I then began to audition and get dancing jobs as a child in commercials and I joined a professional dance troupe for children from New York City. We toured the country performing during the summers."

"Wow! That's impressive." He tooted the chilled bottle back up to his lips.

"After that, I was contacted by various recording artists, locally that is, to help with some of their videos and on stage performances. That went very well and I established a name for myself. Then, about four years ago, I opened my own academy, 'The Sky is the Limit Dance Studio.'"

He couldn't help but feel her enthusiasm and it melded into him, making him happy for her, too.

"Catchy… so, uh, how's business?" He spread his legs far apart and leaned back in the chair.

"It's awesome. I'm very busy, but I make sure I give myself some down time. It's essential." She winked in his direction as if she were conducting some after school special, an intervention on his behalf. He grimaced and rolled his eyes.

I'll be damned if she's gonna be passive aggressive and drop little judgmental hints in my direction and not give it up! If I'm gonna be abused, it better come with some ass attached to it!

"How old are you, Sky? 26? 27?"

"No, not quite." She chuckled. "I'm 33." That confirmed his suspicions. "That's another reason why I need down time. I think I'm in pretty good shape and it's not that thirty-three is old... far from it, but when it comes to athletes and dancers, well, our bodies take a bit more of a bruising, so self-care is crucial."

Why don't you let me take care of your body and bruise up that pussy with some heavy poundin' from my big dick tonight, huh? I'll be cruel to the pussy, baby, then kiss it goodnight... I will make you cum so hard your back will cave in... make you think you love me, give you the time of your life like you never imagined...

"I think you should buy those books." She pointed at his stupid collection. "I bet they'll help."

He nodded and polished off the rest of his drink, then looked out the window. The woman was a lost cause. He'd have to whip out his cellphone later and find a Plan B. Lazarist could tell about half way through a date if he was getting laid or not. At this point, this was a definite NOT. Her body language told him that she was closed off. Arms crossed across the chest, legs overlapped. She'd been averting eye contact at various pivotal intervals. The whole thing stunk to high heaven.

Something isn't right. I'm never wrong about these things…I'm rarely shrugged off or turned down by women. She's setting up the scene to say, 'No.' All the telltale signs are there. I know someone got into her head… I ALWAYS choose the right ones. Me and this broad should be leaving right now, heading to my place or the hotel and screwin' each other's brains out. Something isn't adding up…

A few seconds passed and the reality hit him like a ton of bricks.

SHIT! I bet I know what happened…

I bet she called the bald chick… What was her name? Simone? Sherry? Shit-startin' Stacey? No, Scarlet! Fuck you, Scarlet! I know you're behind this shit! Yeah, and now Scarlet is a woman scorned because I chose her friend over her. She cock blocked. For fuck's sake! Sweet revenge from one hunter to another! I guess she got the last laugh…

He played along nevertheless. Besides, at the very least, Sky was proving to be an interesting conversationalist. He had to give that to her. And it didn't hurt that she was easy on the eyes. She had beautiful long hair and a nice smile, as well. But most of all, oddly enough, she had a quality he believed few possessed—she genuinely cared about how he felt…

Minutes passed and hours matured. The rest of their conversation consisted of small talk—still interesting, but uneventful. He felt himself shutting down, his interest in her twisting and turning in the wind… and for all the wrong reasons. The woman liked to talk about hipster type shit, and he was into it too, to some degree. It was hard accepting that this would be an uphill battle with no ending in sight. Would he have to concede? His dick begged him not to.

Not one to so easily give up, he gathered his weapons of mass pussy destruction and formulated a new plan. Honesty.

"All right, baby, look." He shoved the books to the side with a swipe of his arm and cleared a path for him to rest his hands. "I know that you've been sittin' here trying to figure me out, and I've been doing the same with you. You know what I want, Sky, so are we gonna do this or not?"

The woman's face looked downright mortified.

"Oh give me a break with the jaw drop shit, would jah!" He waved his hand in her direction. "I want to take you home. Point blank, period. And before you ask, no, that's not all I wanted, but it's a big component, okay?"

"What else did you want then?" she asked dryly. Her eyes darkened with clear indignation.

"I wanted to get to know you, just as I said."

"Lazarist, why do you think you are privy to my pussy just because you're good looking, and have an expensive car and money? I swear, dating in New York is the fuckin' pits!"

His eyes grew wide at her choice of words. What a raunchy little thing she was… and she looked so sweet and innocent.

He couldn't help but crack a devious smile.

Hmmm, this honesty strategy seems to be doing the trick. This is getting interesting again…

"I don't think I'm privy to your pussy. I'm privy to conversation and getting to know you. How do I get to know women I'm interested in? I fuck them, Sky. That's just how it is. I need to know if we're sexually compatible or there's no need to continue."

"Oh, what baloney!" She chortled, leaning forward and shaking her head. "You're the type of guy who will get me to your pad, screw me, and I'll never hear from you again. So here's the answer: No, I am not sleeping with you tonight, Lazarist."

"What about in the morning?"

They both looked at one another and burst out laughing.

"You aren't shit, you know that?" She giggled a bit more. "I'm serious though… no sex on the first date. I'm not that type of woman."

"Type of woman? I'll have you know I've slept with *many* ex-girlfriends on the first date and my second ex-wife I slept with on the first date, too. See? We ended up being together. You're making this too complicated."

"And look where they're at now! Gone like common sense and virginity on prom night. Like VH-1's Unsung Heroes… those women are a distant memory!"

Damn, she's funny, too.

"All right, you've made a good point."

"Why, thank you."

They stared at one another for a long while, and then he reached across the table and took her hand. Grasping it tightly, he hooked her gaze.

"I know that this showdown wasn't your idea… but regardless of how it all started and who planted the seed in your head, you completed the race and got over the finish line. I respect that. I'm not going to give up though, Sky. I'm going to keep on working on you until I get what I want. We're going to fuck. And we're going to fuck *soon*. Obviously not tonight, but it's coming. Trust me on that."

She slowly stood to her feet, grabbed her purse, and slung it over her shoulder.

"By then it won't matter… because you'll already be head over heels in love with me. Let's go. It's a lovely summer evening and I want to take a walk with you."

He looked up at that woman and realized a few things—things that could never be reversed, taken back, or denied…

Sky had stolen control… He hadn't seen her crawl from the back and take the wheel, but somehow, she'd managed and now here he was, in the back seat and panting in disbelief. He liked the fuck out of her. She had been playing him the whole time, knowing exactly what he was up to but worst of all, that shit about falling in love? The broad might just be right…

LEO

CHAPTER SIX

Success Has Many Fathers,
Failure is an Orphan...

...Several days later

LAZARIST FORCED HIMSELF to sit on his bed and focus on senseless YouTube videos that involved foolhardy stunts, pranks, and nostalgic uploads from television shows he used to love as a teenager... the stuff he used to enjoy before things had gotten out of control. Constantly shifting his body beneath the black sheets and readjusting his laptop, he grew impatient and restless.

"Shit..." he mumbled, stressing about all the things he should've been doing.

I should be at the club right now...

I should have at least gone through the mail...

I wonder if Shelby ever found that shipment of parsley?

But he had to admit, he was sorta enjoying himself. It had all begun on one evening a few days earlier, after leaving the bookstore, hand in hand with one of the most remarkable women he'd ever encountered. Ms. Sky Jordan. She'd challenged him to go home after work and do nothing, and she meant nothing work related, for at least five days straight.

He wasn't even allowed to see how many virtual strangers had hashtagged Fallen Angel on Instagram. Nope. She'd been very specific about the directions, and he wasn't one to pass up a challenge. He sat up a bit straighter, pressing his back against his headboard and pushed play on a video entitled, 'Fart Spray Prank Goes Wrong', while reaching for his glass of merlot. Five minutes later, he had tears running down his face—he was laughing so hard.

"Jesus! I wouldn't have stayed!" He cackled, his stomach hurting oh so good. Just then, his doorbell rang. All of the muscles in his body tightened. He glanced over at the clock. 3:42 A.M. Sliding the computer off of his lap onto the unoccupied side of the bed, he flung the sheets back and slid his size thirteen feet into his Brooks Brothers velvet slippers. Then, he grabbed his silk black robe from a hook and made his way a floor below. He stared at the front door, knowing damn well who was on the other side. *What's the problem this time?*

He cut off the alarm system and took a deep breath. Undoing the three locks, including the deadbolt, he swung the door open and came face to face with David Zander. The man was wearing his old, worn trench coat, standing slightly hunched and gripping a plastic grocery sack full of Lord knew what. One hand shook ever so slightly and his blue eyes looked bloodshot, dark bags hanging from them, an all too common sight as of late. Silver and black stubble dotted his chin and cheeks, proof of a lack of a shave for at least a week. Reaching into his pocket, the man pulled out his old eyeglasses. Placing them across his face, he gave him a twisted smile, exposing slightly yellowed teeth.

"So, uh, ya gonna let your father inside or just keep starin' at me, you son of uh bitch?"

LEO

...30 Minutes Later

LAZARIST SAT AT his kitchen table and crushed the can of La Croix sparkling water before tossing it several feet to the recycle bin, getting a slam dunk. His basketball skills may have been rusty, but he still had it. His father, now freshly showered and donning an oversized clean shirt and pants, sat opposite him, slurping kosher chicken soup and nibbling on a piece of French bread.

What an enigma of a man. Hatred grew within Lazarist, more with each moment for the specimen better known as 'father.' His heart was breaking a million times over and worst of all, this shit never got any easier, no matter how long the sordid mess had been happening. In fact, no matter what and despite his best efforts, things never changed. They remained the same like a vintage family video played on repeat… the nightmarish kind.

"Your mother still seein' that guy?" the man questioned in between slurps, his brow arched.

"What does it matter, David?" Lazarist tossed up his hands indifferently. "I say this to you all the time. You two have been divorced for over twenty years. Let it go."

"She's my wife!" the man yelled, pounding his bony fist against the table.

"No, she's not," Lazarist stated calmly, leaning back in his seat. "Mom has moved on, okay? Eliza wants nothin' to do with you, so here you are, one child left… *me*… and I'm hanging on by a thread."

"Your sister is a cunt." Dad took another heaping spoonful of his soup, shoveling it into his mouth before giving it a hard swallow. His mouth hanging open now, detachment in his eyes. "My mother, your grandmother, she uh, she told me not to marry a Gentile… worst mistake of my life. She never liked your mother… fuckin' half Irish, half Italian entitled bitch… Catholic, geesh! I shoulda married a Jew. Jewish women are loyal. Now my kids are all mixed up…"

"Here we go again, right? I'm so tired of this shit…" Lazarist dropped his head and shook it.

"My marriage is ruined. I gave your mother everything, but look where it got me?" The old man chuckled. "If I'd married a Jewish woman like my mother wanted me to, things woulda been different."

"Now that's a first. I hadn't heard you word it quite that way. This time you must be trying to entertain me, right? Keep me invested in this idiotic conversation. Lest I remind you, David, Mom converted for you. Funny how whatever doesn't go with your narrative you conveniently omit. You're not in court... I'm your son."

"My son?" The old man chuckled. "You call me by my first name half tha fuckin' time. How's that for respect? You judge me... judge and jury. You've always been so fuckin' smug, you fucker you!" Lazarist rolled his eyes and grinned. His prayer was that the bastard would be gone sooner rather than later. "May as well treat ya like it's court since you sling your hand around like a gavel. And your mother was full of shit, all right? She went back to Catholicism as soon as she'd kicked me out!"

"So what? She still made that sacrifice for you. But again... you're stuck in the past."

"And you're not?"

Lazarist's smile faded. He blinked a few times, gathering his thoughts, trying desperately to steer clear from any triggers that would work him up. When it came to his father, however, it didn't take much.

"Dad, I know that most of the time, when I offer you money, you don't take it. Not because you don't need it, but it's a pride thing with you. This isn't right though. I even told you that you could pay it back. We can draft up a contract if you want." Lazarist was practically pleading... imagine that? Begging someone to take his money.

"No. The answer is still no."

The old guy turned away and crossed his arms over

his chest in defiance. Dad's social security check wasn't enough to make ends meet, but it was better than nothing. The man would use a bit of it every now and again to get a hotel room, food, a new shirt or two, perhaps some warm socks but the rest of it? It was anyone's guess what was going on and how it was being spent. Lazarist had a theory though. There were whores who walked the streets. He was pretty damn convinced that his father was blowing it on hookers.

"I want you to take the money I've been tryin' to give you, a check... not cash. I want you to see your psychiatrist that I had you go to a while back and get back on your medication. And I want you to take that money and put it towards an apartment for deposit and first month's rent. This is important! Winter will be here again before you know it, and you'll be in trouble. It's not safe ... you bein' on the streets. You've already been mugged, beaten up... This has to stop."

His father waved him off and huffed.

"It's safer on the streets than that fuckin' shelter, and I don't want your money! Stop actin' like you care about me. Ya don't! I was richer than you at your age, you know that, right? I don't need your pity!"

The man shoved his bowl out of the way, causing the soup inside it to violently slosh about. Lazarist looked at that bowl for a spell, watching it slowly achieve its calm, become placid.

Be like that soup. Don't let him upset you... keep your cool...

He crossed his ankles and kept insisting, "You need

help. I tell you that every time you fuckin' come here, David. You are sick. You've been sick for a *very* long time. You keep bringing up mom. Well, that's why your marriage ended. Mom loved you." Dad rolled his eyes in disbelief. "She did… and a long time ago, you loved her, too. Things change though, right? Sometimes it's our fault, sometimes the blame points in another direction, but at the end of the day, it doesn't even matter because the shit is squashed. It's done. The ending has been written and you've gotta accept it. But your kids? We're forever."

"Forever? Neither one of ya appreciate anything!"

Lazarist couldn't believe his ears.

"Really? That's why Eliza, who had been a daddy's girl up until the big blow up, wants nothin' to do with ya… 'cause of this shit right here! You sit here and call your own child a cunt. What kinda fucked up shit is that? You are the reason things are the way they are. YOU and only YOU!"

Lazarist stood to his feet and went to pull out a small carton of creamer from the refrigerator, then set it on the counter. He could hear his father sniffing, as if he had a bad runny nose. Then he heard the spoon hitting the bowl once again. The old man had gone back to eating.

"I'm going to tell you one last time. Get some help before it's too late. You're going to die in the next year or two at this rate."

"Good! And I don't need help from nobody…"

"Then why are you alone and homeless?"

"You're one to talk! How many times ya been married? Four?! Snubbin' your nose at me... geesh! You go through women like underwear! I've heard about you, boy. You're the same now as you were so long ago. I've watched you in action your entire life! Real piece of work you are!" Lazarist kept his back turned towards the man as he prepared his coffee, biding his time, begging for patience. "Can't blame ya!" The old man laughed, a loud, cackling witch-like giggle. "I guess you're like your old man back in the day, huh? A real ladies man. I had my share... I had my share... Where do ya think you get your looks from, huh?"

"I look like my mother."

"You don't have my nose or mouth... but you've got my eyes! That got the ladies all the time. Your mother has hazel eyes, not blue! That blue is from me, ya cock sucker. You're tall... got your height from me, too. You're taller than me, but it's my side of the family that's got the height. I'm the reason you're a success... that fuckin' club of yours..." He could hear the old man tapping his fingers against the table. "It should be condemned... if they really knew who was fuckin' runnin' the show. All of that drinkin', partyin' 'nd shit. Nice lookin' place, though."

His father burst out laughing again, the sound oddly out of place. "You're a demon, ya know that, Laz? A mean son of a bitch... heartless. So different from how you were as a kid... so different..."

Lazarist slowly turned around, holding his empty coffee cup. His fist shook ever so slightly as he glared at his father.

"You're a paranoid schizophrenic, Dad with bipolar disorder. I am not going to fuckin' argue with you, of all people, about your perceived reality of my life and my choices. You—"

"Choices? We all gotta make choices, don't we, boy? All this money… this beautiful house! All those sexy women you bang night after night, the cars, the boats, ya got it all. And still, your life is fucked up!" The man pointed a finger at him and laughed so loud, it echoed. That laugh—Lazarist loathed it with a passion. "I can see it in your eyes, Laz. You're miserable. You've got amazing business sense. You're charming as a feather in a cap but when it comes to everything else, you're an idiot! I *begged* you not to follow in my footsteps, boy! I know I was a bad example, so I told ya to not to do it! I told you not to get married the first fuckin' time, the second time, the third and the fourth!"

"I've only been married twice."

Confusion danced in the old man's eyes. His smile slowly faded before he turned away abruptly to stare down into the bowl of soup.

"Yeah, you're an idiot… 'cause of the women… You always wore your heart on your sleeve, you know that, Laz?" his father said mildly, his smile now sad. He stirred the remaining bit of broth with his spoon. "You were such a softie as a kid… fallin' in love just like that." Dad shook his head as he snapped his fingers.

"Every time I turned around, you had a new girl-friend. Your mother said as long as you kept your grades up and didn't get anybody pregnant, she'd leave ya alone. Well, you made honor roll a lot, played basketball, had your friends... and the girls. Everything was fine I suppose, right? Then, you went and got hurt... found out what it was like to be used..." Darkness grew in the old man's eyes. "I know that feelin'... you say I wasn't around sometimes, but we talked. You must not remember... but we did. Ya called me all upset. A sixteen-year-old kid, all tore up over some chick. She'd dumped ya, and you'd thought the world was ending! I think you met that other broad soon after that..."

"Charity... my ex-wife," Lazarist stated dryly.

"And that ended badly and now you *hate* women. You hate your mom, too, don't ya?"

"What?" Lazarist wrinkled his nose in confusion. "I don't hate my mother. I love her. Don't you ever say that to me again. Don't try to put your own bullshit on me. My mother is a good person and you know it, especially after all the bullshit she put up with because of you!" Lazarist gripped the mug a bit tighter, his patience almost on E. "Nobody is perfect, but she did the best she could do, especially after the situation you left 'er in!"

"That bitch left *me*! We woulda still been married!"

"She had no choice!" Lazarist slammed the empty mug on the counter and tossed up his hands. "You were constantly working! You were cheating on her, too! You became ill and wouldn't get help. Why in the hell was she supposed to stick around after all of that? And that's just the shit that we know about. Rumor has it Eliza and I have a brother out there somewhere. What kinda mess is that?!"

"I was a good father most of the time! What I did behind closed doors was none of your goddamn business!"

"Good father?" Lazarist spun in a circle and laughed. "You gotta be kiddin' me. You felt like us havin' a nice house and being in a nice school was enough. You weren't even there!"

"Ahhhh! Here we go with this shit again, but you tell me I am livin' in the past! Hypocrite!"

"I just have one question. Where the fuck were you, Dad?! Don't even answer, okay?" Lazarist held up one finger and vigorously shook his head.

"I'm sick 'nd tired of you." The old man fell back in the chair as if he'd been working night and day.

"You're sick and tired of *me*?" Lazarist pointed at himself. "That's rich! I'm sick 'nd tired of you comin' over here any fuckin' time that you please, talkin' shit to me, taking your ritualistic shower and fuckin' up my bathroom with all of your filth! I'm tired of watching you sit there eating, pickin' a stupid ass fight with me, then runnin' off! Coward! In a minute, we'll be hittin' that good ol' repeat button for next week, and the week after that. Play it again, Sam! Rerun after rerun is my life with you, ya know? You're a fuckin' joke with no goddamn punchline. I don't hate Mom, I hate *you*…"

"You wanna talk about the past, fine! We'll talk about it. I took care of you, Laz, before the divorce. You and your mother and sister didn't want for nothin'!"

"You were a hell of a provider, but where were you for my father-dad breakfasts in kindergarten? Where were you for my first-grade play of the 'Three Little Pigs?' I played the wolf! I was so excited and I looked out in that audience and you weren't there!"

"Of course you played the wolf..." Dad laughed sarcastically. "How befitting... That was the future bein' told if I ever saw it!"

Lazarist ignored him.

"How about basketball games, huh?! Ya never took me to a Yankees baseball game and you knew I always wanted to go. You'd promised and never delivered. I hate that! I hate when people make promises 'nd break em, especially to a kid! That's the worst thing you can do to somebody!"

"I can think of worse..."

"Uncle George ended up havin' to do that father-son stuff... time 'nd time again. I didn't want to go with Uncle George. I wanted to go with *you*! What about Eliza's ballet performances, huh? What about when she got married? I had to walk 'er down the aisle. Even though she'd written you off, I knew deep down she was hoping you'd at least show up. You never did."

"Your sister told me right beforehand she wished I was dead!"

"That was *after* you called 'er a bitch for callin' you out on your bullshit! Where were you when I was goin' through all those changes, huh?! I've been very successful businesswise in part due to your teachings, I'll give you that. I'll give credit where credit is due. But my personal life?" Lazarist shrugged. "You're right… totally fucked! And you know what, David? You're also holding some of the responsibility. You played your hand."

"Oh, so I'm to blame now for you bein' unhappy?! You're forty fuckin' years old!"

"Yes, you're definitely part of the equation and my age has little to do with it. You share some of the fuckin' blame! Now take it! My first divorce was one of the worst times in my life. Instead of you bein' there for me, you blamed me when it imploded, sayin' I was too nice to her, kicked me when I was down. You even laughed! Told me she wasn't good enough for me anyway. What kinda… what kinda man are you? Jesus. What kinda father does that?"

Lazarist shook his head, closed his eyes, and took a deep breath. Dad looked lost in the conversation, maybe not even understanding or hearing a word he uttered. Sometimes, David would have periods of lucidity; other times, he couldn't be quite sure. It was the nature of his illness. But Lazarist was going to keep trying nevertheless. He had to.

"You were a kid. Ya had no business gettin' married at twenty-one."

"Yes, I was probably too young to get married, but I loved Charity and you knew it!"

"She was half Spanish, part Italian and Black. It was doomed from the start."

"What?! What does her race have anything to do with it?"

"Those people don't have the same values we do.

You shoulda never been wit' her in the first place," the man stated listlessly. Lazarist rolled his eyes, ignoring the fool. He refused to engage with him about Charity... it was useless. Dad's racism was an underlying, subdued theme as of late. It seemed the sicker he got, the more pronounced it became. It was something that reared its ugly head in times of his mania or high anxiety. He'd never heard his father speak disparagingly of other ethnicities though, until he was an adult. So odd.

"A man takes care of home, Laz. That's what it boils down to."

"Home is just a house if you're not in it..."

"Yeah." He shrugged nonchalantly. "I coulda done more, but it's hard out here, all right? I had a wife and two kids. You've never been married for longer than two years and as far as I know, you're not a father, so what tha hell do you know?! Must be easy to judge me when you weren't in my shoes and lemme tell ya." The man pointed his judgmental finger in his direction. "Your mother was no angel! She cheated, too. I should get a DNA test for your sister. Eliza and I look nothin' alike."

"She looks like Mom, too! Are you serious?! Don't sit there and tell me how I need to walk a mile in your shoes before judging you because that mile would lead me places I never wanna go. Because of you, we lost everything. We were poor when Mom had to leave you! We went from bein' upper middle class to being evicted time and again until Mom got on her feet, went to school part time and worked two damn jobs just to take care of us!"

"Oh, how sad! Your mother had to get up off her ass and work like the rest of America. Cry me a fuckin' river."

"She busted her ass while you, on the other hand, got a powerful attorney to ensure that you didn't have to pay her a dime! Un-fuckin'-believable! What about your kids, huh?! The hell with us, right? You didn't even want to pay child support, then when you decided you did want a relationship with us, Eliza said 'fuck you', but I was still hopin' that we could have something, because I missed you!"

"Well I'm here now, fucker!" the old man roared.

"And here I am, your fuckin' son! After all of these years, I still hate you!" He couldn't stand how his voice trembled. "After all these years, I still love you, too!" Hot, angry tears welled up in his eyes. He hated this… he hated this more than anything else in life. "Your mind is fuckin' gone, Dad. You used to be brilliant! You were one of the best attorneys in New York!"

"Still am…" the old man stated calmly as he looked down at his runover, dirty sneakers.

"You say that you're here with me, but you're not. Yeah, physically you are, but that's it, Dad. You're not really here and ya know why? It's because you won't get help. You're livin' on the goddamn streets by choice! Who does that? You're not a drunk. You're not on drugs. You're fuckin' insane and worst of all, if you took your medicine, went to your shrink, got into that program we talked about last year, you could be back at the top of your game. You could even go back to practicing law. But no…"

Lazarist shook his head. "You just refuse to be controlled, right? Gotta be a rebel at all costs! People are tryna help you, man! You walked in here smellin' like shit! The man I knew wouldn't have been caught dead without a good shave, clean body and hair combed perfectly, an expensive coat and shoes… you were what I looked up to! Even after you rejected me to go work and chase after more women, I still loved ya! Jesus Christ, Dad! You were an attractive, intelligent, highly respected, proud Jewish man who was open minded and loving, according to Mom. And then, you got sick. Something triggered it, something bad happened… things changed. When the marriage was over, you showed your true colors though, David. You acted like you didn't want to have shit to do with us… your own kids!"

"And what a pompous prick you grew up to be…"

"FUCK YOU! Ya hear me?!" He jetted his finger in the bastard's direction as his entire body heated like an oven. "Fuck you, David!"

The man burst from his chair, the damn thing toppling over as his eyes grew big and wild. He stormed up to Lazarist, bringing his face close to his.

"I WAS SICK!"

"Ya still are!" Lazarist yelled back. "Funny how you only admit it when you're losing an argument and let me make something clear to you, dear ol' Dad. I don't hate you for bein' sick! I hate you for not caring that you're sick and doin' somethin' about it! All of this coulda been avoided." He waved his arm. "If you'd done what you were supposed to, you'd *still* be married to Mom because we all know that you're still in love with her and want 'er back. You'd still have your career and your family. But noooo! Ya just couldn't and wouldn't do it. Had to do it *your* way. Well, your way sucks."

"I loved your mom, boy… I did. That's true," Dad stated calmly as he took a few rocky steps back. "Your mother was pregnant with you before we got married. Did you know that?" Lazarist tried hard to remain unchanged, unmoved. He *hadn't* known that… but it hardly altered the facts. "That's the only reason why I married 'er so fast. We got married right after she found out. You were late bein' born, so she was able to play it off. Nobody knew. My mother didn't like 'er." The old man smiled… an evil, horrid smile. Dad got joy out of saying those words. "Your mother wasn't a virtuous woman. Your mother, son, was a whore. She'd fucked so many men before I came along… A fuckin' prostitute. I saved her from herself."

"Get tha fuck outta my house!"

Lazarist snatched the old man's arm and shoved him towards the exit. Walking a few steps behind him, he made sure the old man didn't try anything. Lazarist unlocked the front door and swung it open as his heart beat frantically in his chest. He knew none of this would matter in a few hours. Dad would either forget the conversation even occurred, or he'd chalk it up as some dream he'd had, versus the actual reality. And then, the fucker would be back… taking a shower, eating food, complaining and saying shit that made absolutely no sense.

The old man slowly walked over the threshold. When his father turned back in his direction, his mouth opened to say something, Lazarist slammed the door in his face. He stood there for a long while, fisting and unfisting his hand. The hot, angry tears filled his eyes once again. Not just because Dad was a wreck, a walking mess… but because Dad had been right.

He *had* become in some ways like him, hardened, disconnected, hating the world, not trusting people—*especially* women… and he hadn't even seen it coming…

LEO

CHAPTER SEVEN

Wishes for a Horizontal Dance...

H E LEANED AGAINST the wall and stared at her.

It was obvious Sky didn't realize he was there. She hadn't even looked his way as her body swayed and gyrated in ways that didn't seem humanly possible. He couldn't believe her talent. She was fucking amazing…

The woman moved to Beyoncé's 'Partition' like she was made of liquid vapor and flowing ink. Donning black leggings and a gray crop top that read, 'FOREVER YOUNG', she reminded him of a doll he wanted to play with… to risk it all to own and possess. Long black hair swung to the left then to the right as she contorted her body in insanely beautiful ways, doing a dance routine all by her lonesome. Minute after minute passed, and he was certain he'd been holding his breath for when he exhaled, it felt like a great relief. And then their eyes met. She smiled at him, walked over to the stereo, and cut it off, bringing the song to a shocking and abrupt end. He left the wall and approached her, slowly clapping his hands.

"You're good… you're *really* good." He slid his hands in his pockets and sized her up, scanning her from head to toe. How he wanted to flick his tongue along her collar bone and taste her salty sweat, to lap it up like a spring in the middle of the concrete jungle he called home.

"You say that like you're surprised," she said with a wink, then went to grab a bright red hand towel, her feet moving gracefully on white sneakers. Dabbing her face and neck, she then chugged down the rest of her Gatorade, emptying the bottle.

"No, you've read me wrong. I'm not the least bit surprised, but seeing is believing. And now," he said, grinning, "I'm a believer."

"So, what are you doing here at my church?" She chuckled, playing with his words, twisting them around in a whole new way. Perhaps this was in fact her church, and she worshiped the ground she walked on… "I thought we were supposed to hook up later tonight?" Her gaze landed on a clock hanging on a wall.

"You're correct but you see, I was in the neighborhood. I wanted to see you… you know, an animal in her natural habitat. I am a bit surprised actually though." His brow rose as he looked towards a wall of windows, nothing but the city stretching beyond them before he set his eyes back on her.

The sun will begin setting soon…

"Surprised about what?" She set the drink down and began to stretch her arms and legs. His cock jumped; the damn thing grew teeth and tried to get at her like some chained up, gunpowder fed Pitbull…

"I thought you'd be giving a lesson or somethin'. I was surprised to see ya alone, actually."

"Well, you must've just missed them. Class ended about twenty minutes ago." He nodded in understanding. "So how'd the five day exercise go? Today was the last day and I promised you I wouldn't ask you until it was all said and done. I'm ready for the full report. Wow me!"

She stood before him, head cocked to the side, looking beautiful.

"The 'life-work' balance?" He smiled and shrugged. "It was okay… It was a struggle, ya know? I hate to admit it, but the first day I failed. I ended up hopping on the computer and taking care of some emails and makin' some calls after hours. The second day, I left work on time, but when I got home I went through some unpaid invoices and signed off on some contracts, then updated some spreadsheets. The third day, I left a little late, but I got on the computer and just chilled. I drank a little wine, snacked, vegged out…" Thoughts of his father arriving and spoiling everything came into his mind, but he shoved those aside. "The fourth day was perfect. Left on time, turned off my phone, watched a couple of my favorite movies of all time."

"And what are they?"

"'Fight Club' and 'The Dark Knight.'"

She laughed.

"Figures… and what about the fifth day?"

She drew closer to him and looked up into his eyes, the attraction growing impossibly stronger at that moment. When he wrapped his arm around her waist, she startled, but didn't push him away. He slowly bent down to kiss her and soon her stiffened muscles relaxed in his grip. After a while, he turned her loose, cupped the back of her neck, and kissed her nose...

She felt delicate, yet sturdy. He liked how her skin and bones melded together, the contortion of her strong muscles...

I bet she looks absolutely gorgeous spread-eagled... or her fucking legs behind her head as I plow her pussy with all of my might. Shhiiiit... I can't fucking wait to find out...

"The fifth day I went out with some pals of mine. My friend, Tobias, was having a barbeque. But, uh, I'll be honest... when I got back home I—"

"Worked," she finished his sentence, then sauntered away towards the other side of the dance floor. She bounced with each step, as if warming up to perform.

"Yeah." He dropped his head, nodded then smiled. "I did. I was actually becoming more stressed knowing that things were piling up, that I wasn't there physically as much. Some of my employees fucked shit up while I was away... See, that is why I micromanage so much. We're all human, ya know? But somethin' always goes wrong when I'm not there. It became a problem. Still working on it, trying to find that happy medium, but I'm a little closer to my goal I think. It takes practice I imagine. Old habits die hard."

"Well, it seems you didn't do so bad for your first

try… It became easier over time, am I right?"

She gyrated her hips back and forth as if hearing a song in her head. It was driving him crazy. Every move she made gave him a rock hard erection. She was an erotic muse in the flesh, without even knowing it.

"It did. So, uh, as I told you…" He glanced down at his watch. "I figured we could go out for dinner. Are you hungry?" She dramatically rolled her eyes, let her head fall back, then walked back in his direction.

"Famished." He smiled at her theatrics… cute. "Well, I was thinkin' of something a bit more upscale than the bookstore." She grinned and jetted out her tongue in a playful sort of way.

Watch out now. I can put that thing to good use…

"So, I'd like to take you somewhere nice tonight. I'll let cha get home and get changed, then come get you, all right?"

"All right… still 6:30 P.M., right?" She bent down and grabbed a bag, drawing his eyes to her ass. It looked like a pumpkin perfectly placed inside her pants.

"Yes, still 6:30 P.M."

"You know what, it's already late so why don't you just take me home, let me get cleaned up and changed, and we can leave from there?"

He tried to curtail a grin, but to no avail. Being at her place, near a bed, could prove to be optimal indeed…

Yes, baby… let the big, bad wolf inside your house. I'll be gentle, I promise…

"Sure, yeah. That's sounds good." He removed his phone from his pocket and typed in the name of the restaurant in order to get the number. "This place can get pretty packed so I better call and make a reservation."

"Oh, where are we going?" She stood straight and hooked the bag over her shoulder.

"Victor's Café on 52nd Street."

"I've seen that place time and time again but never had dinner there. When you said upscale, you weren't kidding." She smiled, looking as if she were genuinely impressed.

Minutes later, he'd secured them a table and they were inside his car, heading over to her apartment. It was a balmy late summer evening and the scent of grilled meats and exhaust fumes filled the air. He turned on his stereo to drown out the honking cars, and the sounds of Sam Smith's, 'Too Good at Goodbyes' came on the air.

"I really like this song." She began to hum along and slowly rock back and forth in her seat to the rhythm. "It's sad… but pretty. Sam Smith is so talented. I have all of his music."

"You like him, huh? I haven't heard too much by him… but I've heard enough."

"Well, I guess they wouldn't really play a lot of him at your nightclub. He does ballads mostly… love songs. The songs you've heard, did you like them?"

"He's all right."

The woman snatched herself away from him as if he had some horrendous, life-threatening, contagious, airborne disease, and eyed him up and down as if he were out of his mind. At this, he burst out laughing.

"What?" he tossed up his hands. "I mean, he seems a little overrated if ya ask me."

"You just lost points… a lot of 'em. Boy, bye!" She turned away and waved her hand dismissively.

"What in the hell?" He cackled. "Shit, I was just bein' honest. You want me to be honest, right?"

"Always." She smirked, eyeing him up and down once again.

"I usually am. Like, for instance, I find it sexily odd that after all that dancing and sweat, I don't smell any body odor coming from you… and I find it strange how, as feminine as you come across, you seem to have no qualms standing practically soaking wet in front of me… Well, not anymore, but you were."

…And you will be soon again. Soaking. Fucking. Wet. I'm gonna make that pussy rival a goddamn waterfall…

"Hmmm, does that bother you?" Her brow arched.

"Not in the least. It's just different is all." He sat straight, proud of himself, as if he'd scored the points back that he lost in the whole Sham Sam scandal.

"You're not honest all the time… Nobody is."

"I'm honest *enough*." He ran his hand along his chin and stole a glance at her from the corner of his eye.

"Well, you've already failed my honesty test. Not sure how you can redeem yourself in that department at this point." She looked straight ahead, crossed her legs, and sat there like her word was bond.

"What honesty test?"

Like I give uh shit! Women and this bullshit… just fuckin' silly. Here we go with the games women like to play… for fuck's sake.

"I told you the banana nut bread at the bookstore was delicious. Actually, it is the worst bread ever baked... ever known to mankind." He couldn't help but smile. The woman was a true piece of work. "It's the only bakery item that I've ever purchased from them that wasn't absolutely delicious. It's almost like some cruel joke. Instead of you tellin' me you didn't like it, you played it off, said it was amazing so that you could get into my good graces... then into my pants. I know your type, Lazarist."

"Ohhhh my!!!" He said in mock fright. "I'm sooooo scared! She knows my type, everyone! Run for your lives! You know my type, huh? Well goody goody gumdrops for *you*. Got every guy pegged, right?" He burst out laughing. "Well shit, baby, you missed your calling. You should drop the dance shoes and go work for the FBI. They're always in need of a few good paranoid women."

"Say what you will, but that whole entire lie, simple as it was, told me right then and there that you were full of shit."

"Hmmm, I see. And why would I choose to lie to you about such a thing, Ms. Jordan?"

"Because you're a control freak. You *have* to have things go a certain way. You also are a brat and you're bossy."

"And yet here you fuckin' are... in my car with me. Imagine that!" He cackled.

The woman rolled her eyes.

"Admit it. You must have your way, especially when

it comes to women. You'll say *any*thing to get what you want... just like *most* guys but with you, you don't give up."

"Okay sweet cakes, two things we need to address, aiight?" He held up two fingers. "First of all, toots, how do you know I don't like my banana nut bread dry 'nd crusty as fuck, huh? For all you know, it may have been... may have been so delicious to me that I was speechless!" He had to catch himself as he tried to control a burst of laughter. The memory of the horrible food was enough to make him want to gag again, perhaps even throw up in his mouth a bit.

The woman shook her head, then laughed.

"You're ridiculous..."

He reached over and took her hand.

"But you like me, don't you?" She grimaced and wrinkled her nose, turning away like she didn't want to answer. "You do!" He burst out laughing. "I know you do. All right, back on track though. Point *numero dos*! Secondly, my dear, how do you know that I didn't know what you were doin', huh?"

She snatched her hand away and turned the radio up. He turned it back down, then cut it off completely as he pulled up to her apartment building. She reached for the door, but he grabbed her arm and turned her back towards him.

"I'm serious... answer me. How do you know I didn't already realize that you were on to me, so at that point, I was just tossin' everything in the ring and tryna see what would stick?"

"That's the oldest trick in the book. You get caught with your hand in the cookie jar and you try to mind fuck a woman, tell her that, 'Oh baby!' Her voice dropped a few octaves as she attempted to imitate a man's tone. 'I knew you were standin' there, honey! I was just playin' with you.'"

He smiled ever so slightly, then nodded.

"Okay, but I did know you thought it was disgusting and I went through with my scheme anyway. Do you know how I knew?"

"That's ridiculous."

"You already called me ridiculous…"

"Well, it bears repeating. Now how? This bullshit outta be good," she said with a smug smile.

"Because you hadn't touched yours…" Her smile slowly faded. "If you thought it was all that fuckin' wonderful, you would have at least pinched off a bit. Now see, in the art of mindfuckology and manipulation 101, which I am King of the Jungle at," he said, pointing at himself proudly. "You have to play the part, baby… and play it well. First thing first, young grasshopper, never ever let 'em see you sweat. You save that shit for behind closed doors… curtain call. You don't become king by wailin' and bein' all soft and squishy in the middle."

"Oh… so you're cut off from your feelings and are unemotional? A genuine sociopath! Goodie! Look, Dad! I've hit the jackpot! This guy here is emotionally bankrupt. Whoopee!"

She thrust her arms in the air and cheered, causing

him to burst out laughing.

"No… just the opposite, actually, honey." He reached for her, leaned close, and traced his lips along the side of her warm, soft face, then planted a kiss along her jawbone. "I'm *too* emotional. I've just learned how to hide that shit really fuckin' well. It's a matter of survival. There's a difference. The second rule you need to learn, sweetie, is that you can't play a player. You're not in my league."

"Who the hell do you think you are?" She chuckled, though he could see she was hardly amused.

"I'm serious, and I don't mean this in a bad way, okay? But you don't play dirty. I do. I'm well-seasoned in filth. Now, I'll give you your props, you're a worthy opponent." He waved his finger close to her face. "But you still need training and even then, you'll never be like me. Guys like me are born, not just made. If you want to beat someone at their own game, you have to *become* him and learn all the rules. And since it would be unbecoming for you to *ever* turn into a motherfucker like me," he said, his eyes narrowing on her, "I suggest you not even try. Stay sweet. Now, let's get you inside, cleaned up, and ready to enjoy a delicious dinner."

She chewed on her inner jaw, probably a million strange thoughts whirling inside that mind of hers. When she reached for the door and started to step out, he gently bopped her ass. She turned in his direction like a woman on the verge of annihilation.

"Dear Royal Pain in the Ass, Sir Jerk of Brooklyn, Duke of Hurl, Emperor of King-sized Fuckery, let that be your *first* and *last* time touching my behind without permission. You got it?" She winked.

"Very creative names you rattled off," he said, emitting a loud yawn. "Tell me you didn't like it, though? Tell me you didn't enjoy the way my hand spanked your firm, yet oh so beautiful, rump? I'm just markin' you for later is all... letting you know that's *all* mine."

"Has anyone ever told you what a dick you are?" She smiled sweetly.

"All the time... Speakin' of coveted cocks, I have one too. You wanna see it? It's known as the eighth wonder of the world."

"Save that classy talk for your funeral. Is your stage name Count Cockula, by chance? Because you just keep biting my nerves and you sure have a lot of balls..."

She slammed the door, but he heard her chuckle again as she reached inside her purse and pull out her keys. He turned off his car and joined her, eager to be around her a bit longer... and a bit longer after that.

She's a challenge... she's feisty... I like this shit. I could get used to this...

After a few minutes, they were inside her apartment. The place smelled like Cuban food and roses. What a strange yet pleasing combination.

"Okay, make yourself comfortable." She handed him the remote control and pointed to the couch. "Just give me, uh, twenty minutes or so and I should be ready."

He nodded, finding it curious that she didn't believe she needed at least an hour to get all gussied up. As she hightailed it out of sight, she called out, "Help yourself to anything in the refrigerator should you get thirsty!"

He then heard a door open and close… then lock. He smiled at that. Precautions…

In his mind right then, he clicked and locked, too… He heard the sound of his front door opening and closing, locking then unlocking, time and time again when David, his father, would arrive at his doorstep. Sometimes the man would show up disheveled; other times, overly joyous, practically singing. Sometimes, his eyes would be bloodshot as if he'd been up for forty-eight hours straight, but the demented bastard was always pushing… prodding… poking the lion. David knew just what to say to make him fall apart inside, to turn and twist him on and off, jab the knife in that much deeper.

'You're a ladies' man… soft-hearted… never should've married her… you hate your mother… your mother was a whore… your mother was a whore… your mother was a whore…'

He headed to the large couch and slumped down onto it, holding the remote. He tossed it from one hand to the other as his heart thumped with pain, his brain full of stuff that felt like blades scraping the inside of his secret, private thoughts, carving them out like pumpkin seeds and casting the gummy mess onto the floor. He squeezed the remote a time or two, like a stress toy, but instead of turning on the television, he just sat there and closed his eyes. Cocking his head to the side, he sniffed the air…

I love the fucking smell of her apartment… The odor of cooked food, comfort food no doubt, despite her obviously watching her weight for work 'nd all. I can smell her, too... her distinct scent...

He groaned as he heard the muted sound of her singing against the crash of the water pouring from her shower. Strangely, he didn't picture her naked at that moment; he pictured her happy... and that turned him on.

What would make her happier?

He wasn't certain, but he definitely wished to find out.

She thinks fast on her feet... she's smart... and the way she dances, wow...

He slowly got to his feet and began to look around, but was careful to not touch. In the corner he spotted a small bookcase filled with novels, some worn out and dogeared, others looking practically brand new. Thrusting his hand in his pocket, he took note that she appeared to really like the color blue, which appeared all over the place—on her throw pillows, in the abstract art on the walls, and on several containers that were various shades of blue, some with plants growing from them, others with odds and ends inside. He kept nosing around, here and there. Her coffee table had an assortment of magazines on it. He sat back down and thumbed through them.

Let's see... She reads Essence, Dance USA, People, Wired, Architectural Digest, and Time magazine...

She has eclectic tastes in reading periodicals, I see... good, good... well rounded...

He spotted an ink pen without the cap on the table, too. That sort of thing grated his nerves.

His attention was drawn to three small milk crates bursting with hats and ballcaps in particular—everything from the typical black and white New York Yankees fare to the diamond studded denim ones with intricate and cool designs. He stretched his legs and ran his hand slowly up and down his thigh as he heard the water shut off. Closing his eyes, he imagined her stepping out, one foot at a time.

I bet her bathroom is mostly blue…

Seashells? Nah. Nautical? Hmmm… probably not, doesn't seem the type. She seems like she'd have ballet slippers or something like that as decorations in there. Maybe theater masks, shit like that… Mermaids? It's a possibility.

He envisioned it all in his mind, painting various scenarios. The walls of her bathroom, the scent of the soap… He could envision her feet rubbing along an ultra-soft floor matt.

It's probably fuzzy. Chicks seemed to like fuzzy shit…

A door opened and he quickly craned his neck in the direction of the sound. He hoped to get a peek of something forbidden… unclothed toasty, brown flesh for his eyes to feast upon. A blur dressed in a dark red robe raced past and entered another door, then locked it at the speed of light. The prey was pretty fucking fast…

Flashes of him waiting patiently for his first ex-wife to come out for prom when they were mere kids entered his mind. He'd been excited to go out and spend the day and night with his beautiful girlfriend. They'd been looking forward to it for weeks. Mom had splurged on a limo and all on his behalf. He'd been in love then, helplessly in love...

He'd never had that sort of feeling ever again...

He hung his head, missing that pure, sweet love... the kind he felt when he knew he'd do anything for someone, even die if he had to.

His love for Mimi had been different—so very different. It was nothing like what he'd had for Charity, not even close. With Charity, there was nothing she could do to make him stop loving her, not even when she'd stopped loving *him*...

He rubbed his hands together, feeling a bit uncomfortable as those old thoughts resurfaced. He hadn't thought about prom in over a decade or more; yet, it had been one of the happiest times in his life.

Funny how something fresh and new could trigger something old and heartbreaking.

But instead of running away from it, hiding it from the world, he sat there and forced himself to *feel*...

LEO

CHAPTER EIGHT

A Lion Protects the Pride...

I T HAD BECOME quite apparent to Lazarist that had Sky been wearing a paper bag, she'd look just as lovely. She knew what looked good on her, though, and how to piece an outfit together. As they sat inside Victor's Café on 52nd street, one of his favorite spots to enjoy Cuban fare, he took that opportunity to delve deeper into all that was Sky, and for him, actions and observations were always the best teachers. He kept studying her as he placed his napkin across his lap. Her clothing interested him... it told him so much. The outfit didn't look terribly expensive. But why would it have to be?

This woman sweated and beat the air with her feet and hands for a living. She was in great shape—she worked hard for that.

She sat there reviewing the menu, wearing flowy black pants that gathered at the waist and a black sheer top layered with a lacey camisole. Around her neck hung a simple silver chain with an opal pendant and she'd brushed her hair in an updo, a sloppy ponytail which exposed matching opal earrings.

But her smell was what kept him inching closer... and closer. Whatever she'd sprayed on herself, he liked it. Resting his hand against hers, he smirked as she looked at his pinky finger touching her thumb. Her eyes soon drifted back to the menu... but she didn't move her hand away.

He leaned in closer, so close that when he breathed, a loose strand of her hair swayed a bit.

"May I ask what you're wearing? Your perfume..."

When she turned to him, it seemed like the perfect distance to initiate a kiss. He stared into two dark brown pools of light... Damn, was she beautiful...

"Bombshell by Victoria's Secret."

"Victoria's Secret?" He nodded in approval. "I have a thing for certain scents. A woman who smells nice *really* turns me on."

"Well, I'll make sure to wear Le Horse Manure next time. If you were any closer to me right now I'd be pregnant... now scoot back."

They smiled at one another and he burst out laughing. Readjusting himself, he picked up his menu, though he already knew what he wanted. Her. But she wasn't an option right then...

Soon, my little pussy cat... soon... soon... soon...

Moments later, the waiter came to give a run-down of the specials and explained to the newbie, Sky, that side dishes were à la carte. The place was particularly crowded that evening, though he wasn't terribly surprised—their food was pure perfection.

"Let's seeeee." She teetered about in her chair as if she were dancing. He found it rather cute and amusing. "I'll haaaaave… you know what? Just let me get the fritas cubanas and I don't need any wine… just water with lemon is fine."

She closed the menu and handed it back to the waiter.

"And you, sir? Nice to see you again by the way." The man smiled.

"Nice to see you, too!" Lazarist was darn right alarmed. Never in his entire life had he taken a woman out and she picked the least expensive thing on the menu, as well as refused a drink *and* his advances all within the same hour. Should this turn him on or should he question her sanity? He'd heard of such things but figured they were fables, something written in books of make-believe.

"Mr. Zander?"

"Ahhh, yes, sorry… I will get the assorted appetizers for two. I want her to try that." He didn't miss the smirk that crept across her pretty little face. "Then you can bring out my usual, the ten-ounce black angus skirt steak with plantains."

"Ahhh yes, the churrasco con chimichurri."

"Yes. I would also like a glass of your Cuba Libre."

"Of course."

The waiter took their menus and left, but Lazarist was still whirling from the realization that Sky was no ordinary woman.

"So, tell me more about yourself…" He clasped his hands together. "I know how you got started dancing, I know you grew up in Brooklyn, too, but tell me—what do you like to do in your downtime besides read and go out clubbing with your friends?"

"Well." She cocked her head to the side. "I actually don't like to go out clubbing too much. I do it just because." She shrugged. "You know, to sometimes be with the group. I pretty much got that all out of my system in my twenties." He nodded in understanding. "I enjoyed school as a kid. I was a bit of a nerd, I guess you could say."

When she smiled that time, her nose wrinkled in a real cutesy sort of way.

"My father was big on that. He only had a high school education and worked really hard to support me."

"Oh… you're an only child?"

"Yeah. It was just, uh…" She ran her fingers over the tablecloth. "Just me and him…" His brow arched in interest, and he hoped she'd continue and explain where the woman who gave birth to her was. "My mom and dad split up when I was real young…" She lowered her head for a spell. "She had, uh… a bit of a drug problem."

His heart hurt for her. He cared. He hated that she had that experience, but perhaps, like so many things in his own life, it had only made her stronger.

"So, you know, it was just me and Dad… and he's a really good father but boy, was he overprotective!" She grinned and traced the rim of her glass with the tip of her finger.

"I can imagine! Shit, if I had a daughter I would probably be, too… especially one as beautiful as you." The color of her cheeks deepened in a blush. She looked adorable. "I'm serious… I bet that was tough on him. Single fathers don't get enough credit, but look! He obviously did an excellent job."

"I'd have to agree." She smiled wider then, exposing all her pretty teeth. "He worked a couple of jobs to make sure we had a decent place to stay and he was always on me about schoolwork and he encouraged my dancing… rarely missed a recital. He did it all. Cooked, cleaned, everything. Um, you mentioned if you were a father you might be overly protective, too. I already told you that I don't have any children, and obviously, based on your statement, you don't either but you know, you stated you'd been married a couple of times, so why is that?"

He licked his lower lip real slow as he gazed into her eyes, not quite convinced he wanted to delve in that topic yet—not because he was opposed to such discussions, but damn it, he was trying to build a special rapport with her. If he went the honesty route, she might be offended. If he told a lie, she might be offended, too. He sat there and tossed around his options for a bit…

Never had dating been so complicated for him. This woman forced him to think outside of the box, to change up his typical patterns of courting behavior. She demanded more right out of the gate. He detested her for that, because now, this became a game... a game he was determined to win.

"I just don't want any. I don't think I'd make a good father." There. He'd said it. The cold, honest truth.

Silence. It killed him that she said nothing. She just stared at him. She wasn't frowning, she wasn't smiling, she just sat there, looking through him...

"Okay. I respect that." And that was it.

But, he knew better; it wasn't over. It was just over for *now*...

Soon, their food began to arrive and it smelled and looked wonderful, but there was one problem...

"Hey, Mateo!" Lazarist raised his arm and snapped his fingers before the guy got too far away. The waiter paused, his brows lifted in surprise, and he returned.

"Yes, Mr. Zander, is there something you need?"

"Yeah, baby, the right food! This isn't ours."

Lazarist chuckled as he pointed to the plates.

"Oh no! I'm so sorry. I'm so, so sorry."

"It's all right..."

But as the waiter went to pick the plates up, one of them slipped out of his hand and almost landed in Sky's lap. She leapt back, averting the disaster as the plate slammed to the ground and broke in a million pieces. Food scattered everywhere and all eyes landed on poor Mateo. The guy was now turning red, sweating, his short, choppy black hair in full focus as he dropped to his knees, scrambling to get all the pieces up. All of a sudden, Lazarist heard screaming and yelling in Spanish. A big guy came barreling out of the back, pointing his finger at him and letting him have it.

"What are you doing?! This is the third time today, Mateo! We're sorry, sir! This guy should be fired! You coulda hurt somebody!"

The man continued to scream and holler at the guy, and it simply became too much.

"Ahhh, come on, man. Relax. Geez." Lazarist tossed up his hands real easy like.

I know how the restaurant business is. This isn't how you handle this. This isn't how you talk to employees. You take their ass in the back and speak to them in private.

He wasn't fluent in Spanish, but he understood enough of it to realize that poor Mateo was being ripped to shreds, just like the pulled pork over a bed of rice. Sky jumped to the floor in her pretty, flowy pants and helped the man, scooping up food, vegetables, everything, and tossing it on the tray. Mateo scrambled about, crying silently.

"No, it's okay, ma'am. I have it. Please... sit down and enjoy your meal."

"It's fine," she said. "Could have happened to any-one. It's no big deal."

Look at her... wow... that's beautiful.

Lazarist stood to his feet and pointed to the big guy.

"Hey, my friend, can I talk to ya ova here, please?"

The man looked a bit confused but obliged as they journeyed over to the kitchen. Lazarist rested his hand on his shoulder.

"Look, I know you're probably the head chef, and you spend a lot of time and energy makin' sure this food is perfect. And it *is* perfect; you're the best. But lemme tell you something." He pointed in his face. "Your ass needs to stay back here and let management take care of this, all right?"

"Sir, you do not understand! This guy has done this several times this week. We've had to pay dry cleaning bills. We've gotten bad reviews on Yelp and Trip Advisor because he is messing up the—"

"People fuck up and it is a domino effect, I get it. I run a restaurant, too, all right? Now sure, I have people who take care of a lot of the stuff but sometimes things go awry, and I own it. I know it is stressful, and I know you're fed up, but you did *far* more damage goin' off on that kid like that in front of all of these customers than he did by leaving the wrong order and then droppin' it on the floor. I've been comin' here a while, all right? I've had this guy as my waiter more times than I can count. He has never done this before… so maybe…" Lazarist shrugged. "He's havin' a real shitty week. Maybe his fuckin' grandma is sick, or he flunked a college exam. Who tha fuck knows? Just give him the benefit of the doubt. Maybe offer him a couple of paid days off, especially if he's been real good and loyal, comin' in on time and all of that up until now."

The chef looked at him sternly, like he wanted to rebuff his words, but then he nodded.

"Yes… okay… you may be right."

"Good. Now go on in there and keep cookin' these

fabulous meals."

The chef smiled, though still obviously angry, and retreated to the kitchen. When Lazarist turned around, he gasped. There stood Sky, her arms crossed, and bits of rice and smashed vegetables all over her knees.

"You're a good man. Still an asshole, but a good man," she told him.

He burst out laughing as she spun around and walked away, taking her seat back at the table.

The next hour was spent with his stomach hurting. He hadn't laughed this hard in what seemed like forever. The woman was rattling off story after story of some of the trouble she used to get into with her friends. Boy, were they wild. He loved it. He convinced her to share a bottle of wine with him, and that loosened her up a bit. He was no longer focused on fucking her... Okay, who was he kidding? Yes, he was, but it wasn't the only thought in his mind. He just didn't want to leave. He wanted to sit there until that restaurant closed and they got kicked out. He wanted to hear her talk all damn night, let her share her life with him. She'd even leaned over and kissed his cheek a couple of times., and he liked that... No, he loved it. He'd held her hand and inter-twined their fingers. He was feeling things... strange, hurtful things that he didn't want to feel...

This was the type of woman he could get into, the kind that grabbed his attention and held it for dear life.

"Well." She sighed. The place had pretty much cleared out. "I better get going."

"Awww, so soon?" He grinned.

"Yeah, I have to teach a class in the morning."

"All right, let me take care of this bill."

"I had a wonderful time tonight by the way, Lazarist." She leaned over again and this time, gave him a sweet peck on his lips.

"So did I." They stared at one another for a spell, then he waved Mateo over. The man still looked beaten down by the world.

"Are you now ready for the check, sir?"

"Pull up a chair." The guy looked downright confused.

"Uh, I'm on the clock. I can't really—"

"Mateo, sit down. Sixty seconds isn't gonna get you fired."

The boy swallowed, dragged a chair from a nearby empty table, and sat down, looking super uncomfortable.

"You made a mistake. You shouldn't have been spoken to that way. Now, I know you don't know me, but I've observed you for a long time. You are always on your A game. What's goin' on, man? The chef back there said this has been hard week for you."

Mateo lowered his head and remained silent. "Man, I'm serious. Ya think 'cause you don't really know me, that I don't care? Look, there are people in my life I've known practically since birth that I don't give two fucks about. You know why? Because they have no idea how to treat anybody. They're maggots. Then there are people like you, people who bust their ass in this business, work like dogs and take home a little check, tryna make ends meet. I wasn't always wealthy, Mateo. I know what it's like to struggle. I went from wealth to havin' nothin', and then earned it for myself later on in life. Nothing is fair in this life; we get what we get. I haven't seen you drop a fuckin' spoon, let alone an entire plate and mess up orders. What's happening?"

He leaned forward and cradled his hand around the man's neck. When Mateo looked back up, he was crying.

"Ohhh," Sky cooed. "Don't cry!" She handed him her napkin. The boy quickly took it and dabbed his face.

"Thank you… uh, it's been real hard, ya know? I don't have no place to live… I leave here and I sleep on the streets. The shelters are full. Me and my brother, I'm raisin' him, we got evicted. I was only $42 dollars short but couldn't come up with the rest of the money in time. I'm tired, man! That's why I keep messin' up. I'm fuckin' exhausted! I can't tell anybody here any of this or they'll start treatin' me funny… start thinking I can't cut it. I think I've got enough in tips tonight though to get us a hotel room. I'm just tryna get back on my feet. I've never been homeless before. It's crazy, yo!"

Lazarist snatched out his wallet without a moment of hesitation and plucked out all the cash he had on him…

"Take that. It's about $235.00. Get your and your brother's asses in a hotel tonight, get some dinner, get clean, and for God's sake, get some sleep. Tomorrow, come by my club, The Fallen Angel, 'round 4:00 P.M. Tell Heathen, that's one of the bouncers there, that you've got an appointment with me. Here's what we're gonna do."

He shoved the cash in the boy's hand and curled his fingers around it. "You're gonna interview as a waiter for my restaurant." Mateo's eyes grew wide. "You have to, because I already know this place is gonna fire you tomorrow. I could see it in the head chef's eyes. They feel like you've cost them too much. It's a business decision for them; it's not personal, but that's how these things work."

Mateo dropped his head again, this time crying even harder, but nodded in understanding. "Shit…" he murmured, choked up.

"I am then going to give you a pay advance once you get through the screening and training process, because we both know you're gonna do well. Take that pay advance, use it to get you and your brother a decent apartment. In the interim, because it's gonna take you a couple of weeks to get trained and straightened out, I am going to take care of you stayin' at a hotel for those two weeks. Then, I want you to tell me how much your rent is once you get the new place and I will pay the first few months' rent and utilities so you can save up a little and get on your feet."

"Nooo! I can't take that from you! That's too much, Mr. Zander."

"It's not too much, all right? I want you on my team. We're helpin' one another out. I need an extra waiter, and that's the truth. Business has improved. I want you to have a good job and I want you to be able to come to a boss you can talk to. Doesn't mean I'll never curse your ass out." Mateo laughed sadly. "But I can promise you this much, I'll *never* humiliate you like that in front of people, all right?"

"I can't thank you enough!"

"Thank me by showin' up tomorrow. On time." Lazarist shook his finger in the boy's face, then got to his feet. Sky and Mateo followed suit.

"I'll be there! I'll be there early, Mr. Zander. I promise!"

Mateo practically leapt into his arms and hugged him. Lazarist stiffened up, not used to men doing such things. He smiled weakly, his gaze drifting to Sky who was hiding a smile behind her hand. At last, he placed his credit card inside the bill and Mateo took it away, then brought the receipt back.

On it, Lazarist wrote out a $100.00 tip and a note that read:

Mateo,

No matter what punches life throws, fight back.
It's much harder for a problem to get the best of you,
if you always stand with your dukes up. Don't you
EVER give up on yourself again.

Lazarist Zander — Mr. Boss

LEO

CHAPTER NINE

The Lion's Lair...

"SOMETIMES I FEEL like I'm floating deep inside of my destiny..." she murmured the words, whispering a tapestry of mental musical notes into a silky web of fantasies.

Spreading her arms wide like a bird, she flitted about like streaks of light reflecting off mirrored walls. Like swaying ribbons tied around cherry blossom tree branches, she rose and fell to the beat of her heart. Sky closed her eyes and drifted there for just a magical spell or two. It was the strangest sensation, wishing to do the strangest of things while standing in that man's beautiful home in Brooklyn. She danced here, there, and everywhere, and as she did, she looked around in awe. She'd dreamed of owning a home like this. A place with enough room to have a child grow from eight to eighty and still not have discovered all the corners to the moon.

In the backyard she could envision a yapping white dog with a rhinestone and burgundy leather collar named Sweet Disaster or perhaps Cupcake. And within those walls... those big, wide walls, perhaps even a small indoor swimming pool, an indoor oasis for two. Like Heaven on Earth, a place where one could delight in a sensuous whisper or the sigh of wood bending beneath the pressure of praying knees. Her eyes welled with happy tears as she treaded lightly on her delusions, but she was careful... She did it all before he returned with their wine. What a pity it would be for him to catch her in a strange trance, to find out she was blissfully out of her fucking mind...

In love.

She was falling for the fucker. Despite his over the top behavior at times, Lazarist was an absolute sweet-heart. He would give a perfect stranger the shirt off his back. His generosity ran deep, and she wondered how someone who on one hand could be so harsh, a bit sexist and verbally combative could then be so loving and write a $10,000 check without blinking an eye. He took her all sorts of places, but more importantly, they discussed every topic under the sun. The bastard was smart... and dare she say it, wise beyond his years. In some ways, he was quite childlike, delighting in the silliest of things like whoopee cushions and childish spider pranks to which she'd been on the unfortunate receiving end.

But in other ways, he was one of the most sensuous, romantic and sexy men she'd ever encountered. He would text her 'good morning' and 'good night' like clockwork. He showered her with elaborate flower spreads and unique gifts. She couldn't even count how many flowers she'd received at the studio alone, and he'd given her a cocktail ring, too. That gift was too much... so expensive. She'd tried to give it back, but he refused.

He was wining and dining her, delighting her with his conversation. He'd made time for her in a schedule that was jam packed from dusk to dawn. For someone so busy, and she knew that he was, it was amazing all the time and energy he was investing in her... and they hadn't even made love yet.

Love... there is that word again.

She hated what was happening to her...

That's what drives me crazy about this! If he doesn't want more, then why is he doing all of this? He is acting like he is my man... I even think he was jealous when he came to take me for lunch last week and saw me dancing at the studio with Antonio...

Men like Lazarist had women at their disposal. Everywhere he turned, there were plentiful options. Women threw themselves at him – and she'd yet to be on a date with the guy without noticing a lady or two giving her the evil eye... probably someone he'd fucked and dumped. She didn't dare bring up the topic—then he'd know she was interested in such notions with him and he could play her to the hilt. He'd already given her rule number one: Never let them see you sweat. She'd spoken to Scarlet the previous evening.

The woman warned her once more to keep her legs closed and trust her intuition. She'd had excessive pow wows with Scarlet about this very thing and they both agreed that she must continue playing the game. Thus far, it had been working. She realized she could find out way more about him through his interactions with others, so she listened to everything he stated regarding such relationships quite carefully. They talked about their families and friends – and he was rather open, discussing in great lengths his mother, his sister, his ten million friends, but he never mentioned his father... Strange. She didn't bring it up either, but made a mental note of it. His communication style was crystal clear – if he wanted her to know something, he openly discussed it in great detail. This part of his life was inexplicably missing. Something was amiss...

She plopped down for a spell onto the couch, bursting with nervous energy. Oddly enough, he'd left her all alone like an abandoned child... trusted her to not be a grab and dash type of hoodrat she was certain he'd heard about, though he was too polite to utter such.

Well, she'd take that back. He wasn't polite at all. He just gave her a little more credit than that. Meanwhile, he still craved the sweetness between her legs and though he was brash and bold, he was no fool. Lazarist stopped short of crossing that thin line between pushing the envelope and distasteful.

Nahhh, he doesn't look at me and see that... I'd have picked up on it by now. The White guys that fetishize about getting in between some silky, Black thighs... he's not one of them.

Perhaps he saw her as some sort of princess, and she had to admit, he often looked at her like she was. She'd catch him stealing glances from his bright blue eyes, the dark, thick brows arching above them making him look dangerous and sexy. That intense stare of his… oh boy was it intimidating. She loved every damn psychotic minute of it. It was cute and predatory all at once.

She'd been enjoying him, perhaps too much. He had the gift of gab. Their conversations ranged from the nonsensical to the political and thought provoking. They'd fallen asleep on the phone…

And he'd asked to make love to her twice since they'd known one another, but her response was always, 'Too soon…' He never kept pushing, but he was becoming more and more desperate as they spent so much time together.

The sexy text messages… and yes, the childish dick pic he'd sent her last night…

She didn't respond to it, let him dangle in the wind. She wouldn't admit it to him and stroke that already huge ego of his, but damn it, he had the right to be cocky about such a specimen. It was big and thick, a motherfucker that promised to make a woman walk funny for at least a week, so she sure 'nuff hit save and kept that bad boy for safekeeping and posterity. Grinning like a naughty little girl, she chewed softly on her fingernail.

I like him so damn much. This is going to end in disaster if I'm not careful. What have I gotten myself into?

Lazarist walked about with his chest poked out, moving like a storm. His voice was full of animation, passion and depth, like a volcano in mid-eruption. He watched her like a hunter... and when he'd kiss her, he'd breathe slow and hard. The warm air from his flared nostrils would tickle her neck as he wrapped his big, strong arms around her body and pull her in a tight embrace. He loved with every limb of his body, consumed her with the slightest touch. She could feel his heartbeat as she'd rest her head against his broad chest, and he smelled good. He smelled *so* damn good, like warm vanilla bean libido... *libido?... negro... hero...* She toyed with the words in her head, constructing them in strange ways as her thoughts played tricks on her.

Back to negro... Black... ebony... African American... Yes, and then some. All kinds of people congregated at his club. It was a true free for all, a Rainbow Coalition for the masses.

She knew he was someone worth running from, to protect herself from indeed, but she couldn't quite turn away from this man who was larger than life. No matter where she'd turn, he'd still be right there, and she couldn't escape. Where he ended, she began. Where she began, he continued. He'd been a lover since birth; he had the type of natural sexiness that ran in the veins like heroin... She'd seen it first at the club on the evening they met when she watched his tattooed fingers slowly twirl a white, shiny cane. Back and forth he twisted the thing, like a magician doing tricks, putting her in a trance.

They had an instant attraction—one that made her

feel so out of sorts, she couldn't wrap her mind around it. The chemistry was intense, and yet she held back time and time again, playing Scarlet's warning in her head. It literally hurt to keep denying him. She'd sweat, her pussy would throb with need, but she played that poker face like she was the Las Vegas champion. In the end, she believed it would be worth it.

She heeded the advice because something within her wanted him...

Wanted him so... damn... badly.

She refused to be easy, and she soon realized that Scarlet was right, regardless of her motives for cockblocking. If you wanted a lion like Lazarist, you had to make him chase you. No wild beast like him appreciated a meal that fell into their lap. They relished the ones that had them jumping, yelling, falling about and putting in the work.

Make him chase you. Make him chase you to the edge of the forest... but not beyond. Make him sweat, make him so hungry that by the time you offer yourself on a plate, he eats everything in sight, then licks the plate clean!

Her mind delved in and out of possibilities, remembering how her friends would always tell her she overthought everything, that it was downright nerve-wracking. They'd warn her that not everything needed to be evaluated.

But this matter did. She didn't want to be one of many... a trophy on his shelf, a plaque on his wall, a notch in his belt.

Maybe he's got a thing for Black women...

That idea piqued her interest. Was she the first or one-hundredth Black woman he'd dated, courted, dragged home like a caveman and eagerly tasted the fruits of the forbidden? Was she a new temptress or his Saturday night special? The sort he preyed upon as he pried dark, rich thighs apart before eagerly dipping his hard White cock deep into the ocean of an African American Goddess of his choice. Fetish? Fantasy? Or his Forever? She shook the notion out of her mind and reflected further on the matter that caused her to be alone in the vast house in the first place...

Trust.

Lazarist had invited her over and upon her arrival, when he asked what she liked to drink and he didn't have it, he insisted on going out and purchasing the Cabernet Sauvignon Washington State wine. It wasn't anything expensive; most places sold it for less than twenty bucks but he stated it was the principle of the matter. Despite her protests, her telling him it wasn't that big of a deal, he insisted and promised to be right back as soon as possible. So, he headed off to the liquor store down the road, leaving her in the company of a roaring fire, a bowl of fresh cherries, select cut deli meats, premium cheeses, and a small chocolate fountain that flowed over various pieces of fruits and marshmallows. Music played from the speakers and she danced to it. Bob Marley... Bruno Mars... The Beatles... She danced and danced and danced. What a wonderland he dwelled in.

Look at this damn house...

She burst out laughing as she spun so fast around and around, she grew dizzy.

She'd never seen such a sight... When they talked about big ballers, Lazarist Zander was it, the epitome of such a man.

Suddenly, she heard the front door being opened. With a gasp, she plopped back down on the couch, crossed her legs, uncrossed them, then crossed them back. She tried to look natural, as if she hadn't just been stuffing her face with chocolate covered pineapple wedges, assorted cheeses from Europe, and flapping her wings like a headless chicken.

"Heeeey, babe! I got it!" His smile was as bright as the sun as he drew near, a wrinkled brown paper bag in hand with the neck of the bottle visible. High hopes lingered in his eyes, the lustful kind for certain, but she couldn't help a smile.

"Thank you so much. You're sweet."

He walked past her and placed the wine in the refrigerator, then came to sit next to her on the couch. His smile slowly faded.

"What? What's wrong?"

A look of concern danced in his eyes. He gently leaned over and traced her lips with the tip of his tongue.

"You've been busy at the fountain, I see..." He smiled, then kissed her cheek. "You had chocolate all over your mouth."

Her lips crimped in a smile. Hooking his thumb under her chin, he tilted her mouth to his and pressed his lips to hers. With their hands they explored one another slowly... so slowly. The sound of fabric rising while their eyelids were falling closed made her weak in the knees. He was hard and warm, his presence overwhelming.

Don't fight this any longer... trust yourself. Is this it?

Yes...it's time, Sky, you know it's time. End the chase, let him finally have you...

Within the blink of an eye his shirt was removed, exposing an extensive canvas of intricate designs in royal blues, emerald greens, candy apple red, and midnight blacks. From the neck up, he looked like Wall Street; from the shoulders down, he was a wild man, a modern-day Tarzan in the flesh. He wanted what he wanted when he wanted it. No ifs, ands, or buts about it.

Spoiled like curdled cow's milk left in the sun, generous like God to Adam and Eve, strong like fathers who openly love their sons, calculating like jewelry thieves who escaped capture time and time again, smart like runaway slaves who'd steal away into the night. Lazarist was all of these things and more, but with beautiful tattoos one must remember what they truly are: scars.

She traced his shoulders and looked up into his eyes while he lowered her onto the couch. They tore into each other like feverish children ripping apart wrapping paper on Christmas morning. Clothing covered the ground like piles of leaves until their needy bodies leaned into one another like blades of grass beneath a stone. Smothered with lust, begging to never breathe again... She danced inside of him, drawn into the intensity of his eyes as he kissed all up and down her neck. He was hungry... oh so hungry...

He'd worked up a healthy appetite for she'd made him suffer... but he wanted the pain. She wasn't for sure, but she was pretty damn convinced that the man craved it like the agony of the needle pricking the flesh and flooding the sensitive layers of skin with copious ink for the first time. She sighed when she felt his nature rubbing against her panties. Shocked at the thickness, a part of her tightened up, scared and excited like the prey that she was.

"I've waited for this for so long... so... fucking ... long. Come on, baby!" Running his fingers through her hair, he mouthed the words, his voice husky, desperate, and filled with intense need.

He kicked her legs open and grinded against her zone, and she shuddered when she felt his hand sneak in between the fabric of her underwear and her flesh, stretching the lace and sliding his finger inside her wet pussy.

"Ohhhh... shit." Her eyes fluttered as he began to work it in and out of her, nice and slow, his eyes not leaving her for a moment.

She bucked her hips to his movements, and he kept dry humping her the whole way, instigating a sensual rivalry within her, working her up into a frenzy. The couch sighed beneath them, and she tried to stay afloat but slipped and slid about as he built up his pace, a torturous slow climb.

"Your pussy is sooo tight, baby. It's gripping my finger, squeezing it. Those sweet walls of yours are hugging my finger like they're in love with it..."

He slid another within her, and the thickness made her coo and wiggle all the more. She was soon crowned with a pillow behind her head, although it took a minute for her to realize he'd done it, slipped it beneath her nice and easy. The tickle of sweat collected against her brow as he slid another pillow beneath her ass, then slowly... so very slowly, slipped his fingers out of her zone.

Sitting on his haunches between her thighs, he looked lustfully at her, then placed his thumb against her clit, circling back and forth. She rocked her hips nice and slow to his movements, an orgasm soon knocking on her pelvic floor door. A hard, heavy hand cupped her right breast and gave it a squeeze. She shuddered when the wet heat from his mouth engulfed the left breast, sucking through the lacey sky-blue fabric.

He teased and pleased her, toyed with her, made her want him to the point of frustration. He kissed all the way down her body, slowly... slowly... slowly... until he reached her valley. With one hand resting against her upper stomach, and his other hand opening up her floral folds, she hissed when the soft, wet muscle from his mouth slipped and slid, sucked and flicked against her clit. She gripped his shoulders, holding on as she wrapped her legs around him, crisscrossing her ankles against his lower back.

While she mouthed things, shuddered and grinded, he slid his hand beneath her back and plucked her from the couch, lifting her into the air. Lavishing her pussy like a gourmet meal, the wet slurps of his mouth made her shake and tremble against his working lips. Holding her close, arm wrapped around her waist, he ate her pussy like the beast that he was, and made his way up his steps to his bedroom. Before they even reached there, she was raining into his mouth… a wet mess of a woman, her screams echoing through his home.

A cold sensation brushed against her back as he pressed her against something hard, soon discovering it was his master suite bedroom door. The thing swung open, and he brought her into the darkness, with only the bits of light from the outside that shone through his window lighting the way.

"Baby… your desires are my command. The sky is the limit. It's time you give me what I want, and I'm *definitely* going to get my lion's share…"

LEO

CHAPTER TEN

The Lion's Roar...

H E WAS NEVER going to admit it.

Besides, pride was involved, and pride was his forte. He kept a stockpile of it on top of a stockpile, and had some in his pantry for an emergency. It was just that serious...

But Lazarist had begun to question his pussy hunting skills. Had he lost his touch? He'd whipped out so many tricks on the broad, he had no choice but to start recycling his tried and true ideas. She was blowing his ego to kingdom come, instead of his dick.

They'd been to the movies, out dancing, he'd taken her to restaurants with names that neither could even pronounce! He had to admit, they laughed way more than they argued, but when a disagreement did arise, it was due to one thing and one thing only. He was hard on the outside but sensitive on the inside, and she was the polar opposite. Perhaps, they could balance one another out.

Days had matured to weeks and he still hadn't cornered sweet little Sky at the back of his cave. Once there, she'd have no choice but to succumb. Once he had her on his property, he had courtside advantage, but she still was making things difficult, toying with him, playing with his emotions. They'd even made out in his car where he finger-fucked the living daylights out of her, but then she gathered herself, pulled her dress down, and waved goodbye, as if the shit had never happened. He was beside himself with roaring rage. How *dare* she!

He'd resolved himself to the fact that she was going to stretch this out until he burst. Yet, although patience was wearing thin and he was growing weary and frustrated, he kept all this frustration bottled up. It was important to him that he remain, at least on the outside, calm, cool, and collected. Internally, however, it was a completely different story. Every time he found himself alone, he'd been jacking off to her photos practically non-stop.

Worst of all, he had no desire to race out and get his 'fix' from some random stranger, or even a tried and true fuckbuddy who'd be ready at the drop of a dime. No. His desires were strictly fixated on her, and he despised her for it. She was the sweet morsel that kept hiding and ducking, slipping away in the night. He'd race after her; she'd smell him coming and flee. He'd creep up on her; she'd roll around under the brush and obscure herself from sight. But now… the wait was finally over…

He flicked on the light in his bedroom, illuminating it just enough so he could take in the details of her beautiful body, and the bra and panties, which looked so good against her skin.

Of course they're blue… she loves blue… how sweet…

I'll beat that pussy black and blue… that's what I'll do!

He salivated at her image, feeling frisky as fuck.

He was in no hurry though. This meal needed to be savored.

"I'll be right back." He pointed to his bathroom door and she nodded.

After discarding the remainder of his clothing, he combed his hair just right. After all, he was very particular about his mane, and even in the throes of passion he wanted to look his best. Spritzing on a bit more cologne, he looked himself over in the bathroom mirror, then reached for the mouthwash and gave a vigorous swish. Once he exited the bathroom, he found her beautifully deposited in the center of his king sized bed, the sheets pulled up to her now fully exposed breasts. She'd already done the honors…

She's no prude. This should be interesting…

He swallowed hard at the sight of her dark nipples poking out. Such lovely breasts she had… he guesstimated they were about a 38C or so, give or take. Rather large for her small frame but to him, they made her even more beautiful. He traced his lower lip with his tongue as he walked to a large curio cabinet in the corner of his bedroom. Opening it, he pulled out two red black cherry scented candles, lit them, and set them on a small desk.

Next, he reached for his white cane that lay against the wall.

"What are you going to do with that? I'm not into being beaten, so if that's what you had in mind you can—"

And then she burst out laughing. He'd hooked it on his erect cock and made the cane swing back and forth as he performed dick tricks.

"Oh my God! You are so childish, Lazarist!"

Her laughter soothed him; he loved hearing the beautiful woman make that sound. Placing the cane back against the wall, he turned on his television and selected several musical playlists he'd created on his computer and uploaded to his TV saved network. This one was titled, 'For Sky.' He could feel her eyes upon him and hear her shifting under the covers.

"Oh, I see you were ready. You really think you're slick! Unfortunately, you kinda are."

He dropped his head and gave a light laugh.

"Of course I was ready. I'm *always* ready, baby."

The first song began to play, 'When We' by Tank and Trey Songz. He liked how she cocked her head to the side, her lips twisted as if to say, 'Really?' He slowly rubbed his hands together and smiled at her, then mouthed the lyrics of the first line.

"When we… fuuuck." He bit into his lower lip, his eyes narrowing on her.

Step by slow step, he approached her, sat on the side of the bed, and opened a clear drawer in his nightstand that looked like two large ice cubes on top of each other. All of his bedroom furniture was black or clear. He enjoyed the contrast, found it masculine, and it appealed to him in ways he couldn't quite describe. After selecting a box of unopened Magnum condoms, a bottle of lube, a small black hand towel and a larger one, he leaned in and kissed her earlobe.

"Rise up, baby. Lift your ass." He flipped the sheets off her and tapped her hip, giving direction. He noticed the small sliver of black hair along her pussy and her pierced navel—so enticing. When she lifted her ass up, he slid the large towel under her, spread it out, and pushed her back down with one hand, while turning on the fireplace with the other. The sudden orange rays of light from the hearth shone in her eyes. Crawling on all fours, he settled between her thighs, noting how her breathing got more intense as her excitement mounted. Propping her head against the headboard, her lips ever so slightly parted, she looked more irresistible than ever. The music flowed, the candles shimmered, and he couldn't wait to savor her flavor...

"Are you ready?" he asked with a smirk.

She nodded, but seemed in a trance. He liked that... she was overwhelmed. Puuuurfect.

He reached under her to cup her soft ass cheeks, giving a gentle squeeze. Layering kisses all over her stomach and inner thighs, he went slow and easy, teasing, torturing her with the sweetest of pecks. Every now and again he looked up into her eyes, and they fluttered far too many times to count. She looked... sexually frustrated. He grinned.

Pleased that the tables had turned in the correct direction, Lazarist took his seat at the throne, once again in his rightful place—the driver's seat, and her ass was riding shotgun. He slid his hands further up and around the curves to her hips and thighs. He closed his eyes and inhaled deep...

She smells delectable... clean... feminine... but like a pussy should. No flowery douches and powders... just the true scent of a woman... beautiful.

Nudging her pussy lips open with a wiggle of his chin, he caught her eye. Her stomach rose and fell faster and faster and he could see her visibly swallow. With hooded eyes, he rested the tip of his tongue against her slit as if to begin... but didn't move.

She wiggled to the left, then to the right, trying to force his mouth to glide and slide against her flora, as if trying to make a machine on the fritz finally work. He chuckled at her frustration and her helplessness intrigued him.

"You're an ass!" she hissed, the prey now begging to be devoured.

Ohhh, look how far we've fallen from the Sky...

"Ask me for it..." He slid his tongue slowly up and down her zone, then pulled away.

Her eyes widened as she fisted the sheets, then she swallowed once more.

"Eat it."

"Use those nasty words you used when you cursed me out the other day... say the word... say *pussy*."

"Eat... eat my pussy," she uttered, her chest now rising even faster.

"Say please..."

If looks could kill…

Her eyes turned to slits as she grimaced.

"Please!"

"That didn't sound too convincing, Sky. Tell me how much you want me to eat your fuckin' pussy! Make me want to tongue fuck this shit until I swallow every drop of you! Now fuckin' say it!"

"Eat my pussy you conceited, controlling, egotistical son of a bitch!" At that, he roughly pulled her to him, and her scream echoed over the music as he jammed his tongue deep inside her. "FUCK! Oh God! Oh my God!"

Working his tongue like a cyclone, he strummed her clit with his thumb. He lifted her higher in the air, jamming her ass against his chest, and shoved her legs over his shoulders, draping them along his back like a cape. Her wetness was unmistakable… a lake grew between her thighs and threatened to transform into an all-out ocean.

"I love the way you ride my fuckin' face! Fuck my face, sexy!"

Working his tongue all over her petals, he slowed down, then sped up, then put his skills on repeat. She gyrated her hips and moaned against him, her orgasm building and building… Oh, how beautifully helpless she looked, caught in his snare. Gently placing her back down on the towel, he reached into the drawer once again and retrieved a vibrating ring and slid it along his tongue. She looked at him in bewilderment.

"What's that?"

Without answering, he lay on his stomach between

her thighs, lifted her legs once again, and ran his tongue all over her clit.

"OH, SHIT!" She screamed as her back arched. Sliding his finger inside her, he gently tongue fucked her while massaging and teasing her clit. The vibration from the ring buzzed against his mouth and his working fingers. She cursed and cried out. The woman was done for...

Target: Identified. Disarmed. Captured.

In no time flat, she was trembling and screaming, her orgasm tearing her apart. Clear nectar poured out of her pussy so fast, he could barely keep up. The big lion had bagged his prey, and soon they'd be mating...

He slid the vibrator ring off his tongue and set it on the nightstand, then pulled her up into his arms and French kissed her. Cradling her body with his, arms wrapped around her, he sat cross-legged, his thighs framing her temple. She rested her forehead on his shoulder, still quivering, still beautifully falling apart. Slipping his hand between them, he played gently with her slick zone. His digits were immediately baptized for she was still cumming, her pussy pooling all over the place with only the towel to soak it up.

She ran trembling hands through his mane, and he so relished her touch, uncaring that she messed it up. All he wanted was to feel her, to let go and immerse himself in the world of this amazing woman. Nothing else mattered but how she made him feel. How she challenged everything he believed by just being there.

By being there ... with him.

When she pulled away, he grabbed her wrist and kissed her fingers... and drowned into her achingly beautiful brown eyes, feeling as if he could look right inside her soul. That pure, kind, compassionate and deep soul.

Something was happening, a deep connection forming, and there was no turning back. He'd waited for her for what felt like an eternity, but it wasn't just that; it shocked him to think the sex had become far less important than he could ever have imagined. Their bodies and minds seemed to crave one another in the worst way, but it was their souls that were running the show.

Running his hands up and down her back, he soothed her while simultaneously rocking his body against hers, pushing her hips up and down, forcing her to slide against his nature. He sighed, his breath hitching when she snaked her arm between them and reached for his cock, as if aiming to get a cookie in a jar. A delicate, soft hand slid against the slick slit, moistened with precum from his excitement. His heart beat all the faster when she shifted and lay on her stomach before him, as if he were some altar, and caressed his cock with both hands. She looked up at him and smiled.

"Ohhhh, baby... your dick is so big... Let me taste it..."

Before he could respond, she slipped him inside her mouth, her cheeks stretched wide as she took half of him in. He shuddered at her oral prowess, the slurping of her mouth, and the way she looked up at him. That could have well been the beginning of his undoing.

Rocking his pelvis faster, he fucked her mouth and gripped the back of her head, forcing her further down. She cradled his balls with one hand and gripped the base of his dick with the other, her mouth receiving more of him as her head bobbed in record speed.

"Your cock tastes so good, Lazarist! Mmmm!" she cried, popping him out of her mouth for a moment. Hot wetness soon consumed him again as she relentlessly delivered premium dome.

He gasped for air and his eyes rolled as his nuts tightened in her palm. She rose for a spell, the head of his cock resting on her lower lip, throbbing with need. He smiled down at her and yanked her up in his arms, causing her to squeal with delight. Placing her on her back, he reached over and snatched a condom out the box. After tearing it open and placing the ripped wrapper on the nightstand, he sheathed himself. Travelling down her body, he administered butterfly kisses and let his hand roam all along the beautiful canvas of her flesh. Flicking his tongue against her swollen pussy, she sighed until she became complete putty in his hands. He finished her off with a kiss along her hipbone, then travelled back up until he reached her lips and crushed them in a kiss. Long, warm arms wrapped around his torso as he gripped his dick and guided the generous head inside her soft walls. She moaned loudly, her mouth open, a look of angst and delight spread across her face.

"Oh baby… please… please!"

Her brows bunched as an expression of weakness crossed her face. He dispensed more of his hungry dick within her tight, wet walls, needing to feel her more than she could ever know. He paused, then slammed hard inside of her and remained still for several moments.

Let that shit sink in...

She gaped, speechless... and he said nothing either, for no words were needed. Lying on top of her, he pressed her down with his weight as he administered slow, deep thrusts.

"Oh my God..." Her voice quaked like she was on the verge of tears, but he knew that was just the slow, wonderful climb to another climax. He was hellbent on making her cum not once, but *several* times, for anything less would be uncivilized.

"Do you like how I feel inside you, baby?" He kissed her neck as he rocked his cock in and out of her.

"Yes!" She ran her fingers all along his shoulders, as if needing to ensure he stayed put.

Don't worry, baby... I'm not going any damn where...

He slowly slid out of her, and her neediness showed in her eyes.

"Get off the bed and stand at the foot of it, facing it, okay?"

She quickly did as he instructed. He stood directly behind her, his groin pressed into her ass. He then pushed her down onto the bed, making her bend at the waist, until her face and breasts hit the sheets. Grasping her by the hips, he guided himself within her. This time, he wouldn't pause. She would feel every fucking inch of him…

"You're going to split me open… doggie style with a cock that big? Shit! And you fuck *hard*… so damn hard." She shook in his arms and reached back, grabbing his wrist. Her shiny, black painted nails sank in his flesh, the sting feeling oh so good.

"Never that, sweetheart. Now why would I want to destroy someone I want to keep fucking until the end of time, huh? I need this pussy to stay in tip top shape! I'm gonna rough it up… bring it to the brink of death… but I promise not to kill it… just *yet*."

He groaned as he pumped hard within her. Her screams were shrill and intoxicating. Her pleasure drove him mad!

I knew she was a fucking screamer! All that backtalk and lip… Damn, it feels good to be so right…

"And when it cums to doggie style, baby, I'm *always* right behind you!"

She screamed out impossibly louder when he thrust hard and deep, wrapping his arms around her waist and squeezing tight. She dug deeper into his arms, drawing blood, drawing moans, drawing life and death and all the stars in the sky. He lifted her legs off the ground and put them in position like a wheel barrel. Shallow thrusts, followed by scream-inducing ones, sent her on her way…

Beautiful, toned, brown thighs coated with her elixir. She dripped all over the place, making a gorgeous mess of his sheets and floor.

"Such disarray, baby! So untidy! I love it! I wanted

you so bad, Sky! So fucking bad! You feel better than I ever imagined… God, your pussy is addictive! You *owe* me!"

He went harder within her and groaned, sweat dribbling down his hairy tattoo-covered chest. The slapping of his nuts against her swollen cunt echoed over the music of Bando Jonez as he sang, 'Sex You'.

Placing her flat against the bed, her legs sticking straight out, he lay on top of her back, pressing her down, ensuring she had nowhere to go and nowhere to hide. Wrapping one hand around her waist, he guided himself deeper within, pumping against her beautiful ass. She sighed and purred like a kitten, then her right leg shook as if she were having a seizure.

"You were sooooo worth the wait, sweetness…"

His chest tightened; his world spun slower until time stood still. Her cumming was the most beautiful thing he'd ever seen. He needed her orgasm as much as she did for he was hooked on giving her pleasure… he needed her to want him… want him *completely*. He held his own orgasm at bay, though it was becoming increasingly harder.

The woman's scent was all over him, hanging in the air, lovely and feminine, turning him on in the most primitive of ways. She looked over her shoulder at him, her eyes glossy with want. Slowly caressing her back with his fingertips, he curled his hand beneath her and strummed her clitoris as he pumped his cock inside her light and easy. The woman shivered like he'd never seen before, cumming again and again. When she'd settled, he carted her back onto the center of the bed. Lying down, they both breathed hard, staring at the ceiling for a spell. He looked over at her.

"Ride me... get on top."

He gripped his dick and caressed it, waiting for her to mount him, perform magic and make him disappear. Without hesitation, she straddled him, cooing and gritting her teeth along the way as she slowly slid down his eager cock.

He prided himself on his dick—the ladies loved it and best of all, he knew how to use the damn thing. He needed to hear Sky moan, scream, yell, bite, draw blood from his flesh... He needed to feel the juice from her pussy trickle down his eager cock and see her fat, glistening pussy lips as he drove himself in and out of her. He needed to smell her store bought fragrance and pussy scent blend together and create its own unique, lovely perfume. He needed to feel her heartbeat against his as he soothed her from another earth-shattering orgasm... one he was more than proud to claim as the reason for her smile and joyful emotions.

She began to slowly bounce up and down on him, her palms resting on his chest as she looked into his eyes. He pumped up while she came down, their feelings for one another releasing, turning loose...

In that moment, his hardness became limber... his coldness warmed... his distance disappeared. The way she looked at him brought his inner beast to its goddamn knees...

Old feelings raced within him, ones he hadn't felt in

so long, he'd almost convinced himself they were a mere fluke or had been a figment of his imagination…

Love.

The look in her eyes was unmistakable. Women had fallen in love with him despite him warning them not to, though he rarely loved them back. That hadn't always been the case; he used to fall in love with the greatest of ease… but he needed to protect himself, so he built a wall. He often had strong connections, enjoyment, and liked quite a few of his lovers very much, but love? That had only been reserved for a limited number in his adult years. He'd turned the emotion off… controlled it… because it was too damn painful to just be himself. The real him didn't get the respect he deserved. The real him was taken advantage of and lied to. No, it had to stop. He had to reign like the lion he was and come down hard… He had to earn his stripes and rule with a hard, sharpened claw. But it was draining… so taxing… never how he truly wished to be…

He loved too hard, naturally…

He'd give his life for the undeserving, too willingly…

If you never fall in love, you can't get hurt… but if I never fall in love again, I STILL hurt…

Could he finally break his own rules and allow this woman into his heart?

He groaned, a loud sound, then gripped her tight and rolled her onto her stomach to mount her from behind.

He was now an enraged animal, a monster looking down at the one who caused him so much distress, he couldn't see straight! She captivated him, made him change his way of thinking on several issues. She'd danced into his life, ripped his heart out of his chest, then teased him. She'd won…

She'd stolen the crown right off his fucking head while he was wide awake…

She screamed out as he jammed his cock deep inside her, his anger at her and love for her blending together…

"LAZARIST! SHIT!" She reached behind herself, pressing her hand onto his thigh, trying to push him away.

"Fuck! I *hate* what you've made me do, Sky! You told me this was going to happen, but I didn't believe you. I didn't want this… but it's too late!"

She gave him a strange look, then let her hand fall away as he manhandled her pussy. Her body violently jerked beneath him.

"Baby, I'm in love with you…" The words escaped his lips before he could stop himself.

He exploded then, his orgasm making his brain swell and his heart skip several beats. He yelled and beat his fist against the bed as he jerked about, squeezing her to him so she could never escape, never get away. She clawed at the bed, her hair a wild, tangled mess, which somehow made even more beautiful. His dick kept releasing, the condom undoubtedly filled to the brim with copious cum. His head spun, and he saw stars as the energy drained from him and his body rested on her, his dick throbbing inside her lovely walls. Breathing hard, he managed to caress her arm, soothing her.

Perhaps it was an apology of sorts for roughing up her pussy as he climaxed, but he simply wasn't able to help himself...

Leaving her, he wobbled to the bathroom, slamming the door behind him. He looked at himself in the mirror, fighting laughter and tears simultaneously.

Oh, the humiliation.

He just needed a moment alone... a moment to collect his thoughts. She was quiet out there... oh so quiet... but he could have sworn he heard her giggle. Perhaps it was all in his mind...

"Fuck! Shit! I feel like a fucking fool!"

He angrily turned the faucet on. When the water burst free he thrust his tattooed hands in the stream and splashed water on his sweaty face.

"What if she doesn't feel that way about me, too? Then I'm right back at square one! I told myself I would *never* let this happen again. First Charity, then Mimi, now Sky! Fuck!"

He turned off the bathroom light and returned to the bedroom, only to find Sky sitting against the headboard, perched there like some little queen, messing with her phone. A big, greasy smile was spread across her happy little face.

Oh, how he loathed her...

He crossed his arms and glared at her.

"What are you doing?" He walked around the bed, then slid under the sheets next to her.

"Sending Scarlet a text message..." She giggled.

He wasn't amused.

She HAD been out here laughing...

"And may I ask what you're tellin' her?" He tried to look over her shoulder and take a peek, but she gave him the gas face and leaned away, blocking his view.

"Hold on..." She laughed again, her fingers flying across the keyboard.

And then, something quite strange happened, she handed him her phone. He took it, curiosity gripping him, and she shrugged, that smile still on her face. Fluffing her pillow, she made as if she were going to sleep and completely turned her back to him. Shaking his head, he proceeded to read the text messages between her and Scarlet...

Sky: *Girl! I had to give in. We just got finished.* 🛏️

Scarlet: *I knew it! I hadn't heard back from you in hours. I hate u bitch. Was it good?*

Sky: *Is Roseann Barr batshit crazy? What do YOU think?* 😜

Scarlet: *BIIIIITCH! I need to live vicariously through you, with your boyfriend stealing ass! I GOT QUESTIONS! How big is it? Can he work it? How many times did you cum, bitch?*

Sky: *1. At least 8 or 9 inches. BIG AS FUCK.* 🌶️ *2. Yes, the White boy has moves and that tongue? GIRL! OMG!* 😀 *Never came so hard in my life. 3. Came at least 5 times. No lie. Damn he is good!*

Scarlet: *Have you told him?*

Sky: *No I am not telling him. His ego is already huge.*

Scarlet: *No, not that.*

Sky: *Told him what?*

Scarlet: *What u told me last week????*

Sky: *Nope. But he just came out the bathroom so I'll tell him now. By the way, he told me first.*

Scarlet: *BIIIITCH! ARE YOU FOR REAL?! YOU ARE IN! Guys like him don't do that – you got him, bitch! SHARE THE BAG! If it wasn't for me you wouldn't have gotten this far. I require a 40% finder's fee. Wingmen's Lives Matter! Well, wingwomen.*

Sky: *LOL. I'm about to hand him the phone since he is being nosey so he can read it for himself: LAZARIST, I LOVE YOU, TOO…* 😍

LEO

♌

CHAPTER ELEVEN

Money Can't Buy Me Love...

L AZARIST SAT IN the café by himself, nursing a cup of coffee and typing away on his computer. He'd told himself that he was going to go to Manhattan, get away for a bit and work. There'd be no distractions, just him and the music from his computer, the people talking, the cars going by, and the big world all around him. He took a seat outside in the courtyard of the Intelligentsia Highline Coffeebar located in the Highline Hotel Chelsea. He'd never been before, but his girl-friend—

He paused and smiled.

Girlfriend...

He was still getting used to such a notion in the pleasantly odd turn of events. But anyway, Sky had recommended it, saying it was her little spot to just sit back for a spell, especially in the warmer part of the year. She'd been on him once again about work-life balance because he'd been backsliding.

Initially, he'd protested, claiming it was all in her mind, but just when he thought he had her convinced, she pulled out receipts. The woman was keeping tabs on him! His comings and goings... she'd used an app to track everything. How dare she! The hours working were once again creeping up, and though they still spent quite a lot of time together, she insisted on him making a change for his own health and wellbeing.

'I love you... I don't want to see you lose yourself again. One day, Lazarist, you are going to wake up, look around and wonder where the days went. By then, it'll be too late...'

Perhaps if he were not at the club, but out in the fresh air enjoying a different environment, it would be better than no change at all. So, he'd conceded and agreed to try. After all, at least it was a compromise of sorts. He glanced at the time.

I need to call Mom sometime today... check in on her...

He wasn't certain what made him think of his mother right at that moment. Perhaps he'd picked up a scent that smelled like her apartment, or someone wore a similar perfume. Whatever it was, she edged her way into his mind and he placed her in high priority.

He kept on typing for quite some time, updating various bits of information and seeing to different tasks. After a while, his cellphone rang. He answered it with a smile.

"Well, hello there. What a nice surprise."

"Hi, sweetie," came the sultry voice on the other end. "The class just let out. I'm going to pick up a salad, eat it real fast, then head over to Fox's and look for a dress."

"Over there on Kings Highway?"

"Yeah, that's the one. Since you said we were going to that show I wanted to look nice." He smiled into the phone. "I mean, I have a few dresses already but nothing as fancy as I'd like. Besides, I can wear it other places too. I've been needing something new that is a bit more upscale."

"I'm certain you'll find something nice. And I can't wait to see you in it... then take you out of it."

She laughed on the other end.

"Your mind is always in the gutter."

"No other place I'd rather be. Anyway, as far as the musical, I think you'll like it. When was the last time you saw a Broadway show?"

He tapped the table with his fingertips.

"Oh, goodness, Laz, it's been years. I've never seen Phantom of the Opera, though. That'll be a new one for me."

His smile grew larger. He loved doing things like this, taking people to places they'd never been, showing them things they'd never seen. It had to be a matter of control for him, kind of like being a teacher or a tour guide; there was power in that, being the one in the know while the rest followed his lead. But, he also just enjoyed pleasing people, treating friends and family to a good time, seeing their faces light up with delight.

"I can't wait tuh take you, baby... it's gonna be great. Do you want my credit card number for your dress at Fox's?"

"No! Why would you ask that?!" He was taken aback

at her response, as if she was deeply wounded by such a proposal.

"Why tha hell are you flyin' off the handle? It was just a question. I just thought it would be a nice gesture is all! What are you tryna prove, Sky?"

"No, the question is, what are *you* trying to prove? I have told you several times, Lazarist, that I do not need you to do that for me."

"Do what for you exactly, Sky?" He flopped back in his seat and rolled his eyes, soon remembering why women got on his nerves and were oftentimes a lot of hassle.

"Pay for everything. I make a decent amount of money where I can purchase my own clothing, okay? Now seriously, you've bought me enough stuff. It's just stuff, right? Clutter... *things!* Is that what we need more of, Lazarist? Items? Shoes! Hats! Coats! We only have two feet. What do we need thirty pairs of shoes for?! I have seen too many apartments to count that look like an episode of Hoarders. Yes, I like pretty dresses; I like nice jewelry, too, but time is valuable. It's the most expensive thing in this world and once it's gone, we can never get it back. Stop flashin' money at me and flash me your time! Flash me you takin' on your day and having fun! Flash me your vulnerability and not your Mr. Boss man antics."

Her words hit him hard. They stung.

"Unbelievable. I offer my girl a fuckin' piece of change to buy herself a fuckin' dress for a fuckin' show that I fuckin' invited 'er to, and get chewed tha fuck out!

You're somethin' else! I don't have time for this shit!"

"You need to calm down. All I am saying is—"

"I need to calm down? Try lookin' in the mirror! Now, unless there is something pressing you really must say, I am hanging up. I hope you're finished, because I really need to go."

"Oh, that's real interesting! You never need to suddenly get off the phone when I'm praising you, complimenting you, or sayin' all the things you want to hear... strokin' that big ol' ego of yours. When I say something you don't like though, tell you the truth, suddenly, the phone needs to go dead. Look, baby, there are too many things in this world, and not enough love and fun. Nice things are... well... nice, and I appreciate them, baby... I do." Her voice softened, as if she realized she may have come on too strong. Perhaps his silence just then led her to that conclusion. "You're so thoughtful, and yeah, I love so many things you've given me but if you spent ten bucks on a matinee movie for me in some dump of a theater, I'd have a good time there, too.

"I just want to be with you, Lazarist... *You're* the fun, baby! You're the party in the flesh! You're the main attraction, not your money." They both went quiet for a while as her words sunk in deep. "You must notice how people gravitate to you, right? Your laughter is loud and big, your presence swallows up a room! People love to be around you not just because you're rich, but because you're funny, you vibe well with crowds, you come across as down to earth and in the know! You are

Lazarist Zander, self-made millionaire, sexy beyond belief, and best of all, you're all mine. I'm not tryna hurt you. I just want you to live your life… *enjoy* it! You've earned it, honey. You deserve to clock out sometimes…"

"I'm all yours," he said, but he was hurting. He did his damnedest to ensure she didn't hear the pain in his voice. Her words brought it all home. It was now crystal clear…

He'd been overcompensating, tossing more and more at her due to something he didn't wish to admit: he was afraid to lose her. Now that he'd gotten her, the thought of her drifting away caused him so much anxiety that he didn't dare even go there in his mind. He was petrified because he was in love, and so afraid that she would see his inadequacies, find something within him that she didn't like… perhaps a weakness?

"I'll let you get back to what you were doing." He forced a smile.

"But I'm the one who called *you*." She chuckled. "All right, well, I'll call you later on today. I look forward to seeing you tomorrow."

"Me, too." He blew her a kiss over the phone and she returned it, then he ended the call. He sat there for a long while, mulling over her words, playing them on repeat. She'd told him off, and loved him through the verbal ass-kicking. Nevertheless, he knew he wouldn't be able to stop…

That's just one of the ways with which I show my love… I buy things… The things are the leaves I wrap around the forest floor for protection… camouflage. Don't look at me too closely; look at the things, my pretty distractions… It makes me feel good to do it… the shiny stuff, the diamonds, the nice smelling ointments and perfumes… I had them as a child, and then they were gone, so I busted my ass to get them again, and then some… and I have that right. I have made certain that I will never be broke again! Wise investments… ownership of property… plenty of money in multiple bank accounts. It's called stability. Money talks in this city. Broke people don't have a voice. I had no voice! I roared, but no one heard me! NO ONE GAVE A DAMN ABOUT ME AND MY MOTHER AND MY SISTER!

Now people listen! They fear me when they see me coming! They squirm during business negotiations because I let nothing slide! I am not a pushover! I am not soft! I AM NOT A FUCKIN' PUSSY! They give a shit about what I have to say now! My money does the talking!

He looked around him and when he lifted his gaze to the sky, the sun almost blinded him. People walked about with their briefcases, luggage, and shopping bags, looking straight ahead, aiming for their destinations. They were all over the place, milling about. The world was passing them by. They didn't get to see the whimsical flag waving at the top of one of the buildings that he just now noticed—it had a pink flamingo on it. They didn't see the adorable little blond-haired girl crying as she pointed to her pretzel that had fallen on the ground. He turned in another direction and swallowed. It was so beautiful… just everyday people, with stories of their own, a hurried lifetime shoved in one single day…

They all had beating hearts inside of their bodies;

they had dreams and ideas, girlfriends, wives, husbands, children and friends who loved them. Where were they rushing off to? Perhaps home? Was their house empty like his? Only filled with the vile rantings of a madman who showed up at his door every now and again at three or four in the morning?

No, he surmised most people were not like him. Most people had someone to hug, someone to miss, someone to care about. And now, so did he...

And she fell upon him like the sky, her words cutting to his core. He'd never let her know how deeply wounded he was, but it didn't matter. What she'd said was true.

He was missing out...

He was missing out on the heartbeat of the city...

The heartbeat of the world...

Too busy trying to collect all the riches in the universe.

He swallowed the last of his coffee, packed up his laptop, and headed out of the place with a plan of action ready to be shot out of the barrel.

Today was officially declared a 'Fun Day.' No work allowed.

He was going to walk around the streets and go into stores he'd never paid attention to; the lousier they were, the better. He was going to speak to the owners, say hi to the customers, and buy something cheap and poorly made, and love every second of it. He was going to order a nice big greasy slice from a street vendor cart and enjoy every horrible bite of it, too. That was something he hadn't done since he was a teenager, but back then, it was all he could afford. He was going to get himself a tall Coke with ice, or Snapple, either-or. He was going to purchase a bike to go riding in Central Park the next weekend. No! He'd purchase two! One for him and one for his beautiful Sky…

Whipping his sunglasses out of his pocket, he placed them on his face and beat the concrete with determined steps. He looked up at the sky and at the large, tall buildings. It seemed like they were looking down at him too, staring with their hundreds of rectangular eyes, winking at him and blowing him a kiss from their opening and closing windows.

I don't know where I'm going, but wherever I end up, that's where I need to be…

LEO

Mom had on a red apron, the exact same shade of her lipstick. It was always rather comical how the woman made provisions to coordinate herself just so.

"Mom, why do you come over here and do this?" Lazarist chuckled as he sat down in his kitchen and watched his mother putz around, pulling out pots and pans, pretending as though she recalled where everything was from her last time pulling such a stunt. "I invite you over. I send a car to bring ya. I tell ya, 'Mom, I've got dinner covered' and then, you come over here with a big ass bag of food to cook up, your apron on, and the determination to treat me like a child! Why are ya doin' this?!"

Smiling, Mom turned to his sink and transferred a bag of lettuce into a colander, then proceeded to wash it.

"You'll *always* be my baby… you and your sister. Hey." She shrugged. "This is what moms do. Besides, I missed ya." She looked at him from over her shoulder, her mid-length salt and pepper hair hitting her shoulders just so.

"You're beautiful, ya know that?"

She looked back over at him and stuck out her tongue.

"You always lay it on thick when you want something. What a manipulative son of a gun!"

"No, I'm serious!"

"Okay, what have ya done, boy?!"

"What?" He tossed up his hands and laughed. "I can't pay my mother a compliment without havin' a trick up my sleeve?"

"I dunno." She giggled as she turned the water off and shook the bowl, forcing the water to drain out of the small holes. "You've been actin' real strange lately, Laz."

"How so?" He crossed his ankles and cocked his head to the side. He loved having her at his home. Her energy felt good, even when she was going to sock it to him.

"Well, for one, you've been callin' me more. Before, I'd get a call once a week if I was lucky and you were rushin' me off the phone as soon as I'd say 'hello.'"

"That's not true!" He grinned, knowing damn well that it was.

"Like hell it's not. Then, you've been smilin' and laughin' more. I mean, don't get me wrong." She set the colander down on the counter and turned to him, raising her leg a little to rest her foot on the cabinet under the basin. "You've always been silly, super silly, but this overkill."

"So I get shit from ya if I don't call enough, and now you're sayin' it's like the body snatchers nabbed me because I'm treatin' you like the queen that you are! Really, Mom?"

"Don't play coy, Laz. You know what I'm talking about." She walked over to his refrigerator and pulled out a stick of butter. "The flowers... I get enough flowers from ya to open a funeral home, but that slowed down and now, you send little notes and cookies... those tiny chocolate ones I like from the bakery. You know I love those cookies." He nodded in agreement. She most certainly did love those cookies. Anything for Mom... "But those silly little poems and notes you're writing? Hilarious!"

"Glad you like them." He sat a bit straighter in his chair, proud of himself. She placed a small pot on an eye, unwrapped the stick of butter, and dropped it inside. Then, she turned and gave him a look as if she wanted to say something more, but instead she changed the topic.

"So, how's work been treatin' ya overall?"

"Good. Things are going great, actually. I, uh, I've

been leaving on time lately, and getting more rest, too."

The woman looked at him suspiciously.

"Let me tell you somethin', Laz. You were always lazy, ya hear me?" She picked up a spatula and waved it in his direction. "If it didn't come easy to you, you didn't want to do it, but if you were really good at something, I mean, really, really good, then I would have to beg ya to stop, to slow down. You would pounce on it and never let up. That's how I knew you owning this club was good for you. You're passionate about it and you work very hard at it—and then what ends up happening is other things in your life get neglected. But..." She shrugged. "That's just who ya are. I had to accept it. And how can we argue with success?"

"That's true. I do what I do well. That's just a fact." He winked at her, and she winked back.

"The Fallen Angel has been featured in magazines as a great nightlife attraction. The youngsters love it. Anyone who loves ya, truly loves ya, has to accept that you can't let this go. Once you find your niche, that's just it..." She shook her head. "You're in, ya know? *All* in... with both feet. I'm proud of ya, Laz... so proud of you." Mom's voice trembled and he dropped his head, sporting a smile. "Just promise me that you'll make time for yourself every now and again, too. Don't want life to pass you by..."

Boy does that sound familiar... He shuddered at that.

Had Sky somehow wrangled up his mother's number and called to complain?! No... she wouldn't have... would she?

"Thank you, Mom."

She was quiet for a spell, only the sound of the sink water running as she filled a large pot with water and transported it over to the stovetop.

"So, who is she?"

"Huh?" He was shaken out of his thoughts like an apple from a tree. "She?"

"Just stop it, all right? I know you're gearin' up for some big song and dance, the kind where you're pretending to be totally surprised, flabbergasted, taken aback... the drama! What a *divo* my son is! Geesh!" She rolled her eyes, causing him to burst out laughing. "The only time you act like a complete fool is when you're in love. I thought after that stripper who I told ya not to marry, that was it! Now, who is it that has done this to you?"

"She wasn't a stripper. She was an exotic dancer and now is a professional adult film artist," He stated with his finger in the air, then burst out laughing.

Mom cut her eyes at him, hissed, and turned back towards the sink.

"She was garbage! Tried to blackmail you in court... lied about being pregnant, even. What a classless slut. You haven't had any decent woman since Charity, Laz."

"Oh, Mom, come on! Why do you always bring up Charity? We could be talking about the weather, and you'll bring that woman up. That was a million years ago. She's remarried, has kids, and works for some nonprofit place, last I heard. Come on, now."

Mom stood there and glared at him, then began to mess with a loaf of frozen garlic bread.

"How is she, by the way?"

"Really?" He flopped back in his chair, closed his eyes, and placed his hand across his head in disbelief. "So you're really doing this, huh? Just gonna pretend like I didn't ask you to *not* do it."

"She hasn't called me in a while... been busy with her husband and kids, I suppose." Mom shrugged, completely ignoring his feelings about it all. Once Mom had found out Charity had remarried, she was devastated. She'd wanted them to work it out and try again, although they'd both admitted to her countless times that despite the fact they still loved each other, that wasn't enough to sustain a relationship. Surely, Mom had to understand that.

"I dunno how she's doing. I haven't spoken to her in at least a couple of years."

Mom walked over to the oven and tapped her lower lip, trying to figure it out again. She always forgot how that oven turned on.

"Third button to the right..." he offered.

She turned the knob to 350 degrees and then returned her attention to him, looking him dead in the eye.

"You're not off the hook about the 'she' you've yet to identify. Come on, we don't talk all the time, but you tell me *every*thing. What's up with the secrets? What's going on?"

Yes, it was time. This conversation was long overdue.

He pointed to the chair across from him, the same one Dad always plopped in when he'd show up at the oddest times. She sat down.

"Mom, I know after I filed for divorce from Mimi, I was upset and told you I was done… that I didn't want to be involved anymore, but…"

"I knew it." Mom smiled wide, her head held high. "I told Eliza that you were in love again! She said, 'Naaah, Mom! He treats women like shit! He's really done now!' I knew it!"

His smile slowly faded.

"Eliza thinks I treat women like shit?" That was his little sister. How horrible for her to think that of him.

Mom shrugged and grimaced, resting her chin in the palm of her hand.

"Honestly, babe, ya do. I know it's because you've been hurt, but yeah. I mean, when ya tell a woman one thing and then do somethin' else, that's treatin' them like shit. You're a womanizer, Laz. You went from being a hopeless romantic, a real sweetheart, to this mean, awful… shit." She waved her hand, as if it were all too much for her to say.

"No… say it. Tell me."

She hesitated for a brief moment. "You just hurt so badly, baby, that you wanted them to hurt, too… just like you."

Mom's eyes were full of pity, as if he were in need of prayer, as if he were some leper. That wasn't what he wanted! He didn't want to be that man… he *wasn't* that man. That was all an act! Couldn't she see through it? Why didn't she know?

"But I know that was all for show…" He sighed with relief, and his forehead hit the table. He felt her hand as she reached over and rubbed his hair. "You just couldn't take anymore. You were in protection mode. I explained that to Eliza. She saw it as plausible, I suppose. She did agree that you'd changed. I told 'er, not really, 'cause when someone is playing pretend, that's not actually changing. That's just a role, and it's always temporary."

He sat back up. "Yeah, well, that role is over. The wall is down. I met someone and she... she makes me believe in love again, Mom."

The older woman grasped both his hands and squeezed.

"Her name is Sky. She's a professional dance chore-ographer. Mom, she's good, too! She's worked with a lot of big name celebrities on their music videos and she does a lot of work for commercials, things like that. She teaches classes for children and adults, too. She's... she's fucking beautiful! And she's got a good heart. She was raised in Brooklyn... and she's so sweet, and... she doesn't want me for my money. Her actions prove that."

Mom's eyes glossed over, but he suspected those tears that threatened to fall were ones of happiness. Perhaps he was right... Maybe she'd trust one more woman who'd entered his life. Just one more.

"She sounds wonderful, honey." She patted his hands before slipping hers away. "I never want to see your heart broken again, sweetheart. I worry about you, Laz, because when you love, you love so hard that it drives ya crazy. You don't sleep... you don't eat... It's awful watching you explode from the inside out when things don't go right. So I think that's why I understood why'd you taken another approach, though it was drastic and harmful. But I knew one day, sooner or later, because you're such a passionate man, that you'd fall prey to your one and only weakness... and that's love. It's your kryptonite—but you need it."

He sighed and nodded.

"I want to meet her. Can you arrange that soon?"

"Of course. How about next week? I'll ask her what day works for her."

"Yeah, any day but Wednesday. Oh wait! Your birthday is next Thursday! What's the plan?" Getting up from her chair, she made her way over to the uncooked chicken and began to season it.

"I don't know. I was hoping you were planning some big lavish party on my behalf." He chuckled, but he was certain that she knew he in fact hoped a big deal was being made about his special day.

"I've got some ideas, but they're none of your business. Back to what we were discussing for a bit. Ya ready to listen?"

"Yes."

"Good. Let me tell you somethin', Laz." She grabbed the black pepper and began to sprinkle it all over the thighs and breasts. "The problem is, you stopped trustin' your own judgment. After you realized you weren't pickin' the ones that were right for you, you stopped trustin' yourself. That can do some damage to one's ego, 'specially to a man like you. Everything you do, you do it big! 'Fallen Angel', parties, gifts, the whole nine. People see you as the loud one, always in the middle of the action, the center of attention. But, what they don't know about you, something only a mother would, is you don't do all of that for the attention; you do it to make people smile. It's a gift, from you to them. Why? Because that's what *real* bosses do. They give, even when they no longer have it to spare. Because giving, especially of one's time, is the greatest gift of all..."

LEO

CHAPTER TWELVE

The Lion Sleeps Tonight...

"OKAY, OKAY… I get it now." He smirked as he sat across from her on her couch. Sky placed her glass of red wine down on the coffee table and leisurely crossed her legs. She'd been flirting with him for the past ten minutes, but he hadn't yet taken the bait. Instead, he focused on business matters… *her* business matters. "So, the studio is part of that, I see. When are you thinking about looking at other properties?"

"Well, I am not really sure." She sighed and hitched her elbow on the back of the couch. "I would like to relocate the dance studio from Brooklyn to Manhattan, but then my rent would be double the price for half the space." He nodded and took a sip of his wine. "I don't want that. I need every square inch I can get. Rent is no joke in Manhattan though, but damn, the location would be awesome… if I can swing it."

"That's exactly right. The costs may be even triple what you're paying now. I tell you what, I have a friend who's a great real estate agent. I'll ask him to keep his eyes peeled, tell him the budget you wanna stay in, okay?"

"Thank you, I appreciate that." She also appreciated him not rushing to suggest purchasing it for her, to take control like she was certain he was dying to do. Nope. She wanted to do this on her own. It was important to her. He leaned in and kissed her.

Ahhh, yes, the love I've been missing…

She closed her eyes and took it in, the softness, the gentleness of his kiss. When he pulled away, her pink lipstick had imprinted on his lips. She reached out to rub it off with the pad of her thumb, then kissed his cheek. The hairs from his beard tickled her face, and she loved it.

"Thanks for inviting me over tonight." He leaned back into the blue throw pillow, propping his hand behind his head. "It's been a few days since we got to sit here face to face. We've both been so busy. Sometimes a phone call just isn't enough."

"Yeah, I missed you. Had to make time for my baby."

Lazarist smiled at her then glanced around her living room as he often did. He seemed to enjoy looking at her things, her stuff… her collections. His eyes rested on a framed photo of her father she'd just put out the day prior, setting it beside the television.

"That's your father, right?" He got to his feet, wineglass in hand, and walked over to it. Picking it up, he studied it intently.

"Yeah, that's him."

"Wow." He looked at her from over his shoulder then returned the framed photo to the television stand. "I see the resemblance."

He went quiet for a spell—too quiet. She always wondered what was going on in his mind when he silenced himself like that. Lazarist was naturally gregarious—always talking, always joking, always saying something completely unnecessary or slick. When he was quiet, it set off her alarm bells.

"Hey." She raked her fingers through her hair. "Come here... I want to talk to you about something." He made his way over. "You never, and I mean, *never*, mention your father. Is he, uh... is he still living?"

"If that's what you want to call it." The room grew suddenly cold. Lazarist's face turned impassive, blank, and it scared her. The smile was gone in a snap.

Maybe I need to leave this alone. At least, for now.

"Hmmm, okay..." The awkwardness between them hatched from some invisible egg, and now the creature that had morphed from it was racing around the room, poisoning the air with a sadness that was almost palpable to the touch. "So! Next question." She laughed and slapped her leg in a playful sort of way. "What would you like for your birthday? I think it's awesome that your mother is throwing you a party. I can't wait to meet her."

"Oh, you don't have to get me anything!"

The man blushed... but she wasn't buying it.

"You need to stop sitting there acting like it's not important to you! You've been hinting around about your upcoming birthday for the past few weeks!" They both chuckled. "It'll be your day to shine. We both know how you *loooove* that!"

"Nah, it's fine, really. I'm just lookin' forward to all of my friends and family being there… and introducing *you* to everyone." He leaned over and took her hand, his eyes on her as he intertwined their fingers. "I love being with you. I want people to see why I've been so happy lately. Besides, it's time, ya know?"

"I definitely agree." She snuggled up to him, laying her head on his shoulder. She wrapped her hand around his arm and fixed her gaze on her father's photo. "Speaking of meeting parents, I told my father about you…"

"Well, good. What did he say?" Lazarist asked after a few moments of silence. He leaned to carefully place his wine on the coffee table beside hers.

"Well, he's not really certain what to think, quite honestly. I mean, he and I are pretty close, you know? I told him I was seeing someone… let him know who you were. Let's just say he has concerns, but he is still open minded about it all."

"Concerns, huh? Based on what? Race?"

She sighed and sat up, but kept her hand on his arm. It was funny that the man couldn't even fathom why someone would be apprehensive about a woman dating the likes of a man like him…

"No, not because you're White. You're a local celebrity. You're well off. You've been married a couple of times already and well…" She smiled ever so slightly as she cocked her head to the side. "Let's be honest. You have a reputation for being a big-time playboy. He's afraid you might break my heart. He thinks I'm too trusting, as well." At this, the man burst out laughing. "What are you laughing about? How in the world could you find that funny?"

"Because Sky! Your father apparently has *no* idea the hoops you made me jump through… too trusting my ass! You're a man-eater! This soft, demure persona is a ruse! You've got more good sense than almost anyone I know. Play you, my ass!"

All right… that was funny and she couldn't help but chuckle. But, in this case, she owed some of her success to Scarlet, who knew her way around men such as the great Lazarist…

"Okay, point taken, but still."

"Yeah." He leaned in and kissed her forehead. "In all seriousness though, I know what you mean… Well, what *he* means, rather. But he has nothing to worry about…" He pressed his hand against her shoulder and leaned her down on the couch. The leather sighed beneath their shifting weight. "I'm going to take good care of his daughter… *real* good care…" She smiled up at him as he mounted her, pressing his groin between her thighs. She felt his hardness through her jeans, and when her gaze landed back on that photo, she grimaced.

"Uh, hold up… Can you put that picture face down?" Dad's dark brown eyes upon her and his smile proved suddenly unnerving. Lazarist burst out laughing.

Lazarist hopped up and picked up the photo. He

looked at it again for a spell, then placed it face down. When he returned to her, she was wiggling out of her pants, eager to feel him deep inside her. He reclaimed his position, grinding against her panties, then drove his tongue deep within her mouth. In seconds flat he disrobed, his clothing ending up in a heap alongside the couch. Hands roving all over one another, they went at each other like feverish wild animals.

"I want you so bad!" She cooed as he shoved her purple sweater up to her chin and removed her bra.

Gripping her right breast, he engulfed the left nipple as if his life depended upon it. Nails raking up and down his back, she held on as he administered delightful pleasure. He kept the pace, not breaking his stride as he tugged at her panties and managed to expertly snatch them down to her ankles. She kicked the damn things off, her valley now completely exposed for his taking. He didn't bother to journey slow. He held her by the hips and jammed his hot tongue against her slit, flicking and sucking her zone. She clawed at his shoulders as he tongue-fucked her, then slid his finger inside of her ass, making her coo and squirm.

"Baaaby!" He moaned as she came against his mouth, shaking and unable to slow down and control herself.

He crawled back up her body as if he were a wild cat and she were some tree, and sank his teeth into her neck like some blood crazed vampire. She screamed, the pain and pleasure immense as he cupped her breast and pressed his erect cock against her pussy. He yanked her thighs further apart as if he were angry with the world, and then thrust ruthlessly inside.

"Oh God!"

His dick stretched her wide open, his thrusts hard and breathtaking. Lifting himself up onto his palms, he stared down at her with such intensity. His gaze drifted to his handwork...

"Fuck! I love watching my dick goin' in and out of your tight, wet, pink pussy, baby!" She sighed when he wrapped his hand around the back of her neck, forcing her upward to take a front row seat at the fuck show, with tickets for two. "Look at this!" She eyed his thick, long cock thrusting deep inside her, over and over, coated with their mixed juices, and feeling so turned on. He kissed her then with such passion, breaking her concentration and making her heart beat harder and faster. "Sky! I love tha fuck outta you! Tell me this pussy is all mine!"

"It's yours, baby!"

He pounded hard and rough within her, falling upon her in a heavy, tattooed heap, yet never slowing until he hoisted her off the couch and held her tight in his arms. Jostling her up and down on his sword, he moved slow and easy, delivering every delicious inch of himself to her. And then, she saw love in his eyes... a wanting... a need. Wrapping her arms around his neck, she held on tight. Faster and faster he went until he shuddered against her yet keeping her safe in his arms. His groan was loud and primal as he unleashed his seed deep within her; the warmth of his cum felt comforting, sexy, safe...

He pressed his forehead against hers, eyes closed, heart racing a mile a minute, and lips parted, murmuring love spells still unheard but felt deep within. She wished she could stay that way forever... slick thighs wrapped around his tapered waist, feeling his big, juicy dick throbbing within her. She couldn't describe it, couldn't explain it, but she loved making love to him more than any other man she'd ever given herself to...

After a few moments, he gained his composure and made his way with her in tow to her bedroom. Nudging the door open with his shoulder, he placed her gently on her bed and soon, they lay snuggled under the sheets, their naked bodies wrapped around one another, holding tight, for dear life. She laid her head against his chest as he stroked her hair in the tenderest of ways. He kissed her face, smiled, then kissed her as he massaged her shoulder.

"Let me do you..." He looked at her in bewilderment. "A massage... lie on your stomach."

The big man rolled over onto his abdomen. His long legs extended beyond the length of her bed, his feet hanging off the edge. She smiled at the sight. Reaching into her dresser drawer, she retrieved a bottle of almond scented massage oil, flipped the lid, and poured a quarter sized amount into her hands. Rubbing her palms together, she began at his shoulders, working out the kinks.

"Mmmm, that feels soooo good," he slurred with a big smile, his face planted firmly into the white pillow.

"You're still a little tense…" She kept at it, then paused to reach over to her clock radio and turn on some music.

This ought to help…

She rarely used it for such things, but her phone with her playlists had been left in the living room when their tryst had first begun. This would simply have to do.

'Wild Horses' by The Rolling Stones was the song that came on. The sight of her smooth naked tawny body atop his brawny, enormous, tattooed one made her pause. She looked at their reflection in her vanity mirror, taking note of how she was mounting him, like on horseback… or perhaps, like a wild lion roaming the jungle that she'd managed to tame. It didn't bring her delight or carnal pleasure to see him beneath her; it gave her peace, for a part of her believed he *wanted* to be brought to his knees, shot down like a poacher, with an arrow filled with nothing but love. Yes, he wanted this… He wanted to be captured but by one woman, and one woman only…

Her.

"Lazarist…"

"Yeah, baby?" he spoke in a whisper, falling into the groove of relaxation.

"I just wanna tell you that you never have to pretend with me. You can be yourself, and I promise to never tell anyone your deepest secrets. I love you… and lovin' someone means that they can trust you. Everyone needs someone to talk to, honey… even a man like *you*."

She kept on massaging him, going about her way, but

when he turned, the skin around his neck twisted as he looked her in the eye. His baby blues were narrowed upon her, his dark brows furrowed. He didn't say anything—he didn't need to. She just kept on massaging her lover as her heart beat for him and her pussy slid against his ass every time she moved in one direction or another. He slowly turned away, as if shaken from a daydream, and rested his head back against the pillow, but this time, he looked troubled. He didn't close his eyes; he just lay there as the lyrics to 'Wild Horses' played on and on. After a couple of minutes, he broke the quiet...

"I was ten when I knew somethin' wasn't right." He began. "My father started talkin' to himself." Lazarist's eyes stared off into the distance. "He'd become forgetful. My father never forgot anything. Then, he started accusing my mother of cheating. She hadn't been, at least not to my knowledge. Then, some clients started to complain about him... said he was actin' weird and unprofessional at times. He was an attorney."

Stopping her ministrations, she grabbed a white linen scented tealight candle from the nightstand drawer. Next, she lit it up with her lighter and set it down by the radio.

"My father was one of the best intellectual property attorneys in the state of New York. No lie. He was even mentioned in one of those big finance magazines back in the 90's. Anyway, things got real fucked up. He then... he then started to verbally abuse me and my sister... call us stupid mistakes... shit like that.

"He'd never spoken to us like that. He was the best father when we were little, ya know? Real great. He did everything with us. Pony rides, Coney Island and the beach… museums. My father was brilliant, a real smart guy. He taught me so much in such a short period of time. He schooled me about business, explained to me how things work, even at that young age. He went over the importance of money—how to save it up so you could enjoy life. He didn't always drive us to school in his fancy car. He'd make us take the subway sometimes, even the bus, sayin' we needed to learn about the world, to be grateful, and that we should know how to ride the subway anyway so we could get around with or without him. I was thankful for that.

"And he was funny… so damn funny, Sky. He's Jewish, and though he was raised in a pretty strict Jewish home, he never made me and my sister feel like we had to believe the same as him. He said it was our choice. He was real open like that, real understanding. Just a beautiful person… and then… and then it all changed. It all… went down the fuckin' drain…"

She bent down and planted a soft kiss on the back of his neck, and he startled at her touch. He clutched the pillow with those tattooed fingers of his, the ones covered with skulls, the Leo zodiac symbol, and money signs, and it was a shock it didn't burst at the seams from his abusive handling. He began to shift beneath her, then settled once again… becoming still.

"He started doin' things to my mother, too. Stayin' out late, cheatin', lyin'… and then he hit her, smacked her right in the mouth during an argument... right in front of us. He'd never laid a hand on our mother prior to that, Sky, *ever*. My father had always said men who hit women were cowards... and here he was, doin' it. I'll never forget the blood pooling out of my mother's mouth as she stood there in shock, and how enraged I was. Eliza, my sister, started cryin', but I was infuriated. He and I got into it. I lunged at him with all of my might and he knocked me backwards. My head hit the wall and all I saw was blackness. I was just a little kid, ya know? But I was so pissed off, I honestly thought I could take him on. I had to be taken to the hospital for a concussion. Life as we knew it was over... just done with."

He relaxed his grip on the pillow, took a deep breath, then continued. "He kept on, refused to get help for a while. Then Mom threatened to file for divorce, so he finally saw a doctor. After a couple of weeks, he was diagnosed as paranoid schizophrenic."

She froze at that confession. Inside, she was crying for him, but held it all back for the last thing she wanted to do was interrupt. She tried everything within her to keep her composure.

"It was really like something inside of him snapped, just like that. This didn't happen over a few years' span; we're talking a couple of months. No warning whatsoever. After that he was prescribed medication and things settled down for a while. He became more like he used to be... even resumed working again. But then, he stopped taking the meds, said they made him feel funny. The paranoia amped up again. Now, Mom was a whore

TIANA LAVEEN

according to him. Eliza wasn't his kid and I was trying to top him, to be better than him. He said I was tryna compete, tryna be the man of the house... just crazy shit. I became his rival in his mind, an adversary... his own kid, an enemy!"

He chuckled mirthlessly.

"And Mom had had enough. She'd tried to stick it out for us kids, but she couldn't anymore. She filed for divorce, called the police, and had him put out. He's been livin' on the streets on and off ever since. Sometimes he'd get an apartment, and then it would be gone. I offered countless times to help him. Sometimes he'd let me, most times he wouldn't. He's... he's destroyin' me, Sky..." His eyes glazed over. "I can't let him die, but I don't want him to live. He uh... he comes to my house sometimes, in the middle of the night... smellin' like death, like he's been rollin' around in some carcass.

"He takes a shower. I pull out some clean clothes I keep for him and he puts them on and then he sits in my fuckin' kitchen and berates me. It's the same shit, each and every time!" He punched the pillow with all of his might, then burst out laughing... a manic, painful laugh. "He sits there eatin' my fuckin' food, right? Drinkin' my drinks, wearin' the clothes I bought him, and he tells me what a fuck up I am! Ain't that amazing?!"

He chuckled louder, but she knew with each second, her baby was falling apart... She kept on massaging him, going further down his back and along his spine, working out the kinks, the pain... "It's like he *needs* it! You know what's sick, Sky? You know what *really* makes this super fucked up?"

"No, baby… I don't…"

"I let him do it! He's the *only* person on this fuckin' planet that I let say any fuckin' thing to me. I do it 'cause he *needs* it! He'll die if he can't… It's like he's diabetic and I'm his insulin. He doesn't want my money; he just wants me to stand there and let him do it. He wants to kill me… because when he sees me, he sees his former self…and he hates me for being a living reminder of what coulda been…I… I let him do it! I'll sacrifice my own peace of mind, my own sanity to let this goddamn nut tear me down!"

A tear slowly rolled out the corner of his eye and soaked into the pillow. She could barely catch her breath. She felt herself hyperventilating for the pain in his eyes was so horrible, so strong. She wrapped her arms around him and he flinched! He screamed out as if he were dying. She held him tighter… that big lion of a man had turned into a lamb right before her very eyes…

He didn't need her to say anything. He needed exactly what she was doing—touching him, kissing him, crying with him…

"It's one big fuckin' mess, baby! It's a fuckin' mess! Eliza has begged me to stop lettin' him come over and I don't discuss it with my mother. She'd be furious… probably call tha cops. A couple of times I didn't let him in, and I was guilt ridden about it. It was terrible. I kept envisioning him out there hungry, gettin' mugged or beat up, or worse yet, killed. But I can't keep doin' this. I gotta let him go, Sky… that's why I'm all messed up now, because I know I have to. I gotta say goodbye to him."

Yes you do, baby! Yes, you do!

"The man I once knew is gone, and that's the hardest part of this… the hardest part of all! Which one of him was real? This guy, the damn psycho, or the first one, the one who gave me baths and sang to me, huh? I'll never know! I feel like my entire early childhood was a lie—or maybe this shit right here, the life I'm living right this second ain't real, either. Either way, it's a hell of a thing to wake up one morning, look in the mirror and see that someone can make you crumble, fall apart like this. I don't bow down to no fuckin' body!"

He jerked away from her, his eyes full of fire and misery. She pulled her hands away, knelt back on her knees, and just listened.

"But if you put that man in my face… you put that fuckin' man in my face, Sky, and I just… I just wanna make him better! I just wanna make it go away!" he said, waving his hands about. "I can't wash the crazy away, I can't beg the crazy away, I can't fight the crazy away, and guess what? I can't buy the crazy away, either! You wanted to know about my father. Well, here ya go! He's one big fuck up, and his son is a fuck up, too! Ya happy now?! I ain't so great after all! I'm a chicken! 'Fraid of lettin' him go, 'fraid of what people will think if they knew the truth! He's right! I AIN'T NOTHIN'!!! I AIN'T NOTHIN', BABY!"

She cradled him in her arms, pushing his head into her bosom and keeping him there. The man shook and wailed, tearing her up inside. She held him as tightly as she could, and he held onto her as if his very life depended upon it.

"It's okay... Shhh... it's okay, Laz... You *are* somethin'... you're somethin' special! You're the king of my heart!" She soothed him, running her hand up and down his arm.

At that moment, she realized something very important—something that changed how she saw the man she loved—and she knew then she'd never be the same...

Every boss has a weakness; even the strongest of men can be destroyed. The ego is a dangerous thing, especially for a leader who is self-made. The proud lion roars the loudest not when he's angry, but he does so when he's heart is broken, lost in the jungle and has nowhere to turn. Feeling all alone, keeping secrets, afraid of what the masses will think if they catch him with his jeweled crown even the slightest bit tilted...

The lion turns east then west, north then south, but he can't find his way back to his pride. Not due to a lack of sense of direction, but because he no longer knows where home *truly* is anymore and he doesn't trust the world any longer. For the world gave him a doting father, who then turned into a wicked stranger, all in the blink of a vertical pupiled eye...

LEO

♌

CHAPTER THIRTEEN

Birthday Bash, Birthday Crash, Time to Take Out the Birthday Trash

LAZARIST'S MOTHER STAYED in the prestigious Avalon Midtown West Apartments on W. 50th Street in Manhattan, which afforded her a great view of the city. He'd purchased the place for her himself; she and his sister would always benefit from the finer things in life as long as he was around. Her two-bedroom, two-bath home was lavish and beautiful, contemporary with a mix of antique furniture she'd collected over the years. The works of local artists adorned her walls, while exquisitely crafted lamps, Oriental rugs and other precious items enhanced the space.

She was minutes away from everything she could ever need—her doctor's office, her favorite restaurants, and a slew of stores she loved to frequent. The apartment building itself offered a multitude of amenities such as an indoor pool, fully equipped exercise room, and a well-designed sitting area in the lobby for guests and small gatherings. Best of all, it was a secure location, a place that he felt assured she'd be safe and unbothered.

He arrived wearing a silky black V-neck shirt and gray trousers, paired with his favorite Tom Ford loafers. He was rather particular about shoes; perhaps that was why his girlfriend's recent ramblings about 'things' had stung so much. Of course, he'd taken it personally—it was a dig at him, and she'd scraped open a wound. He liked his things, and he would not apologize for being a self-declared male shoe whore. He was what he was, with pride. Wrapping his arm around Sky's, he greeted the doorman with a nod and entered his mother's building for his big birthday bash. He rather enjoyed how the guy had looked his girl up and down for she was a showstopper. He couldn't help sneaking glances at her, either.

Sky looked absolutely stunning.

Wearing a light blue baby doll dress that tied at the waist and a long matching kimono of a similar shade, she was pretty as a picture. Baby blue high heeled shoes covered her feet, tied with silky bows. Small diamond hoops adorned her ears and she sported a diamond tennis bracelet which he insisted she accept as a present—one of many he intended to give her.

Her hair was parted on the side and worn down, the black, deep waves making him seasick with love. He loved it when she kept her hair that way, and though he still had no comprehension regarding hair extensions and the like, nor did he care, he delighted in the way she put herself together.

Yet, regardless of the lovely eye candy he sported and the fact this was his special day, he felt a little out of sorts, as if sensing some sort of trouble was on its way. He couldn't shake it, but chalked it up to a case of bad nerves. For reasons he couldn't articulate, he felt rather somber, too. Sky had also mentioned how quiet he was, though the early morning birthday fuck and breakfast she'd served him in bed had been stellar.

He pushed the elevator button and in they went, smiling at one another. Sky cradled a gold and ivory wrapped box and he curiously stole glances at it, wondering what in the world it could be.

Moments later, they were at Mom's door, and he could smell the delicious food pouring out into the hall enticing him. Classic jazz music drifted out to the hallway and no doubt several people had already arrived, chattering and laughing, already in the groove of the gathering. He cherished moments like this and looked forward to such occasions. He rapped on the door, and it swung open within seconds.

"Heeey!" Tobias, his best friend stood holding a beer and wearing a white turtleneck and blazer. "The king is here!" the man declared as he and Sky entered the dwelling, the door closing and locking behind them.

Suddenly, he and Sky were surrounded by a mob of people, all wearing smiling faces and speaking at the same time. Eliza, his sister, shouldered her way through the crowd, wearing a black pantsuit and her dark brown hair pulled back into a sleek bun. He reached for her and they held one another, then she landed a big kiss on his cheek.

"Laz! So glad you could make it. I'm sure it almost slipped your mind!" she teased.

Several of his friends gathered closer to him, wishing him a happy birthday and pointing out the table laden with beautifully giftwrapped presents and shiny bags, balloons galore and a large punch bowl more than likely with enough alcohol to incapacitate a rhinoceros.

"Hey, Eliza and Tobias, I have someone here I'd like you to meet." He waved them back over as the crowd thickened, forming a wedge between them. "This is Sky Jordan... my girlfriend."

"So nice to meet you." Tobias took her hand and kissed it. "Lazarist has told me so much about you." The man's smile was large and flirty, and his eyes glowed with approval.

"He's told me about you too, Tobias. It's nice to put a face to the wonderful tales now."

"Same here. He treats my son like his own... may as well be his nephew. Great guy you've got there!"

Tobias's cheeks turned rosy as he laid it on thick. He knew they'd have a completely inappropriate discussion about Sky later. Tobias was *almost* as freaky and dirty-minded as he was.

"Hi, Sky. I'm Lazarist's favorite sister."

"She's my *only* sister."

"I'm also responsible for all of his success," Eliza joked again, causing him to smile. Much to his surprise, his sister draped her arms around Sky and pulled her in for a hug. "So glad that I could finally meet you! I've heard nothin' but good things!"

"Yes, and Lazarist talks about you all the time, too!"

The two ladies held on to one another like they were buddies, chatting it up for a bit. He found it interesting to say the least.

"Eliza, where's Mom?"

"In the kitchen." She released Sky's hand and pointed in that direction. "She said she wasn't going to even bother trying to greet you at the door and fight your adoring fans."

He rolled his eyes at the lady's jabs, wrapped his arm around Sky's waist, and led her to the galley. The place smelled so good, his stomach flipped in anticipation. Mom stood with her back towards him, a million pots and pans around her, and several of her friends mixing ingredients in bowls or standing nearby drinking and chatting amongst themselves.

"Mom!" he hollered out.

The woman quickly spun around, burst out laughing, and tossed the wooden spoon she was holding onto the counter. Several of her friends yelled his name and waved, their excitement almost on par with his mother's. With arms open wide, she shimmied towards him, her hair now cut into a shoulder length bob and sporting a camel colored ankle length dress with slits down the sides.

"It's my Lazarist! Nice you could spare a minute from your adoring aficionados and devotees and come visit the host of this festivity." He chuckled as he wrapped his arms around her and squeezed tight. The woman peeked over his shoulder, eyeing Sky. "And who do we have here?" She slid her arms from around his neck and he brought his love close to make the formal introduction.

"Mom, this is Sky Jordan... my better half."

Mom smiled ever so slightly and extended her hand for a shake.

"Hello, Sky. So glad you could come tonight in celebration of my son's fortieth birthday."

"I wouldn't have missed it! I've also been looking forward to meeting you."

Mom seemed slightly apprehensive, and he couldn't blame her. His history was checkered at best, and though he wouldn't classify his mother has overly protective, she loved him... and she didn't want to see him hurt anymore.

"I was just told about you recently." Mom shot him a look of disapproval before glancing back at Sky. "And my son seems to be quite fond of you."

"I'm fond of him, too."

Mom studied Sky for what felt like an eternity. An awkward silence webbed between the two of them, and then he cleared his throat, trying to break it up... whatever 'it' was.

"Uh, would you like to help me get the buffet set up?" Mom turned towards an empty table across the room that was covered in a gold and black cloth with a gold, bejeweled crown resting on it as a centerpiece. "We can talk while we do it… get to know each other."

"Evelyn!" one of her friends called out before Sky could respond. "Which of these is ready?"

Mom pointed to various dishes and bowls—some of his favorite fares, including salads, soups, breads, and the like.

"I would be honored to help," Sky said.

Lazarist leaned down and whispered in her ear, "I love you… have fun." He winked at her before releasing her hand, then made his way over to a cluster of friends who were having a good time without him… How dare they!

In no time, his throat was sore from laughing, his belly burning from the nonstop chuckles as stories rolled out from his loved ones regarding many of his fiascoes in life. One thing Lazarist prided himself on was being able to withstand jesting. Besides, as a lover of a good time and a well-timed joke, he was all for it. There was a thin line though. Cruelty and passive aggressive behavior, backhanded compliments, and the like were completely unacceptable. Pokes at his character were practically unforgivable, but if he was the butt of a joke and it was funny, hell, he would even join in on the fun, roasting himself down to the ground. After all, he was the center of attention during such times, and he was able to laugh at himself, even if the tale wasn't exactly flattering.

There was plenty of this to go around... such as the time he attempted to bake a pie and even told his mother it was child's play... how hard could it be? An hour later, the fire department had arrived and his place smelled like burnt toast. Disaster.

Or the time when he tried to ride a bike for the first time as a child without having been taught, figuring he knew what to do and just how to do it, too. The resulting trip to the hospital had been no fun whatsoever and the laceration across his face had left a small, tell-tell scar on the side of his forehead.

Then there was the time he decided to get drunk and go off at work about some perceived injustice. He was holding a microphone, but it wasn't on so no one could hear him; he simply looked like a maniac standing on the stage, flailing his arms about, and ranting and raving. Someone then uploaded the video to YouTube, and they never let him live it down. The jokes had been fired non-stop...

"Flap like a chicken, Laz!"

"I'm angry as hell, and I'm not going to take it anymore! You won't hear it anymore, either..."

"Is this thing on?!"

He'd tried to hide in his office for a week.

And so the tales continued, his face burning red, the times good as could be. Then he felt a warm arm surround his and the scent of a perfume he'd admired for years. He looked down into the hazel eyes of his mother, who coaxed him down the hall in the direction of her bedroom. He looked about, trying to find Sky, and saw a glimpse of her speaking to his cousin, the two around the same age, standing there smiling at one another and discussing something he was certain had to do with him... or at least, he hoped so. Once inside mom's bedroom, the place dripping with style and class, she closed the door, crossed her arms, and stared at him.

"Damn you."

"Don't start." He pursed his lips together, ready to have an argument if need be.

"Damn you twice! Damn you three times! I like her. I like her a lot." He burst out laughing, a weight off his shoulder. "I wish I could say otherwise, but I can't. I just pray to God that Sky doesn't end up like Mimi or all of your other ex-girlfriends... trash."

"Mom..." He grimaced as he rested his hand on his hip. "Why must ya go there?"

"Because that's where all the roads lead, despite me advising you for years to take the ones less travelled. In any case, she's wonderful. She's articulate, she's nice... very good... yes, this is very good." Her eyes narrowed as if she were calculating the sum of something complicated and had just realized the answer. "Seems to have a good head on her shoulders. I'm still investigating," She crossed her arms and lifted her chin, her brow arched just so. "But thus far, I don't pick up anything off-putting."

"That's good to know."

"Let me ask you something that I've never asked you before."

"What? If I have a humble bone in my body?"

Mom shook her head and smiled.

"No... and I already know the answer to that but why bring down the mood by poking fun at my first born? Anywho, and this isn't a problem—you know me better than that—but have you ever, and I mean ever, dated a White woman seriously, Laz? I have seen White women you were just usin' to the pass the time, but I am talking about ones you've actually called your girlfriend?"

"Well I had—"

"Because there was Charity." Mom started to count off her fingers. "And she was multiracial. Then there was Deborah, who was African American, I believe. Then there was Tiffani, who was biracial, and then there was Kimberly... she was that Nigerian model. And then there was Alisha, who was half Japanese and half Kenyan... and then there was—"

"Okay, I get it!" He chuckled. "For your information, yes! I have had several White girlfriends, but it's obvious that I enjoy the—"

"Melaninated queens, too." At this, he burst out laughing.

"What?! Mom, where are you gettin' this stuff? When have you *ever* used that term?"

"I saw it on Facebook!" she stated emphatically, causing him to laugh even harder.

"Mom, did you know—"

Just then, someone rapped on the bedroom door. Whoever it was kept knocking and knocking.

"Hold that thought," Mom said as she walked over to the door and opened it. Tobias stood holding a wine cooler, a look of concern on his face.

"Shit." The man visibly swallowed. "I can't... fuck it to Hell. Lazarist, I think you better get out here..."

His heart sank. The look in Tobias' eyes said it all.

Dad is there...

Lazarist could feel it in his bones. As he and Mom made their way out of her bedroom, he walked up the hall and stiffened, his muscles locking up as if instantly frozen.

"Jesus! Are you serious?!" Mom screamed, her voice shattering the otherwise peaceful surroundings. The woman slapped herself on the forehead and marched towards the scene of the crime, a scowl on her face fit for a villain. "You've got some nerve!"

"Mom, don't," Lazarist called out, stepping out around her, his footsteps echoing.

Everyone stood around quietly and the music was now at an almost undetectable volume. Heat spread from his head to the soles of his feet. Every part of his being was on fire; the anger and hatred married and gave birth to him...

He shot a glance over at Sky, who looked more con-fused than concerned. He turned back in the direction of the uninvited guest, his jaw and fists clenched.

"Happy birthday, my love..." Mimi said, standing in a short red dress with a plunging neckline, her tits practically spilling out of it. Long black hair flowed down her shoulders and back and four-inch strappy heels sparkled on her feet. She held a huge satiny red package with a big white bow on top.

"What the hell are you doing here?"

"It's your special day, and I wouldn't miss this for the world…"

CHAPTER FOURTEEN
The Devil on D-Day

H ER HEART RACED like wild stallions in a field during a torrential storm—or at least, that's what horses looked like in the old western movies. Sky was a city girl, Brooklyn born and raised; what the hell did she know about wild horses? Her brain was a whirlwind of perplexity and anguish as she teetered the line between playing it cool and blowing her cool.

Girl, there's people standing around here... don't show your ass...

Calm. Cool. Collect a bitch in the elevator and clean her clock!

She stood there gripping a crisp celery stick covered in homemade ranch dipping sauce, playing a role when all she really wanted was to use her fists. She'd never been much of an actress—what you saw was what you got, like it or not. But, with no mother in the home to show her a bit of feminine tenderness, she had to learn the shit on her own. Though, at times such as these, she tended to forget all of that.

She ogled the woman standing half way across the room who was smirking something vicious. Her breast, waist, and thigh ratio mimicked Jessica Rabbit on silicone overload.

What in the plastic surgery hell?

Sky sized the bitch up. She wouldn't be too hard to take…

Her man was in the throes of a verbal showdown, slinging curse words here, there, and everywhere until he yanked the busty bombshell by the arm and stepped out into the hall, slamming the door behind him and disappearing to Lord knows where.

She has to be an ex… but which one?

The bastard had so many…

My love? That woman called him, 'my love.' Bitch, that's not your love. That's my man and that just might be your Emergency Room bill, too!

Just then, Lazarist's best friend, Tobias, approached her.

"Don't worry," the man said with a thick European accent, as if reading her mind. "He'll take care of it."

"Tobias, who is that?" She jammed the celery in her mouth, though her appetite had been crushed as soon as the woman arrived.

"Malicious Mimi." He chuckled and shook his head. "Supreme bitch. That's his second ex-wife… horrible person. Back 'nd fourth to court they go… she just won't stop. Lazarist will put her in her place. No worries!"

Her heart started to race, but she sported a smile

nevertheless as he tossed up his hands, nicked a baked chicken wing from a silver tray, and waltzed away back into the crowd. Her curiosity climbed to record highs as she stole peeks at the closed front door of the lovely apartment, wondering what was going on between the two.

What type of person does that?!

The music was soon turned back up and people began chatting once again, making no mention of the woman, at least the ones within earshot. Lazarist's mother, however, was sitting on the couch with a friend of hers, her expression tense as she clutched a cup of coffee. Sky cracked her knuckles over and over and debated on slipping into the bathroom and dialing up Scarlet. Hell… maybe even invite her over so they could tag team on a mothafucka…

No… you don't need to call her. You've got this. Keep it PG and classy, Sky. No one needs to see your Angry Black girl thug side. She chuckled to herself, though she struggled to muster up much humor regarding the matter.

She reached for a potato chip and jammed it in her mouth, then chased it with a swallow of something divine. The champagne had been poured into a gold flecked glass, the drink probably costing the same amount as her damn monthly rent.

Great! The ghost from Lazarist's Birthday Past has arisen…

Mimi, you don't know me… I will turn into Leslie Jones up in this bitch and Ghostbust your injected, ant-built-bodied ass right into whatever crypt you rose up from!

LEO

"IT'S YOUR BIRTHDAY. Of course I would be here, baby! Look at you, with your sexy self! Still rockin' hard, huh? Turned the big four-oh!"

The succubus looked smug, her twisted expression making him all the more infuriated. Entitlement at its best.

There they stood in the hallway a few feet from Mom's apartment door. He tried to keep his voice down and not attract attention, happy to hear the music start once again and things moving on inside the place. He hated scenes like this. His mind conjured up images of the ceiling caving in and falling in on the bitch, causing her to plummet ten floors down. He delighted at the notion.

"You weren't invited. Go home."

"Awww! Is that any way to treat your wife?" She smiled—a forced smile.

"Ex-wife... a mistake for certain. In fact, I would say, besides the time when I bet on the Dodgers when I was seventeen, you were the worst mistake I ever made."

"Oh, honey." She reached for him and ran her fingertip along his chin. "I was the best pussy you ever had."

"Not even worth five dollars... a crack-whore could've given better head and for a lot less aggravation."

"Crack, huh? What about when you snorted a line of cocaine out the crack of my ass, you freaky, narcissistic son of a bitch?"

"That was one time… Never touched the shit again, and I was drunk off my ass… didn't know what I was doing, pun intended. Let's not forget that you're the one who'd purchased the shit and brought it home. You're the one on drugs, Mimi, not me." He coolly crossed his arms over his crotch. "And how many fake pregnancies, dead parent stories, and the like will you hatch up to get what you want? You've run out of time, and you don't even cross my mind."

Her smile faded, but just by a smidgen.

"Enough of this sweet talk. Look! I brought you a special present. Don't you want to know what it is?" She smirked as she tilted the gift box from side to side, as if this were a game—a joke he'd get a real big fucking kick out of.

"Cyanide? Rat poison? If so, the best gift you could give to me is for you to stand here and ingest it. If it's not either of the aforementioned, shove it up your double-fisted, Mimi does Miami ass! I don't want it! I paid for whatever is in it, anyway. You don't work anymore, remember?! Lazarist foots your bills, right? Being the opportunist that you are, I should have suspected nothing less. My family and friends tried to talk me outta dealing with you, but I didn't listen. You have a looong history of this sorta shit! But oh, no, I gave you the benefit of the doubt… thought you were being unfairly judged because of your occupation. You bein' a whore was the *least* of my problems."

"I hate you, Lazarist." She seethed. "I hate you because you don't know what love is! I loved you and you know it!" She pointed her blood-red, dagger shaped nail in his face. "Come on." Her face suddenly morphed into some disturbing joker-like expression. "Don't you wanna eat this pussy for old time's sake, baby? Damn, you could eat some pussy! Lick it good like a cat at a milk bowl... purrrrr!"

"I don't want your pussy or any parts of you, Mimi. Don't you have any self-worth? Geesh! This is pathetic! How fuckin' sad!"

She sneered, her lip twitching. They glared at one another until she raised her arm and smacked him across the face. He barely flinched, but he could feel the burn from where her hand had landed. He shook his head.

"Don't you *ever* put your goddamn hands on me again. First and last warning."

He pressed his palm against her shoulder to turn her away, but she screamed out, causing him to immediately let go. The last damn thing he needed was the police being called, and the woman was definitely not above making false claims against him to further her agenda. She pointed her finger in his face, her red painted lips twisted as if she were disgusted, her forehead crinkled like an old brown paper bag. She looked like she was itching for a fight.

This is what she wants. She is trying to egg you into hitting her. She wants your ass locked up.

"You want to add domestic violence to the list?! You're a big guy shoving a little woman! Who do you think they'll believe?" she threatened, proving his suspicions. "Now, I suggest we have a talk about finances. I was going to wait until after your party, but since—"

"Get tha fuck outta here! You can take me back to court a million times. It's over! At the end of this year, you get your final check and not a penny more. We don't have any dependents. You are fully able-body."

"You know what? You're gonna go crazy just like your father." She cackled as she twisted the knife deeper in him. "And I can't wait to sit back and watch. As far as what's owed to me, that's a lot. If it weren't for me, you wouldn't have all that you have, Laz."

"That's complete bullshit."

"I helped you with Fallen Angel. I—"

"You didn't do shit but berate my employees, walk around there like the queen bee, and get on everyone's fuckin' nerves! They actually admitted to me recently that they'd thrown a private party when I came into work the day our divorce was final. A fuckin' fancy farewell! The wicked witch is dead shebang! They tried to act all somber about it 'cause I was upset, but Heathen later told me that that same night they had an actual party over your ass! Jesus! Everyone hates ya, Mimi. You can't get work in the industry anymore because of your bad reputation. So instead of gettin' a normal job, you wanna leech off me and you can't stand it that the free ride is almost over."

She rolled her eyes and yawned. "You want to be on my payroll without doin' a bit of work. Not gonna happen. If I'm not fuckin' ya, I don't care about ya, I don't love ya, or you don't work for me, you don't get *shit*! Those have always been my rules, and they serve me just fine."

"Yes... you and your impossible rules. Everyone must follow the big boss' rules! Mr. Self-Important." She dramatically rolled her eyes. Carelessly tossing his gift box on the floor, she crossed her arms over her breasts "And as far as that divorce party, why in the hell should I care? Those flunkies you hire—ha! Worthless! They hated me because I was always a better manager than you. You've got a bleeding heart for sob stories."

"Yeah, and I fell for yours, too... a bunch of lies and bullshit. I shoulda believed your ex-husband when he tried to warn me about you. Look, I'm done, okay? I am askin' you for the final time to leave, Mimi. We've got nothing to say to each other and I refuse to let you ruin this for me, cause a big ass scene."

"Oh, but I have *plenty* to say to your new sweetheart..." His eyes narrowed on her. "You want to bring my morals into question? Let's try yours out for size. Yeah, that's right. I heard you've got a girlfriend now... not a bitch you just fuck." She shrugged. "I would expect nothing less from you. You keep quite a few in rotation. But I've heard this is *serious*." She grinned wide. "And the word on the street is that she's a charming, pretty, innocent little thing... a dancer... how sweet!"

"My relationship is none of your business."

"Oh, sure it is when it comes to matters of negotiations. I doubt that she is in any way privy to your dark deeds, Lucifer... oh, sorry, Lazarist. Don't you think she'd like to know about who she's *really* dating? So madly in love with?"

He kept his composure, but his head was throbbing. Hard.

"How about I march right on back into my dear sanctimonious mother-in-law's lavish abode, find tha bitch in question, and let her know that her doting, generous, gorgeous, big-dicked daddy is nothing more than a filthy—"

"GET OUT!" The woman burst out in a fit of laughter as she bent low, picked up the present, and turned to walk away. As she made her way down the hall, she glanced over her shoulder with a huge smile.

"Lazarist, I suggest you call your attorney and extend my alimony, dear. For when it comes to my motherfucking coins, I always reach for the sky…"

LEO

CHAPTER FIFTEEN

Feed You to the Lions...

LAZARIST HAD DOWNED two Heinekens, one Corona, and a glass of red wine, and he had no plans on slowing down. He'd cursed out a bastard passing by who looked as if he was trying to take a leak against his club wall, and swore to yank a motherfucker's vocal chords out of his goddamn mouth if he didn't quiet down. That had been the DJ setting up and arguing with his girlfriend on the phone, loud enough so patrons could hear. His temper was shorter than usual that day, and the littlest of things set him off like a rocket.

Things had been… tricky, to say the least. A looming dark cloud hung over his head, the kind he wished he could ignore, but he knew Mimi all too well. She was a Pitbull in a skirt—once her teeth were in you, it would take an entire football lineup, wrestling squad, and hockey team to get her to turn you loose.

Tobias sat across from him in his office, the place filling with second hand smoke. It was early afternoon,

and tonight they had a special comedian being featured—a guy he'd never heard of but he was assured the
fella was a big damn deal. Every seat was sold out, but
instead of basking in the money fall, he chewed on the
events of the last few days, seething at the thought of it
all.

The gold and ivory cake with the large jeweled crown
from the bakery had looked less impressive after Mimi
had dropped in like a shart and shit her negativity all
over the fuckin' place. He had cut a rug with his baby,
forcing big smiles as he danced to the music but inside,
he was all twisted up and enraged. Sky had even given
him the perfect birthday gift – a pair of Tom Ford shoes
he'd been eyeing for a couple of weeks.

Mom had gone out of her way to make his special
day fantastic. Everyone had showed up, even some
people he hadn't seen in months. He'd tried to push
Mimi out of his mind during the party, but it proved
damn near impossible. It hadn't helped that Mom was
going on and on about it, and Eliza had thrown flames
on the fire by working the older woman up in a frenzy.
He'd hoped everyone would just stop talking about the
piece of shit; after all, that was what she wanted, all that
attention.

Tobias crushed his cigarette into the ashtray. The
man had come by just to say hello, as he did from time
to time.

"Had to explain to Sky that my ex is greedy and out
for my blood. Isn't this just fantastic?!" He threw up his
arms in exasperation. "Mimi has come up at least three

times since the party... Jesus. So now my girlfriend's dealing with a guy whose father is a basket case and an ex-wife who is foul beyond belief. Nobody needs this shit right now. Especially not her."

He hated the look on his best friend's face, especially the way his black handlebar mustache twitched and swung up and down as though invisible, microscopic children were using it like a seesaw.

"Shave that fuckin' shit off..."

"Huh?"

"That stupid mustache you've grown out over the past few months. Looks like a fuckin' toupee glued to your upper lip."

Tobias grimaced and shook his head.

"Look, you bastard, don't take your troubles out on me." He laughed, drawing a grin from Lazarist. "Anyway, how's your father doing? You haven't brought him up in a while until just now."

"The last time I actually spoke to him, like discussion wise, we got into it worse than usual. I'm done, man." Lazarist leaned back in his chair and waved his arm in disgust.

"I hate to say it, but that's probably for the best, Lazarist."

"He stopped by the other night, Sky was over and she was sleeping, none the wiser. I didn't even bother lettin' him in, especially not with her there. I saw him on the camera and told him to leave. He tried to start up and I cut off the speaker and the lights. I can't fuck with him anymore. I just can't. Fuckin' toxic. I'm so fucking sick of people."

They were quiet for a spell.

"All right, man," Tobias said, breaking the silence. He clasped his hands together and leaned forward. "Problem number two… What are we going to do about Mimi? I haven't seen you this happy in a while, but if what you told me is true, then she's going to really mess shit up for you. I am certain she means what she said."

"Oh, there's no doubt she meant what she said. You can take that to the bank. Here's the thing, though. She always told me that I taught her well about investments. I got to thinking about that long and hard after she pulled the shit she did at my birthday party. So now, I have a special gift for her, just like she had for me—only this one is a gift that will keep on giving. I'm gonna fuck *all* of her shit up, Tobias… Ya hear me?"

"Shit… what are you cookin' up?"

He passed Tobias a glass of Scotch and leaned against the desk.

"Check this out. She's got assets, shit she doesn't know that I know about."

"She told the judge she was broke."

"Exactly." Lazarist smiled and steepled his fingers.

"How did you find out about this?"

"I hired a private investigator. He found out in less than twenty-four hours. She tried to say she was destitute. She's full of shit. She has like three sugar daddies in rotation, and she's been stockpiling my shit like she's tryna build a fuckin' fort with it. She bought some property out in France, too, but she has it in someone else's name… sneaky whore. I'm goin' after every damn dime she didn't tell the judge about. She perjured herself! This could even include some jail time… You walk into the lion's den, you never leave. She shoulda kept her ass out of my way."

"Shit!" Tobias swiped his forehead; his mouth was hanging open. "I mean, how though? How can you prove all of this? I know that you have the investigator but if it's in someone else's name then—"

"It's simple but you let me worry about the logistics. Trust me." Lazarist narrowed his gaze on him. "It'll be taken care of and the case is being built as we speak. *I* will be taking her ass to court this time. She should've left well enough alone."

"But really, ya know, Laz, you won't have to worry about her if you remove the threat altogether."

"What are you talking about?"

"Why don't you beat Mimi to the punch and just tell Sky the truth? It was a long time ago. You could—"

"Do you realize how hard it was to get that woman to trust me?! Do you have *any* fuckin' clue how long I waited to even be intimate with her? Not because I wanted to wait, but I knew she was different, okay? She was worth the wait. This isn't even about sex. It's about my connection to this woman."

"How did you explain to her about Mimi's debut?" He didn't miss the smirk on the bastard's face. It was a fucking mess. But there was no rewinding time. What was done was done.

"I told 'er that Mimi has an axe to grind and that was

that. I apologized to 'er if it made her uncomfortable. Sky acted okay about it, but I know she wasn't. I could see it in her eyes... It upset her. I don't like it when someone upsets her, even if that someone is me..." They looked at one another for a long while.

"I can see why you love her, Lazarist. This one, and I can't believe I'm sayin' this!" The guy chuckled. "This one just may be the one."

"She *is* the one, Tobias... she really is. When I get a few things sorted, straightened out, I'm going to make her my wife."

"Whoa!" Tobias threw up his hands as if to say, 'slow down.'

"I'm serious. Third time is a charm. This is it. There's not one doubt in my mind. Just the other day, I told 'er that the nightclub was getting a little remodeling. I sent some of the old mirrors 'nd shit over to her studio... those expensive custom made ones."

"Yeah, I know the ones."

"Do you know what she did with them?"

"What?"

"Instead of hawkin' 'em, selling them or even using them herself – and trust me, she wanted them, there was some place over in Harlem – a little dance studio for kids that are underprivileged and she gave those damn mirrors to them." Tobias' eyes grew larger. "Exactly, alright? She cooked lunch for me and brought it over to the club last week when I told 'er I was too busy to break away. Besides my mother and Charity, nobody has ever prepared for me a homecooked meal. Ever. She's helpin' some really talented lady, some singer, with her music video pro bono because she thinks the woman's song has a good message for Black women. I mean, Sky is financially stable, but she's not exactly ballin', okay? She could use the money – but her heart is so big, she doesn't even care. She and my mother, sister and aunt had dinner over there at Gotham Bar and Grill and she kept tryna pay the bill, even though my mother is the one that asked her out.

"My mother fuckin' loves her, Tobias… they talk on the phone for God's sake and text." Tobias chuckled at that. Yeah, it was hard to believe… but it was happening. "My mother hasn't liked anyone this much since Charity – and trust me, mom hates just about *every*one. Sky is the best thing that ever happened to me. She gives me fuckin' back massages, she makes me laugh, she's supportive, she doesn't tease me about me likin' to bite her neck and wanting her to bite mine and she lets me do all kinds of freaky shit to 'er with no complaints – and she's not a former fuckin' porn star in order to do it, either. She loves me, man. I've been waiting a long time for this and it'll be a cold fuckin' day in Hell when I let Man-hater Mimi waltz in and destroy everything. Not gonna happen." He tossed a catalog full of office furniture across the room in a rage. "She fucked with me at the wrong damn time." He leaned in close and pointed his finger at Tobias.

"I would say *any* time is the wrong time to fuck with you." Tobias smiled, then lit a fresh cigarette.

"You threaten me, that's it!" Lazarist threw up his

hand. "She wants war?" He snatched a bottle of cognac from his desk and poured some in a tumbler. "Then she's got it. Lock 'nd load 'em, it's time to blast..."

IT HAD BEEN raining all damn day.

Sky zipped up her gym bag and looked around the studio for a spell before removing her phone from her purse that sat on a nearby chair. She dialed her friend.

Damn. This stupid voicemail again.

"What up! This is Scarlet. Leave a message but please don't make that shit too long because I will not listen to a bunch of rambling that goes on and on like a Tiana Laveen novel. Just get to the mothafuckin' point and don't send me a bunch of text messages either, like you writing a damn thesis because those will be ignored and deleted, too. Some of y'all are fuckin' up my minutes, so make that shit short and concise. I ain't got all damn day. Thank you."

"You *really* need to do something about that voicemail message, Scarlet!" Sky burst out laughing. "You're a damn fool. Anyway, wanted to know if you and Toi maybe wanted to hook up and get drinks tonight. Call me back when you can. I thought you'd be off work by now."

Sky disconnected the call then made her way over to

the small utility closet and pulled out a broom and dustpan. Even though she had a cleaning service come out a couple of times a week, tonight was not their night and she saw some crumbs over near a window, possibly from a cookie.

Probably someone snacking when I told them no food or drinks besides water in here. She went over to the scene of the crime and began to sweep up the mess into the dustpan, humming as she went along. Just then, she heard the door swing open. When she turned and looked, her heart sank. Pure heated anger bubbled within her, along with a feeling of foreboding.

Mimi stood a few feet from her, eyeing her like a venomous snake eyes its prey.

The woman was wearing a pair of yeast-infection-causing jeans, so damn tight, it was wonder she hadn't passed out and died, then rose again like Easter Sunday. Her black high heels were tall, her crop top barely covering the large, manufactured breasts that bounced about within it. Two long, black silky braids were draped down the side of her body, hitting her just above the hip. Light brown eyes shimmered in the light and her mouth twisted in a mischievous smirk.

"Hi, honey, are you Sky?"

Sky placed her hand on her waist and twisted her lips.

She gripped the broom a bit tighter, too… just in case it would come in handy.

"Let's not play these games. You know exactly who the fuck I am. What do you want?" The woman gave a tinkling laugh and began to walk towards her.

"Don't come any closer," Sky warned. Mimi stopped in her tracks. "I'm closed. I didn't invite you in; but of course I and so many others already discovered that you have a knack for coming to places where you're not welcome." Sky sucked her teeth and shrugged. "So why should this be any different?"

"Look, baby, I'm not your enemy, all right?" The woman threw up her hands as if surrendering. Thick, gold bangles clanged together as she swayed to and fro. "We are both women of color in this big wide world, just trying to make it. Unfortunately, we fell in love with the wrong man, and that's the *only* reason why I'm here... to warn you about Lazarist."

"There's nothing that you need to say to me, share with me, or make me aware of, okay? And you can cut it out with the sisterhood of the travelling pants bullshit. Just because you are a woman of color doesn't mean we are on the same team. Hell, we're not even playin' the same sport. Please leave." Sky pointed towards the door.

"Ohhhh, he's got you good!" The lady's eyes narrowed like some serpent's. "Let me guess... your first date was magical, right? He joked a lot, wanted to get you in bed. You, being a good girl 'nd all, probably played the game to nab you a rich guy... acted coy and old fashioned. That only made him want you more. The chase was on. You've probably never had a man of means before, have you?" The woman offered a mock sad expression. "Never mind that. The point is, he is intoxicating."

"Yeah... and I think you're drunk right now. Walk

the line, all the way to the exit, and lock the door behind you."

The woman burst out laughing, but the act was faker than her ass.

"Cute... you're so funny. I can kinda see what he saw in you. Well, kinda." She shrugged. "He's addictive, isn't he, baby? Six feet and five inches of tattooed sex appeal... and he's filthy fuckin' rich. But not all of his money came honest. That's blood money, baby."

Sky swallowed as her eyes narrowed on the woman.

"You're a good girl, aren't you? You probably have a lot of pride, right? You want the best for your community... for your people. You've never dated anyone like Lazarist before. He is definitely different, isn't he?" The woman's voice softened as if she were drifting in a daydream. Sky wanted to run her away, make the woman shriek and bail, but she couldn't. Worse yet, now she was curious as to what this woman was driving at. Worry filled her and this time, no birthday dance would make it go away.

"He can fuck so beautifully, right? It's rough, hardcore music with silk and satin and nibbles and bites against your neck... It's a long, hot, roving tongue against your eager pussy and it's a big, juicy cock that takes your fuckin' breath away—*every.single.fucking.time* he shoves it inside you! He's a beast in bed, with me being a former porn star..." She laid her hand across her chest, her expression proud. "I think that says a lot because honey, I've slept with some truly talented men." She chuckled. "He's perfect... even with that big mouth of his and the terrible temper, like a two-year-old havin' a fit. He's magnificent, in spite of it all. A bit too amazing, right?"

"Spit it out or shut up. I'm sure you've been told that a lot right after the money shot during your movies."

"Oh damn baby, what a funny little girl you are." The woman grinned, her expression tight and creepy.

"A little girl I am not. I'm *all* woman, Mimi. Please don't underestimate me. You don't know me. You don't know me at all." They glared at one another. Sky put her free hand on her hip and cocked her knee, as if resting on the broomstick she had in a death grip. She rolled her eyes and channeled her inner beast.

"Mimi, some of us actually take care of ourselves," she spat, "so we look youthful for our age. We don't look all used up and tossed away like old tissues full of semen. And for the record, please let it be known… I'm a woman who will take this goddamn broom and beat you within an inch of your miserable, worthless, trifling, mothafuckin' cum guzzling, random dick ridin' life. You got it? Don't come up in here thinkin' you are getting Ms. Manners. I'm Ms. David Banner, 'bout to turn into the Hulk, so you've got about five damn seconds to drop a dime or I'm going to dance all over your fuckin' face, stomp you into a one-dollar wine cooler because that's all you're worth. And then I'll sweep you up into this dustpan and toss you out the window for a proper burial."

The woman's expression morphed into one of pure shock.

"Fine. I'll get right to it." She clasped her hands together. "And just so you know, everything I am about to tell you is 100% fact. I gave Lazarist a chance to rectify this situation before I came to you. I have not heard from his attorney, so I believe he has called my bluff. He hasn't answered my calls, either. I have not been faring well in court with him, so if I am going down, so is he. I am going to walk away with something because a loser I am not..." The woman's eyes grew incredibly dark. "You know what they say." She shrugged. "A woman scorned... Anywho, do you remember hearing about the Loren Housing division in Brooklyn?"

"Yes, who didn't? Like so many other historical places, it was taken down by gentrification. Greedy people as usual." She grimaced.

"Yes, exactly." The woman smiled. "Well, guess who was behind that? Guess who bought that property, had all of those poor Black people kicked out and got his greedy big ass tattooed paws on all of that fuckin' money?"

Sky felt her blood running cold. The Loren Housing Project had been one of the few places some people could afford to live. It was also a historical spot; the land once had a large mansion on it that housed runaway slaves who'd managed to make it up North.

"Your lover boy did that. If you don't believe me, look into property records. The online search is free. Remember all of those crying children on the news? Homeless... displaced... They *never* showed the ring master, the guy running the circus, pulling all of the strings. He didn't give a damn about anyone but himself."

Oh God! How could Lazarist do something like that?! What kind of person would do that?! Please tell me this bitch is lying. She has to be!

"You honestly didn't think Lazarist is as wealthy as he is just because of the club, did you?" The woman frowned, then burst out laughing. "So naïve... No, no, no, baby. Now, he's honest about *many* things, but he always keeps a few secrets... that's his nature. A hunter never lets the prey know where all of his weapons are, sweetheart. Just when you think you know him completely, there's some big bombshell he's got squirrelled away, a dirty little secret. Lazarist owns *lots* of properties, but that one right there, yeah... that was his biggest windfall yet."

Sky did everything in her power to not react, to show no emotion.

"I don't believe you. Get out. Now."

She prayed her tone didn't deceive her. The woman smiled so smugly. She turned to walk away, then paused.

"Oh, and one more thing, princess... He'll keep on being your knight and shining armor until you tell him that his shit stinks... He'll keep on treating you like a queen, until you dare to defy his authority... He'll keep on wining and dining you, spoiling you rotten, treating you and your family and friends like you're the best people in the world, until you break his rules. He's a control freak. He's domineering. He's alpha on steroids. He's sadistic. He's greedy. And he will break you the fuck down, Thumbelina. Run. Run as fast as your little dancer feet will carry you…"

At that, the woman turned on her heels, then disappeared out the door, the same way she'd come…

LEO

CHAPTER SIXTEEN

The Day the Sky Fell on the Lion

(What is a King of the Jungle without his Queen?)

S KY STOOD THERE shouting at him in his home, gripping a bunch of papers in her hand. She was in his living room, her laptop secured firmly under her arm. Wearing a pair of yoga pants, an oversized t-shirt, and a scowl on her face, there was no way in hell this would end well. Lazarist had known something was up when he'd tried to call her multiple times but it went straight to voicemail. Sky was mad as hell, but he wished he hadn't seen this coming. Somewhere deep inside, he'd already spotted the writing on the wall. It was his own damn fault for not listening to his inner self, the one that told him to make this right before it was too late. But pride was a hell of a drug...

"And *that's* why I told you I can't stand men like you! You are a true asshole in every sense of the word! Only thinkin' about yourself! Heartless! You had me totally fooled! I shoulda *never* fucked wit' you in the first place!

You ain't shit, you know that?!" She kept on going, waving her finger in his face as she went completely the hell off.

Lazarist couldn't get a word in edgewise. His brain swelled with increased pressure and stress, and he realized something right then. A headache was born, taking full effect. This had only been the first of many Mimi attacks. She'd unleashed the one she believed would upset his woman the most—and boy had she been right. Strange how women were able to tune into each other's weak points so well.

But he'd had enough. It was time to take control of the situation because he'd be damned if this broad, no matter how much he loved her, was going to stand in his living room and go off on him like this without some sort of rebuttal.

"SKY! PLEASE!" His voice boomed as he held his head and pointed towards the couch. "Be quiet. Sit down and listen to me!"

She suddenly drew silent, her eyes narrowed as she seethed, but she did as he asked and plopped down on the couch, while casting him hateful glances from over her shoulder.

"I read everything, you son of a bitch," she began again as she set her computer beside her and slung her purse onto the table. "I didn't let that bitch see me sweat; as you say, I played it cool, but you better believe I left work right afterwards and did my own research. Regardless of the messenger herself being who she is, the message was correct. You can't blame anyone but yourself for this! Those people had nowhere to go, Lazarist, and you displaced them. If you'll do that to all of those people, then who's to say you won't turn on me, too?! There's no possible way you could explain yourself out of this—so don't even bother!"

"Then why the hell are you here?!" He put his hand on his hip, waiting. All she did was purse her lips and shake her head at him in disgust. "I'll tell you why since all you want to do is scream and yell at me, and not let me tell my side of things. You're here because you want an explanation, a reasonable one, so let's cut the bull-shit!" He waved his arm frantically about. "Can't you see what she's doing, Sky? She's trying to drive us apart, force a wedge between us!"

Sky turned away, averting eye contact. She crossed her legs, and her body shook ever so slightly. She looked both enraged and worried. He couldn't much blame her.

"Baby, look." He chanced a couple of steps towards her, his voice low. "Here is what happened with that deal, okay? Yes, those families were put out, but it was happening anyway.

"I had no idea until everything was finalized because the original company buying the property, Sky, pulled out at the last minute. Not because they cared, but because of the bad publicity. I naively stepped in with my money but was unaware of the back story until the very last second. What the news conveniently didn't report is how I rectified the situation after I found out what was happening!"

She slowly turned back towards him—listening now.

Thank goodness!

"I own an apartment building in Queens. I told you about that. The area is actually really nice, and I was renovating it at the time, so a lot of the apartments were empty. I do not take care of the management, but it's mine," he explained. "So, do you know what I did?

"I put all of those families in there for six months with all the utilities and everything paid, free of charge, and then I gave each family $1500 towards their moving expenses once that six month period was over! It was way nicer than where they were at, so yeah, it wasn't in Brooklyn anymore but I made sure they had roofs over their heads, all right? It cost me a hell of a lot of money!" The frown on her face slowly faded. "I don't have proof for that besides bank statements, but I'll be *more* than happy to try and dig all of that up, even though this happened almost ten years ago."

Silence stretched between them for a long while.

"I... I don't think that'll be necessary," she finally said, a clear look of relief on her face.

He disappeared into the kitchen, poured them both a glass of red wine, and returned to her. She took it timidly, her hand shaking ever so slightly.

She didn't need to say how she'd intended to break up with him that night. She'd shown him how her nerves were shot to hell and the whole mess was killing her inside.

Fuck you, Mimi. You did this shit! I am coming after your ass with a vengeance!

"So, you see, yeah, it happened... but not the way it

was portrayed."

Sky nodded, but he could see she was still all worked up, irritated beyond belief.

"Let me tell you something… I am going to handle this, okay?" He gently pulled her arm, forced her to look him in the eye. "But it's going to take me some time. So, what that means is, I'm going to have to come clean to you about a few things."

A look of concern creased her expression. His heart began to pound a mile a minute.

"What?" she questioned softly, her tone letting him know she couldn't take much more. He clasped his hands and dropped his head. His robe fell open and he didn't bother closing it.

"I, uh, I'll be the first to admit that I don't like acknowledging things I have done and said that really don't paint me, I guess you could say, in the best of light. Mimi has some dirt on me… and it would only matter to someone like *you*… someone I want… someone who makes me happy… someone I love. So, I'm going to take my friend Tobias' advice and just take her power away. The way to do that is to air all of my dirty laundry, Sky… to tell you everything she possibly could so I could wring this situation out and make it dry."

He gulped his wine down until there was not a drop left and placed the empty glass on the table.

"I'm not sure I'm ready for this."

He shrugged. "I'm not ready for this either, Sky. I don't want to do it… but I know it's better that you hear it from me." He took a deep breath. "A few years ago, right before I met Mimi, I had an affair with the wife of one of the New York Yankees. It was just a rumor, but it was true… not one of my finer moments."

He closed his eyes, rested the back of his hand across his forehead, and flopped back on the couch.

"So… did you think that was okay? What's the story behind that?"

He shook his head. "No, it wasn't okay, but I was thinkin' with my dick, baby. Men, we don't think the way you all do. It's got less to do with emotions and more to do with what we want at any given time. I didn't love her… I mean, I cared about her, but it was nothin' that serious. Bottom line, she liked how I made her feel. She felt neglected by her husband. I was being romantic with her, showering her with attention, and well, she liked my dick game, too. We had a lot of physical chemistry. They ended up getting a divorce over it, and that's when the guilt came in for me, because they had a couple of kids together. I broke up a family… and if there is a such thing as karma, I definitely got mine when Mimi entered the picture. Anyway, I have had more than a few affairs with married women, Sky, but that happened a long time ago…"

"So you lack morals and character. Big surprise."

At first, he thought the lady was serious, but then he saw her lips curl in a grin.

"I'm not like that anymore. I'm serious. That was really selfish on my part. I can admit that now. I'm not making an excuse for it, either, but their marriage had been screwed up way before I entered the scene, but I still take accountability for putting the final nail in the coffin. She'd been the man's wife after all… and if someone was fuckin' my wife, regardless of whatever issues we were personally havin', I'd probably try to kill whoever came between us."

"You're only telling me this stuff because Mimi would beat you to it, right? Not because you really think it's the right thing to do. You'd take this to your grave, wouldn't you?"

He tried to figure out what she wanted or expected. Regardless, though, he was going to continue to tell the truth, no matter how badly it made him appear.

"Yeah, I wanna beat her to the punch. If I'm to be completely honest with you right now, that's exactly right. This stuff doesn't benefit you to know, in my opinion. But at the same time, who am I to say what you would think is important to know about me and what's not?" He shrugged. "I can't really take that choice away from you… and just because I don't see it as pertinent doesn't mean you might not. It shows the type of morals I had, I guess you could say… but there's always more to it than that, Sky. Sometimes, as ridiculous as you think this sounds, it wasn't just about me, all right?

"I like to make people happy, and even though what I did was wrong, that woman had a need, we were attracted to one another, and even if it was only for a few months, I made 'er happy. It sounds fucked up, I get it, so there it is… I've told you, but I'm tryna explain what was going on in my mind, too. Nah, I wouldn't want you to know this stuff though… which proves that

I knew it was wrong. Who in the hell would want to be seen in a negative light? Especially when I love ya so much and I don't want cha to think I'm some scumbag."

His brows furrowed and his heart beat fast. "I'm human, Sky. I'm a man. I've made mistakes… a lot of 'em. I've done a lot of good too though; I just don't go around tellin' people about it all the time. Yeah, I like to show off and be praised, but the shit that really moves me, that makes me wanna ask what the fuck the President is doin' to change this place, to make it so we all can live and survive in peace, I don't broadcast that, all right? I don't tell people about the donations I make, none of that. It's nobody's business but mine and God's."

They sat there quietly for a spell, then she reached for her wine and took another sip. Setting it down, she turned just so and looked him in the eye.

"I'm not innocent, either. Yes, we're both human and we both have made mistakes in the past and you know what? We're going to *keep* making mistakes, Laz, in the future. The difference is, we have to learn from that stuff, Lazarist. I know that you genuinely care about people… and that's what matters to me." She placed her hand over her heart. "What's important is that you learn from the past, don't keep repeating it, and try to do better in the future. See… I saw you, so I know who you really are. For a minute, I lost balance… I stumbled, baby… Mimi got me off track." She smiled sadly. "But I know what you do under the bright blazing sun, and I know what you do in the dark of the night.

"I saw how you helped that poor guy Mateo at the restaurant. I saw you pickin' up gourmet food in your club one night and walking outside to give it away to the homeless at two and three in the morning."

He had no idea she was aware of that; it wasn't something he shared. To Lazarist, despite him enjoying being in the limelight, going onto social media posting pictures and updating statuses of, 'Look what I did' seemed rather unnecessary, and took the authenticity right out of the act. When he gave, he gave from the heart, not to receive accolades.

"I watched how you talk to your mother and sister, how loving and funny you were with them." She reached for his hand and squeezed it. "Your mother has told me so many things about you, stories that only a man with a good heart would do regardless of you being, well, human, and fuckin' up from time to time. Yeah, when Mimi took me off guard like that, I reacted without thinking."

"Right... and exactly what happened when you first came over here is what she wanted!" His voice trembled as he pointed in the direction of the front door. "She wanted to take everything from me! And by everything, baby, I mean not just my money. It's you..."

She leaned forward, caressed his face, and placed a gentle kiss on his lips.

"I get it now... I do. And I believe you. I understand that she wants us to break up. She wants what I have because you don't want her anymore, and she wants your money, too. Instead of being angry with her, you should feel sorry for her."

"Pssht!" He rolled his eyes. "Fuck her, ya hear me? I am not wastin' one damn prayer on her ass! Feel sorry for her my ass!"

"Laz, I'm serious. Listen to me. She's the type of woman who will *never* be happy. That's why she's gotten so many surgeries, told so many lies, and started so much shit… because she can't stand to be alone with herself."

She reached for him and kissed him again as he sat there agitated, pissed that this woman, who he'd give his life for, was showing compassion for the enemy. What kinda sick world was this? He pushed his head into her palm, eager for her touch. Sky was so beautiful… such a lovely soul.

"People who can tolerate being alone like themselves, Lazarist. They are a fan of their own company. When you see a woman who can never be without a man, be without people around, this points to their insecurity. Being on their own scares them, baby. Because when you're alone, you have to face yourself… you have to see all the parts of you, the ugly and the pretty bits, and not just the external stuff.

"People who can stand themselves, like you and me, we struggle, too. It doesn't mean we always like ourselves twenty-four-seven, and it doesn't mean some days aren't hard and taxing… days when we question our worth. It means, like, when I dance by myself… when the class is gone and I'm alone, it's just me and the music, ya know? It means I can stand it… it means I can step into my own space into this world and be all right.

"Maybe I think I'm having a bad hair day. Maybe it's worse than that… Maybe I wonder why my mama chose the drugs over me and my father." He slowly looked up at her, and her eyes glossed over. "I think about that, ya know, even at my age. She's been gone so long, but sometimes… sometimes I'm all alone, a little girl, dancin', tryna find my mama…"

A tear fell down her cheek and he clutched her tight to him, hugged her hard. She wrapped her arms around him.

"But no matter how good the music is or how hard I dance, she never shows up. I'm a motherless child… and ain't nothing going to change that."

Her body rocked against his as he soothed her, ran his hand up and down her back, kissed her wet cheeks and simply loved her…

"And I think to myself, as I spin 'round and 'round, that she's probably dead or in some institution. And I know that I must have some of her traits, too… and that makes me imperfectly beautiful. All of that still makes me her daughter, no matter what. Despite everything I've been through, I don't mind bein' alone with myself, Laz. Matter of fact, sometimes I prefer it."

She slowly pulled away from him, a big smile on her face.

"I know you don't, Sky. I love how independent you are. It attracted me even more to you."

"Right, but Mimi can't stand it. That's why I told you to feel sorry for her. She's broken to pieces. She's runnin' on a full tank of hatred and because there's so much nastiness in the world, she never runs out of supply. She can fill up almost anywhere. You just happen to be her station of choice right now. She can't stand not being perfect... not being wanted, being rejected by you. Because somewhere deep inside of her, she was rejected, too, but she never got help for it. She never processed it, honey. She turned it on herself and let a bunch of different men fuck her on camera for money. I am not even against porn, per se, but if you gotta take drugs to do it, then it's not for you."

Sky was brilliant. Her compassion and intelligence mixed together and created the thing his mother called 'wisdom.'

He still felt Mimi could go fuck herself, but he kept that thought to himself this time...

"I don't mind havin' flaws. I'm in pretty good shape, but I have some stretch marks on my hip." She smiled as she pointed to her thigh.

"Tiger stripes, baby... they're tiger stripes."

She burst out laughing at this. Then, she kissed him again.

"I have marks. I get pimples sometimes, especially when it's that time of the month or I've eaten too much dessert. I get angry when I should just chill. I chill when I should be angry. I used to look at my father sometimes and hate that he was so protective; so much so, that when I finally *did* get of age to go out and do my own thing, I went wild. So yeah, we all have a history... no such thing as perfection."

"There's no such thing as perfection... but you're

perfect for *me*."

He picked her up in his arms and she wrapped her thighs around his waist. Moments later, they were outside, standing on his bedroom balcony, the lights of Brooklyn shining bright. Muted Spanish music from some nearby joint could be heard playing, voices carried in the city, and the zooming by and honking of cars became their symphony. They stood there in each other's arms, kissing, talking, smiling at one another. He undid the tie along his black robe, allowing it to fall further open, exposing his nature. Her eyes immediately dropped to his cock and her lips curled in an appreciatory grin. Wiggling discreetly out of her black and blue striped yoga pants, she cast them aside. He moved the grill a little to help obscure the dirty deeds he had in mind...

Sitting on a black iron chair, he coaxed her to straddle him.

"Damn!" She hissed as she worked her pussy down onto his rock hard cock. He pumped upward to get deeper. Their eyes locked on one another, they fucked each other in slow motion. He gripped her hips, needing more of her in the worst way.

"No, no, no... don't run from it, baby...just relaaax..."

He bit into his lower lip as he increased his pace. Her hips had risen ever so slightly, putting a gap between his thrusting and the impact. Wrapping one hand around her neck, he pulled her in for a kiss. Their tongues danced along one another's, the heat-filled exchange making his heart beat damn near out of his chest. Crisscrossing his arms around her back, he secured her in place then moved as fast and hard as his hips would allow. She screamed and cried, falling apart against him as her pussy nectar coated his pumping rod. With gritted teeth, he huffed, his anger and lust merging together. Sins from the past had reared their ugly head and threatened his sanity... and his sanity was named 'Sky.'

He couldn't tell her how crazy he would have gone had she left him...

I would've lost my fuckin' mind!

"I love you so much, baby!" he yelled as she came against him. Her legs shook as he slowed down, giving her a moment to release. "You look so beautiful..."

He gently kissed her forehead. Her soft, sweet moans escalated his need for her for his own ecstasy was contingent upon making her happy... making her feel good all over. They fell in love with one another all over again, their bond tight, bound in steel, metal, and the history of tortured pain. She was the street savvy good girl, and he was the bad boy with a heart. Together, they'd rule the world.

He groaned and jerked as his climax caught him un-expectedly. Feeling the fire all inside him, he emptied within her, jolting and falling apart beneath her beautiful, limber body.

Pulling her shirt up, he bathed her breasts with his working tongue. The taut nipple was his dessert as he enjoyed the sweetness of her flesh. The heat of her pussy hugged his throbbing cock and he never wished for this to end. The feeling of desire, ownership, and loyalty blended together as they once again became one.

Yes. Ownership… what a thing to say to a woman, but he knew it was true. He was a collector, a lover of 'things', just as she'd accused him of so long ago, and in the most beautiful of ways he declared her his favorite item of all. He would do everything to protect her for she was his… all his and his alone.

His eyes narrowed with a sudden, insane burst of jealousy when the thought of her with another man crossed his mind…

What if she'd left him after hearing of his sordid deeds? Surely, she'd move on, find another guy to fuck… dance into the lucky bastard's life and make the sky rattle with a thunderstorm, so that he, too, would fall under her spell.

"Ah!" she screamed out as he used the last bit of his erection and pumped within her hard, until he couldn't go any further.

Perhaps it was insecurity that made the big, brave lion do such a thing… remind her that he'd found her first. She belonged to him now, rightfully so…

He gently kissed her shoulder, then bit lightly into her neck, and she purred.

She purred so beautifully…

She's mine. Anyone who tries to take my beautiful dancing doll away from me will live to be sorry. I'm generous with my money, not with my mate.

Men kill over money. Men kill over power. Men kill over pussy…

He seethed within as images of Mimi jumped within his head—all the horrible things she'd done to him, said about his family, and now this!

How dare she show up to Sky's job? That's a lot of damn nerve.

And then, he smiled. He grinned so wide, he almost erupted in a chuckle.

They say elephants have a long memory, but cats are vengeful creatures. Thus, the ones that cross them, the ones that betray them, the ones that try to steal their joy, take away their shiny, pretty things will suffer... because the lions rule the jungle for a reason—they are brave, they are fearless, and they fight to the death.

And most of all, just when you think you're safe, you're not.

They never forget a mothafuckin' thing, and once you're on their hit list, you are forever their prey...

LEO

CHAPTER SEVENTEEN

Take You on the Ride of a Lifetime...

LAZARIST SKIPPED HIS way out of the courtroom. The latest scheme had failed miserably for Mimi, who was found to be a parasite to the court system—the judge said as much.

As he made his way to his brand new white Porsche, a little belated birthday gift to himself, the bloodsucker chased after him, her silver heels sparkling against the cement as she weaved about in the parking lot like a fruit fly around a bowl of apples. He could see her in his car reflection as he got ready to open the door. Her chest heaved up and down, her twisted, demented expression a thing of victorious beauty. He slowly turned in her direction and grinned, showing all his teeth.

"Hi, loser!" She reached to smack him again, just as she'd done on his birthday, but he caught her wrist and squeezed. She winced in pain, giving him delights that she could never fathom. Tossing her arm down as hard as he could, he smirked at her.

"Wouldn't want to mess that hand up, would you? That's your good hand, the one you use to count other people's money."

"Lazarist, you're going to be very sorry about what you've been doing to me! *Very* sorry!"

He crossed his hands over his crotch and jammed his tongue against his jaw to stop a foul curse from escaping. Shaking his head in disbelief, he gave himself a moment to calm down and stop from causing a scene that would truly land his ass in jail.

"You just can't get enough, can you? I know the dick, the nice dinners, the tongue work, the exotic vacations, the expensive jewelry, the spa dates for you and your friends, the big house and the money were good, but good Lord, baby!" He threw up his hands, his face hurting for he was grinning so hard. "There's more fish in the sea!" He cackled. "You've fucked half of 'em. You should know all of their names by now! Nemo, Flipper, Jaws, hell, since you're bisexual, Dory, Ariel the Little Mermaid, and a fish called Wanda, too!"

"Fuck you, Lazarist! I am *not* walkin' away empty-handed. You know me better than that!"

"You usually walk away with a face and fist full of jizz… but I understand. Not gonna happen this time around. Listen, lady…" He began to count off his fingers. "First, I file for divorce from you after discovering your insanity and the way you enjoy drama… you keep shit goin' and flowin' like laxatives and plumbers fixin' broken johns. Second, you keep the courts all jammed up with these ludicrous court cases against me. They're tired of your shit, too. You've had three different attorneys on top of it all.

"Third, you go to my fuckin' girlfriend's place of business and tell her half-truths to stir up trouble—but instead you drove us closer together, as if that were possible. You inadvertently proved that we have that kind of bond. Finally, you have the fuckin' audacity to step to me in this parking lot after your case was thrown out of court! Just like when I threw you out on your ass! This is my last warning to you..."

He paused to rein himself in. "Look at me now! Fuckin' look at me." He did not continue until he was sure her eyes were looking into his. "Trust me Mimi Bianca Bryson, you should be grateful for it. I don't give multiple choice or multiple chances. The only multiples I supply are multiple orgasms, which you'll never receive from me ever again for as long as you shall live. I am stingy with the warnings... so this is your last one. You're pushing me, baby..." His eyes narrowed on her as he tried hard to hold it all together. "But I'm not going off the edge. I'm going to turn around and bite you where it hurts."

He swung the door open and got in his car. The fresh smell of the new vehicle was invigorating.

As he pulled away, leaving her standing there, he immediately dialed the private investigator he'd hired some time ago.

"Hey, Mark! It's Lazarist Zander."

"Hi, Lazarist. How's it goin'?"

"Great. Just watched another two hours of my life roll away, time that I'll never get back due to the ol' insane ex-wife. I need to move on this. Like I told ya, she won't let up. I know this isn't the end, so I need everything ya got to help shut this shit down once and for all. Despite it being inconvenient and time consuming with these ridiculous trumped up money grubbing lawsuits, she's wreaking havoc in my relationship; she's also been callin' my fuckin' mother and getting into it with her, and I can't have her trying anything else. I wanted to get a restraining order, but then I realized that I may need to build a case in order to prove her instability. She'll just get more strategic with a restraining order, anyway. I've heard about her in action. It wouldn't be her first time being told to back the hell off and she treated it as if it were a mere suggestion. I need this to end, all right? Like yesterday!"

"Got it. Completely understood! Just give me another five days or so, and I should have the report complete. She gets around, doesn't she?" The guy chuckled. "She's got a real bad shopping habit too. She's goin' through money like water and she still has *plenty* to burn."

"Of course she does, because it's not just about the money for her, Mark. I realize that now. Even if I were broke, she would be harassing me. She doesn't like that *I* was the one to leave *her*. That was a shock and a blow to her self-worth. She can't face the fact that I've moved on and I'm happy. *Real* happy. She's out for blood, man, but I'm not backing down from this. I was built for shit like this… I will hit her where it hurts. She must've forgotten who I am. I'm just the bastard to remind her. Call me Ginkoba." While Mark burst into laughter, he fixed his ring on his pinky finger and pulled out onto the street. "All right, I'll check back in with ya next week. Hold down the fort and lift every rock. I want to know *every*thing she's been doing; hell, even the last time she farted. I want it all!"

"Will do, boss! Talk to ya soon!"

Lazarist disconnected the call and made his way to Fallen Angel. He had a mountain of shit to take care of, and tonight, he wanted to quit on time.

Because he had his own private dancer now, waiting for him at home…

LEO

"OKAY, NOW PUT your foot on the brake… No! That's the accelerator!"

Their necks jerked as if they'd been attached to tether poles before the woman came to an abrupt halt. Lazarist braced his chest as if he were having a heart attack and rolled his big blue eyes, laying on the drama in his customary way.

"And I thought I only *worked* with actors! Apparently, I've been sleeping with them, too! Just stop it, all right?"

"You're gonna kill somebody, Sky."

"We're in this big ass parking lot alone at midnight, Laz! Who tha hell am I going to hit?"

"You just gave me whiplash!" He rubbed his neck as if he really needed medical attention. A call to 911 was perhaps in order as he sat there looking helpless, getting on her very last nerve. Sky sucked her teeth and rolled her eyes as she kept her hands on ten and two, gripping the wheel a bit harder to stop herself from hitting him upside the head.

"Look, you told me you'd teach me how to drive. I might not even decide to after I get my license, but I want it as an option. You agreed with me, and now here you are acting like I'm supposed to be a professional, like my ass has NASCAR credentials after ten minutes in this dark parking lot. And you're barking at me like some dog!"

"Well, call me Scooby Doo, damn it, because you're treating my ride like the damn mystery machine! I'm about to be a *real* ghost if you have it your way and your friend Velma's blind ass runs us into a damn pole!"

She hissed and shook her head. "Real funny, Laz... real funny!"

"You're going to destroy my Lexus. I took this one out of commission because I knew it would be the easiest for you to learn on. It's not a stick, it drives easy, and it's intuitive. I tell you what, in all seriousness, okay? Let's go to the junk yard and get you something tomorrow. Something that costs about five hundred bucks or so. That way, I can feel better about whatever happens. You can tear it up and I won't lose any sleep over it. Or better yet, let's just go buy you one of those electric scooters. Owww!"

She plopped him upside his head. He grinned and rubbed the offended area, then took a deep breath and pointed to the steering wheel.

"Okay, Sky… fine. Let's start again. Take it out of park." She reached for the gear and did so. "Put it in drive. No… that's neutral… Why are the windshield wipers going?!"

The damn things swished back and forth faster and faster, making a blurry mess across the glass.

Oh, no!

Laz reached over in a huff, shoved the gear in park, turned off the wipers, and burst out of the passenger's side door like a cyclone. He marched around the car, his suit jacket swinging like he was a tall George Jefferson. Before she knew it, she was swooped out of the driver's seat and placed on the passenger's side faster than her head could spin.

"Oh, so that's how it is?!" The man put the car in drive and began to leave the parking lot. "Laz! You hear me talking to you! Stop driving this car and give me another chance!" He slowed down, still looking straight ahead.

"Sky, do you know what your problem is?"

"Yes, I somehow decided to fall in love with a man like *you*!"

"I said your problem, not your blessings." At this, she rolled her eyes. "Your biggest problem is that you don't follow directions. I can't work with people who don't fuckin' follow orders. Just let me be in love with you, and that's it." He waved his hand dismissively. "I'll get you enrolled in a driving class, first thing in the morning. I promise. I'm throwin' in the towel."

"I *do* follow directions, Mr. Hot Under the Dog Collar! Still barkin' as usual! Secondly, I don't want to take a driving class when you can just as easily teach me. Throwing in the towel? So now you're a quitter... how sad."

Suddenly, the man looked up to no damn good. He ran his tongue over his lower lip and eyed her as if she were the last chicken wing in town.

"Fine. Challenge accepted. I'm going to teach you how to drive a car, *all right!*" He lunged at her, reached over her body in a flash, and suddenly the passenger's seat flew back, forcing her to practically lie down as if she were on the floor. "Turn around and get on your knees."

"I don't know what you're talkin' about. This isn't any kinda driving lesson that—" She was stopped short as he slid quickly over to her and mounted her from behind. "What... what are you doing?!"

She shuddered when she heard him yank his zipper down and felt his big, warm hand glide against her back, then slide down to her leggings. He yanked them down to her knees, and her panties came next. A cool breeze chilled her exposed ass but was soon replaced with his pressing groin. The softness of his pubic hair made her pause but the hardness of his big fucking cock against her crack made her swallow. He roughly kneed her thighs apart.

"This is how you drive a car! Put the shit in drive!" Her body trembled more violently when his tongue glided against her lower back then traced around the tip of her ass crack. Digging her fingernails into the seat fabric, she squelched a scream when his tongue darted in and out of her asshole, twisting and turning, fucking her with it like he loved every damn second.

"Oh my God! You're so nasty! You filthy son of a bitch!" She squealed... but damn, did it feel so good! He increased his pace, then stopped, leaned against her back, and gripped her breasts, giving a hard squeeze.

"You put your hands on ten and two, just like this! Tonight, you're gonna learn how to drive a stick shift though, baby! I changed my mind!"

She screamed out when he impaled her very soul. Fingers shaking as she tried to get a good grip, the seat and car rocked so ferociously, it was a wonder the damn thing didn't fall apart.

I guess Toyotas really are built to last!

His groans were loud and guttural as he thrust deep and fast within her. Her breasts ached from the way he gripped them, the pain and pleasure merging into a delightful cocktail she felt a tinge of shame for enjoying. The heat from his mouth tickled her neck, then the dull pain of his teeth scratched her skin. Their moans intertwined as he loved her down. His sex was so damn delicious...

"Bring it back! Bring that ass all the way the fuck back!" He slapped her butt cheeks hard, commanding her to rock her hips into his domineering plunges. Bright lights soon shone in the distance, and she stiffened, fearful they'd be seen out in public having a go at one another. But Lazarist kept right on; in fact, he didn't even slow down…

"Lazarist! Someone is coming!"

"So!"

"So?!"

"Let them come. That's damn sure what I'm trying to do!"

He took a fistful of her hair and yanked, causing her to moan and sigh as he glided his hand against her pussy, petting it, rubbing her folds and clit with precision.

"Oh God!" she belted.

"I know all the buttons to push… all the ways to make you get up and go… Laz knows *all* the ways to rev up Sky's engine… Tonight, I am showing you how to drive a motherfuckin' car. Cum on!"

Her pussy rained down upon him, and she shook at the realization that she was squirting, falling apart beneath him. Her right leg trembled uncontrollably, her back arched, and she clawed at the air, desperately needing to hold on to something as she fell hard into an orgasmic abyss.

"Second gear!" he roared, jolting her out of her soft, fuzzy place.

With a firm grip around her neck, he jostled himself

hard and jack rabbit fast within her, never slowing as the car that was approaching drove slowly past. Lazarist had told her this old building rarely had any visitors, the structure on the property being condemned and shut down for months. She was relieved to see that the car kept on going, and couldn't believe that her man truly didn't give a shit about who saw him fucking in the middle of nowhere.

She hollered when he practically knocked the passenger's door off the hinges, shoving it open. Cold air tickled her exposed flesh as he hoisted her around her waist, his dick still deep inside her. With careful steps, he placed her hands against the hood of the car, then continued to ruthlessly fuck her.

She was in too much shock to speak...

Too turned on to tell him 'No' or 'Stop', she caught his image in the reflection of the car window, the way his lips were turned as if he were angry with the world...

Her nipples grew hard from the coolness of the top of the car. Her body slid violently up and down it as he growled, huffed, and tore her pussy up, manhandling her in the most wonderfully ruthless of ways. Soon, she felt the nudge of his chin pressing into her shoulder blade...

He's almost there...

She smiled in anticipation.

She sighed as his teeth pierced her skin and the warmth of his cum filled her valley. A few more deep thrusts, and he fell upon her, breathing hard against her back until she heard the jingle of his belt...

"And that... my love..." he stated breathlessly, "is how you drive... a car... a Sky-dancer Cadillac Supreme, to be exact..."

CHAPTER EIGHTEEN

Dancing to a Different Tune

S KY WALKED AROUND Lazarist's lavish home office, eavesdropping on his conversation. The man's frustration was more than evident, especially with how he kept swiveling back and forth in his leather chair like he was on some amusement park ride.

"Well shit, how much longer? …Yeah, I understand that but she… okay… I know that… okay. All right, Mark… another week. Damn!" The man gripped his forehead as if he had a headache. "Man, you really gotta put this in turbo charge… All right, yeah, I know it takes time for what I requested… I'll try to be patient but that's not my strong suit… yeah… okay… talk to you later."

Lazarist disconnected the call and picked up his drink off the desk, chugging it.

"Who was that? What's wrong?"

"Nothing, baby… just some business shit. So, are you ready to go?" He spun around, a big smile on his face.

"Yes, I'm ready, but I want you to tell me where we're going first."

"No. That'll ruin the surprise, baby. I've already told you that. Come on now, just relax and enjoy." He got to his feet, looking dapper in his Brunello Cucinelli dark suit. He'd paired it with a rich red tie that caught the light just right. As he stepped around the desk, she could see even his socks had a bit of red in them. What a capricious but nice touch.

"Why do I have on this expensive dress you bought me? Come on! Just tell me, Laz, damn! Okay, just a hint. Please?!!!"

She stomped her foot like a brat, hoping he'd break down and blurt whatever surprises and secrets he had up his sleeve.

"I am not telling you anything, baby, but you *do* look amazing! There's no doubt about that."

He laughed lightly as he buttoned his suit jacket and polished off the last drop of his liquor. Going to a mirror that hung on the door of a small closet in his office, she checked out her reflection. She was dressed in a high collar, red and black, long bodycon dress with an Asian feel. One long slit ran up the leg, and her shoes were made of black silk, tying up the leg, reminding her of platform ballerina slippers. Laz had placed a bright red ring on her right hand and a teardrop red pendant necklace that was so beautiful, she'd been rendered speechless. She didn't know what type of stone or jewel it was, but it was gorgeous.

To pull the entire look together, she'd pulled her hair up in an elaborate braided bun adorned with two black chopsticks she'd negotiated down to half the price from the little Asian shop around the corner from her apartment. Lazarist messed around on his phone for a spell, then made his way towards the door.

"I'm going to take a piss and then we can leave. I'll be right back…"

She could hear his footsteps until they faded out. How she loved the look and smell of this room. Nosing about, she hoped of finding clues he may have accidentally left out in regard to their secret rendezvous.

It's so comfy in here…

She felt close to him when she was in his office. It exuded his essence, summed him up perfectly.

The place was decorated in rich hues of ebony wood, gold, and marble. On his desk sat a large gold glass that held various expensive pens he'd received from around the world. He kept things pretty tidy, but the place was still filled with knickknacks, odds and ends, making it interesting. He often burned candles that smelled like tobacco and turned on a diffuser containing peppermint essential oil. He said it relaxed him.

Ever so faintly, throughout the entire house, the speakers pumped out music. This time, it was 'Trip' by Ella Mai. She began to sway her hips to the sexy music and snap her fingers. Dipping her hand in his box of coveted gold covered chocolates, she unwrapped one and popped it into her mouth, then tossed the wrapper in his clear glass trashcan that sat next to his desk. She rolled the smooth chocolate along her tongue until it melted against her palate.

These are so damn good…

Bopping about, swaying to the music, she moved to and fro and began to peruse his book collection. Most of them were about land ownership, investing, the history of New York, a few true mafia books, the biography of Hugh Hefner, and a couple that looked as if they were strictly for reference—old thesauruses and hardbound dictionaries with gold binding and such. One book caught her eye, however, for it stuck half way off the shelf, as if it were about to fall to the floor. She pulled the black, thick, and heavy book out of its place and read the title.

'The Black Pussy Vortex' by Dr. Saint Aknaten. She shook her head and cracked up at the title, then flipped through it, landing on a portion that had been highlighted with a yellow marker.

Every King must have a Queen if he wants to rule and reign.

… Pray for your prey, gentlemen …

Ask the creator to lead you to her. This could take less than an hour from the time of request, or it might take years. It depends upon the two of you and how open you are to love.

Once you find her,

Hunt the prey.

Fuck the prey.

Marry the prey.

Plant your seed in the prey.

Protect the prey at all costs.

DATE. MATE. PROCREATE.

The Queen runs the show. She just makes the King believe he does...

It's all a game, ego driven bullshit. Why is the Queen the one holding the most influence? Without the Queen, we are nothing.

If you destroy the woman, you destroy the entire civilization.

No nation, no people, no domicile has ever stood the test of time if the Queen was annihilated. The womb is the temple. The womb is your altar. But the womb is made of glass... fragile.

She can be destroyed with words and ill intentions, just as much as she can with cannons, artillery, and sharp blades.

Remember that when you disrespect her... when you cheat on her... when you don't provide for her and your family... when you lie to her... you are destroying the civilization, one dastardly deed at a time...

If you cast her away, do not be surprised if she is discovered and treasured by another. You will not be able to regain your seat by her

side.

Not because she lacks loyalty, but because she has now outgrown you.

Step up your game, mothafucka.

Defend the damn Queen...

Wow... that's wild!

She shook her head as she closed the book then placed it back onto the shelf in the proper way. Just then, King Lazarist entered the room, a coy smile on his face. He slipped on his coat and placed hers on her as well. She had to admit, she felt special. The sneaky bastard was up to something, and he'd covered all of his tracks.

"All right, beautiful. Your chariot awaits..."

LEO

THE GOLD AND white limousine pulled up to the Lincoln Center. The driver soon opened their doors and Lazarist helped Sky out of the vehicle. With a tug of her dress, she got the fabric back in the right position after they'd felt each other up on the way over. He couldn't keep his hands off her, and tonight, like most nights when he was feeling rather amorous, the feeling was mutual. It didn't help that they'd both been drinking, which only whittled down the bit of decorum they actually possessed.

As they walked hand in hand, he caught their reflection in the window and winked.

We look like a power couple... because we are...

He didn't miss the large, childlike smile that spread across her beautiful face, her cheeks plumping like a rosy-cheeked cherub.

"Lincoln Center, Laz! What are we going to see, huh? A dance, I hope! I love it here... haven't been in a long time!"

He opened the building door and she stepped inside, him following close behind. Wrapping his arm around her waist, he kept her secure to him as they waded through the crowd.

"It's time you kick up your feet and relax for a change. Instead of you dancing, you get to watch someone else. Tonight, we're going to see Alvin Ailey American Dance Theater."

Suddenly, Sky stopped walking and snatched her hand away. The poor woman's chin was trembling and her eyes glossed over.

Oh shit...

"No, no, no!" Leaning in close, he embraced her, people bumping into them as they came and went. Resting his chin on her shoulder, he whispered in her ear, "Baby, don't do this. I can't have you crying on me now... This is supposed to be special, ya know? Something to make you happy... I'm tryna make you happy, honey, that's all."

"Don't you see? You did!" He pulled back and looked into her eyes. "I just... I'm in awe right now.

There's no way you could've known..."

"Known what, baby?"

"When I was about seventeen years old, I saw the Alvin Ailey American Dance Theater perform. Obviously it was a different troupe at that time." He smiled affectionately at her. "And it moved me so much. I had never seen anything like that in my life. All of those tempting tan, deep russet, rich mahogany, soft peach, ripe banana with freckles, midnight sky, auburn undertones like sunset at dusk, desert sand, and chocolate bar brown men and women swaying to the music that dug deep in your soul and pulled all you had within and spun you around and around... exposing their unbelievable talent with each fluid motion... I was never the same after that, Laz, in a good way. It changed my life!"

A tear fell down her face. "They inspired me so much! People of color, *my* people, dancing in celebration, telling a story with their limbs... this time not because we had to. We weren't just mere entertainers for an oppressive system that saw us as lesser than... barely human. No, we stood tall trying to caress the sun and bent low to the Earth, attempting to go back to that from which we came. And we were proud! Proud to be talented! Proud to be Black! Proud to live our greatest life!"

He smiled at her and ran his thumb across her cheek, careful to not do it too hard... he didn't want to ruin her makeup.

"I'm a dancer by nature, Lazarist. I was born to dance, born to teach... and I'm so... I'm so happy right now!" More tears sprang from her eyes before she buried her face against his chest. He lovingly ran his hand along her back, soothing her. "Thank you! This was so thoughtful, Laz. It means so much to me."

Her gratitude warmed his heart. His soul was full.

"You're welcome." He tilted her chin up and made her look him in the eye. "Anything for my baby."

He kissed her forehead, wrapped his arm back around her, and led her to their seats. Time went past faster than he realized. Much to his surprise, he was loving the show. They sat holding hands, staring at one another for extended spells of time, kissing, then concentrating on the beauty before their eyes. Lovely dancers contorted their bodies in the most amazing ways. It was spellbinding. He'd seen his baby do similar moves—she practiced every day from the moment she woke up. She did it so effortlessly, with so much grace. He got easily aroused from watching her move like that. Rarely was she allowed to leave his abode without a morning quickie if she dared to let him watch...

Shoving the thoughts out of his mind, he shifted in his seat to get more comfortable. Before long, the show was over and her exuberance thrilled him to no end.

"That was... incredible!" she squealed as they made their way out of Lincoln Center, the crowd spilling all around them. She fanned herself with her program, and if her smile were any bigger, her face might have cracked.

"It was, right? Thanks. I definitely owe you a 'thank you' because if it weren't for you, I doubt I would've gone on my own... wouldn't think I would've liked it but I really did." He glanced down at his watch and cleared his throat. "So, uh, before we leave, did ya wanna walk over to the water fountain? They have it all lit up at night... it's nice."

"Yeah, I'd like that."

She laid her head against his shoulder and wrapped her hands around his arm, squeezing tight. Before long, they stood in front of the fountain, the water glowing with hues of gold. He stood there, entranced, thinking...

"You know, when I was a little boy, my father used to take me and my sister to this restaurant, some Chinese joint, I forget the name of it. It was a long time ago and it's closed now; something else is there. A clothing store I think... Anyway, this place had a little water fountain with koi fish 'nd shit in it." Sky listened, her expression curious. "He would mostly take us there sometimes after picking us up from school. Sometimes we'd eat in, but most times, he'd get carry-out and then all four of us would sit down as a family and eat dinner together.

"Eliza liked to look at the fish, and she'd beg Dad for one. He'd always say 'no', but I remember staring down at the coins, thinkin', 'Wow! That's a lot of money!' One time, my dad told me that the money itself wasn't important—what mattered was what it symbolized. He went on to explain that it was in there because people had made wishes. Some people just tossed it in because it seemed like the thing to do. Others did it because they saw other coins in there and thought, 'why the hell not?' Some though had dreams, and they were so desperate that they tossed their little bit of money into a koi fish pond beneath a battery-operated waterfall, hoping that God would see that and help them out. They'd never admit this to anyone, but somewhere deep inside, they really hoped their luck would change. At that time, me and my sister were just a couple of rich kids who didn't know what struggle meant… *yet*." He laughed dismally as he cocked his head to the side. "But yeah, I never forgot that… wishin' on a star, ya know?"

Sky's hand warmed his back as she rubbed it, soothing him.

"I see love kinda the same way, baby." He turned away from the alluring lights of the fountain and looked at her, holding her close. "Some people do it because it seems like the right thing to do. Others do it because they just wanna be like everyone else… that relationship goals type shit we see posted everywhere… and it isn't even realistic. Every couple has problems, bumps in the road."

Sky nodded in agreement. "But then, there are some people who are hoping and praying that they find their better half… that in this crazy city, hell, in this fucked up world, they manage to run into the guy or the girl that just turns their life completely around. It's not the penny, nickel, dime, or quarter that means much. It's what it means to the person who tossed it into a little aquatic oasis filled with fish. I was all of those people at various times in my life, Sky. When I married my first wife, it just seemed like the right thing to do because I loved her and she wanted to get married… and I wanted to make 'er happy.

"The second time I did it because everyone thought I was the luckiest guy in the world to catch the eye of a big time ex-porn star. Mimi garnered a lot of attention. She's known practically wherever she goes… and I did love her, Sky, but not with the kind of love that warranted a marriage. I did it because, well, I wanted to do what I thought people expected me to do… get me a gorgeous woman who everyone wanted. But she was hollow on the inside, and I couldn't connect with her. Not because of her past job, but because of her past, *period*… You were right, Sky. She does hate herself, and she had it rough.

"No excuse for the shit she pulled, but I know where it came from. Regardless, I made a mistake, a big one because that marriage should've never happened. Even up until the wedding day, I contemplated callin' it off. But my ego…" He shrugged and turned away. "I just couldn't… I couldn't stand to look bad by doin' something like that. I had a lot to learn, the hard way. But I've learned my lesson now… and now, I am finally experiencing the third reason why people toss their money into the pond…"

He dropped down on one knee before her and took her hand.

"Lazarist… Lazarist! Oh my God…" Her voice cracked as her eyes welled up with tears. And so did his…

"I've wanted to be at this stage in my life and meet someone like you, Sky, for a long ass time. I'll be honest and humble myself for ya. I never thought a woman like you really existed, and if she did, I wasn't always so certain I'd deserve her. I love your personality, and you're fuckin' beautiful, too. You're funny, you're tough, witty, soft when it counts… you're a wonderful lover and you're my friend. I can trust ya, and that's real important to me, baby. I've got thousands of associates, but only a handful of true friends because I don't trust easily anymore. I've been through too much, Sky. I'm damaged."

"We all are, baby…"

"I'm a handful, but you managed to hang in there anyway. You love me…"

"I do! I love you so much, Laz."

"I know that you do. I can always see it in your eyes, even when you're sick of my shit." They both chuckled at his words. "I can hear your love for me when we speak to one another… I can feel your love for me when we make love—you give me all of you, never holding back… I am… I am totally in awe of you. This time, I will toss my coins in the small fountain not because I need to be like everyone else, not because of public approval or what's expected of me, but because I want to experience love… *true*, passionate love for a change. The kind that is filled with give and take. No pressure… it's not forced. It just comes naturally."

He swiped a tear from his cheek and removed a blue Tiffany box from his pocket. By now he could see that people had gathered around them, watching. Sky gasped, her tears flowing softly down her face. He opened the box and showed her the ring he'd painstakingly selected—a platinum French cut halo diamond band engagement ring, with a four carat cushion center stone.

"Sky Jordan, love of my life… I have an important question for you. Will you marry me?"

She nodded, her smile bright and big as she continued to cry. "Yes! I will marry you, Lazarist." Her voice quivered.

Standing, he removed the ring from the box and slid it down her finger. The people around them clapped loudly and he heard a few whistles. He wrapped his arms tightly around her, rocking her back and forth, unable to imagine any better feeling than this…

Pulling out a coin from his pocket, he tossed a quarter into the fountain.

Once for the past, two times for the present, and three times for their future…

LEO

♌

CHAPTER NINETEEN

Write a Check Yo' Ass Can't Cash

"YEAH… SO IT only seems fair."

Rubbing on his chin, Lazarist leaned back in the white Porsche's car seat. Chronixx' 'Skankin' Sweet' played through the car speakers. As of late, his love of Reggae music had become stronger. Once upon a time, that was all he listened to, though he'd rather forget the brief spell he'd gone through at age twenty when he'd tried to grow dreads. What a disaster. He credited his love for reggae to its healing powers. He'd had so many breakdowns and hard times in life, the music helped him get through those rough patches. When he heard it, he imagined swaying palm trees, fresh coconut juice, and beautiful bronze women walking in sheer, colorful sundresses along sandy shores. It relaxed him like peppermint incense, long stiletto shaped nails slicing into his back, Sky's open thighs, and money stacking in his account.

"Hmmm, glad you had a change of heart and understand that this is best... for *both* of us," Mimi stated on the other end, dragging him out of his deliberations.

He swallowed a chuckle. He could hear her inhaling and exhaling, imagining her hookah in her hand. Her pussy was probably flooding from the excitement his words conjured up. After all, bringing a motherfucker like him down would be a feather in her cap for certain. "So, you'll be over with the check when, my love?"

"I can be over right now actually. Give me about thirty minutes."

"Okay, great." He could hear the satisfaction in her tone. "I'll be waiting, baby."

And then she disconnected the call. He leaned forward and turned up the music. An uncontrollable smile creased his face. He looked down at his tattooed fingers as he worked the steering wheel, making his way to Manhattan. They symbolized the craziness of his youth, not something he'd do at his current age. Yet, they showed a path he'd taken, one he'd travelled while wearing blinders, living by the seat of his pants.

Dollar signs, skulls, hearts, his zodiac sign, Charity's initials, they were all there... In fact, all the tattoos on his body told a story, too. He'd thought about getting some cover up work, but right then, he appreciated them. They showed he was captain of his own ship, doing his own damn thing...

...It was great to be king...

LEO

SKY GOT OUT of the Uber and walked right up to Mr.
Palsy, the realtor. He'd been referred to her by Lazarist,
and for what it was worth, she could see why the man
was so good at his job—he had the gift of gab, made her
feel comfortable and showed her some of the most
gorgeous properties in Manhattan, some of which she
had no idea were even up for grabs.

It was evening rush hour in Manhattan, and this was
the last property she was scheduled to see. They'd parted
ways earlier, but then he got a call about another
property and told her it was a must see. She felt close to
exhausted; they'd been out for over two hours already,
but it was now or never. Located on 36th Street, the
building had been renovated and had just come up for
lease. This was the opportunity of a lifetime.

Mr. Palsy extended his hand for a shake. "Nice to see
you again, Ms. Jordan."

"Nice to see you, too! So, here it is, huh?" She
looked up at the towering place, loving it already.

There is no way this place is in my budget!

"Yes, here it is! I think you'll find it quite nice and
though it is a bit smaller than your current studio, there
are some upgrades you may find too enticing to resist!"

He winked at her and they made their way inside.
Ten minutes later, she was practically salivating. The
mirrored walls were gorgeous, the windows huge and let
in so much light. There were built in speakers in the

walls and a restroom right inside, so no need to go out into a hallway or another floor to relieve oneself. The floors were in incredible condition and though it was slightly smaller in floorspace, the ceilings were higher, making it feel and look massive.

"This is incredible. I can't even deny it. This is the best property I have seen thus far."

The agent nodded in agreement as he handed her a paper with all of the information.

"I knew you'd like it. That's why, despite the inconvenience of coming back out tonight, I realized I had to show you right away. It just went on the market this afternoon and with this location, it will be snapped up quickly. It meets most of your expectations." He shoved his hand in his pocket, his shoes echoing against the floor as he slowly paced about. "Also, the couch and chairs stay." He pointed to the modern furnishings. "They were bought to stage the place but it was made clear that they are thrown into the price. There's central air... no window units required. As you can see, there's even a water fountain, a small dressing room area, and a unisex restroom with a lock that has a full shower, toilet, and vanity sink.

"It's... it's perfect." She sighed, feeling lost and sorry she'd ever laid eyes on it now. "I saw the asking price though." She breathed deeply and looked at the piece of paper he'd handed her with all the specifications.

"Well, you can always submit an offer that isn't the asking price, Ms. Jordan, but I will be frank with you. This spot is going to go fast and there are probably plenty of people willing to pay the asking price and then some. Why don't you ask your fiancé to—"

"No." She looked at him sternly and shook her head. "I refuse to have Lazarist foot the bill for this. I know that he's your friend and he had probably told you to show me anything that I like, but I have to figure out a way to do it on my own."

She took another deep breath and spun around the place as excitement and sadness merged within her, dancing inside her brain. "I think that I'll, uh, I'll make a trip to the bank first thing in the morning… see what they say. I will review all of my assets again. I want this place. It would be perfect for my classes; the new students I'd get from this central location would make sure it *more* than pays for itself over a short period of time. I'll figure it out…" She was speaking more for herself than for him. "I'm going to do my best. And I'm going to do it… on my *own*."

LEO

I KNEW THIS mothafucka would come around…

He kept playing those words in his mind, knowing that that was exactly what the demonic woman was thinking. Mimi certainly believed she had him by the balls. Starting lawsuit after lawsuit had to be exhausting, and she was determined to keep stirring the pot, causing trouble in his private and professional life. Despite losing in court, she undoubtedly still believed she had the upper hand.

Time to make the truth do what it do...

Lazarist stood at Mimi's apartment door in Manhattan and rang the bell once again. He seethed as he reminded himself that this was the extravagant place he'd paid for.

The door swung open and there she stood, half naked. Mimi's long, ebony hair was tucked behind one ear and she donned black, lacey lingerie that reminded him of a sheer swimming suit. She'd paired it with a matching, ankle-length robe she'd left untied for his viewing pleasure. Her 40DD breasts were hanging out, the pierced light brown nipples standing erect and at full attention. Lazarist twirled his white cane and winked at her.

"Come on in," she said in a flirty tone.

He entered, and she closed and locked the door behind him. To his left, the fire was roaring and some soft jazz music was playing, all the trappings for a fuck-a-thon. By the fire lay a white bearskin rug, with a bowl of strawberries and two glasses of white wine next to it.

"Have a seat." Mimi's voice sounded so sweet, just like it used to when they first met. Her facial expression was soft, and she smelled nice; the rich, aromatic perfume hit him as soon as he walked past her. He made a few steps towards the fire and sat on the couch, still twirling his cane. Mimi, however, sat on the bearskin rug, her knees far apart, exposing a glistening pussy. She leisurely picked up her glass of wine and brought it to her ruby red lips. Taking a cutesy sip, she placed it down, green and gold greed dancing in her light amber eyes. With a slow hand running down the length of her leg, she patted the rug.

"Why don't you come on over here and sit next to me, Lazarist?" She cocked her head to the side and smiled. He slowly got to his feet, then sat on the bearskin rug, his back poker straight and his ankles crossed. He smiled at her, then removed his checkbook from inside his blazer. He placed it to his left and her eyes landed on it, her lips curled in a grin. Then, reaching back inside his blazer, he removed a packet. She looked surprised, curious even.

"Thanks for letting me stop by at such late notice."

He picked up the glass of wine, looked at it, then placed it back down. There was no way in hell he was drinking anything offered from her. The woman might have slipped a drug in it, something to get him drunk, zoned out of his damn mind. He'd be lucky if the only thing he did after landing in that position would be snorting cocaine off the crack of some whore's ass.

"What's that?" She pointed to the folder that was sealed closed.

"Oh, this?" He pointed to it and chuckled. "Just a little surprise." He grabbed the checkbook. "Oh, damn, I forgot my pen. Do you have one handy, baby?"

"Yeah, of course." She got to her feet, a big smile on her face, and sauntered off. As he sat there alone, he looked about at all the luxury items she had…

My money bought that vase… My money bought that painting, that chair, that table… It bought all of this shit! She had money when we met, but she never could've afforded to live here or have any of these furnishings. She deserves nothing that's in here!

He swallowed down his rage when she returned to him, offering him a sleek gold pen, one fit for a king.

She lay down, running her hands along her breasts and licking her lower lip.

"You wanna fuck, Lazzy baby? One more time for old time's sake?"

He smiled and focused on his checkbook, opening it up and finding a blank one to make out to her.

"Nah, I think I'm good, Mimi."

"You sure, baby? All this good, juicy, yummy pussy… this tight ass that you love to suck and shove your big, fat dick inside?" She inserted her finger within herself, working it in slow circles. She pulled it out and sucked it, then gave him a hooded glance, her lips curved enticingly. "I won't tell your little girlfriend with the funny shaped breasts, I promise." She cackled.

"Those are called *natural* breasts, baby," he stated calmly as he proceeded to write the check. "You haven't seen or felt any in so fucking long, you forgot what they're supposed to be like. I happen to prefer hers. I like a *real* woman, inside and out." He shot her a brief glance. "A little plastic surgery is all right, but I think you went a bit too far. That's none of my business though, right? I mean, hey, if that's what you want, that's what you want, right? Who am I to judge?"

"Well." She shrugged. "I am a real woman, baby…

suit yourself. But the Lazzy I know would *never* pass up a chance to get his cock sucked. Let me taste that cum shot, baby…" She began to crawl towards him on all fours, her eyes centered on his crotch. He raised his hand to stop her.

"Don't, Mimi. We're not fucking. You're not gonna suck my dick, I'm not eatin' your pussy. We're not doing *any*thing like that at all."

"Awww!" She laughed. "Poor Lazzy bear got a girl-friend now he can't have any more fun! Boohoo! You'll be begging for this ass soon enough… She can't handle a man like you. See, you and I are the same… we're freaks. She's a sweet, innocent thing. She doesn't know how to please a man like you… but I do." She pointed to herself.

"You know what?" He got to his feet and snatched the folder off the floor. "I was going to do this different-ly, but you just can't let me be great." He chuckled. "I can't stand one more second of this so let's just get the show on the road."

"What are you talking about?" She looked up at him, still on her knees like a dog begging for a treat.

"You've been on your knees a lot lately, but unfortu-nately, it wasn't to pray to be a better person." Her expression turned to confused. He dropped the pen down on the rug, placed the checkbook on the nearby coffee table, and tore open the envelope. "Here is a copy of all your assets…"

He flung the big stapled report down on the floor. She grabbed it and thumbed through it, her face contorting, her brows dipped. Her complexion reddened, and his heart raced with excitement.

SHOW TIME, BITCH!

"What's this?"

"Don't play fuckin' stupid with me, Mimi. It's all the property you own, some of it before we were even divorced, others before we were even married, which you neglected to discuss or admit to owning during the divorce proceedings."

She looked frantic, vexed, enraged. He pulled out another report, and another, then flopped them down on that bearskin rug. She scrambled around on her knees, her big breasts swinging as she grabbed each one.

"That's all of your bank accounts… the ones in and out of the country. You've got a nice little nest egg, don't you? Been wringin' mothafuckers dry since 2015!"

"How'd you get a hold of these?! That's illegal! This is my private—"

"I don't give uh fuckity fuck! Don't grovel down there and talk to me about laws, rules and regulations when you've broken each and every one! What *you* did was illegal! And that's lie to the judge so you could get more money from me. I have paid so much alimony to you, I could literally own two brand new, fully loaded yachts by now! Not to mention all the free shit you're getting from all your sugar daddies! They're married, too. I wonder how their wives would feel about knowin' their husband is throwin' their savings at a lying whore?"

He grabbed his cane and began to twirl it faster and faster as fire danced in her eyes and within his soul.

"Did you honestly think this would end well?! You thought you could take ME down? Lazarist Zander?! That's hilarious! You thought I was gonna let you blackmail me and treat me like some pussy?! You must've forgotten who tha fuck you were dealin' with, Mimi!" He dumped the rest of the contents out onto the rug and sat down on the coffee table, crossing his ankles leisurely as he watched her squirm.

"If I still smoked I would light up right now. Seeing you losin' your fuckin' mind with these courtside tickets is a real treat!"

"Shut up! SHUT. UP!" she screamed so loud, the vein in her neck protruded. Her eyes were huge as she looked over the documents and all the photos of her out and about, exposing all her dirty deeds.

"What? You don't wanna play with your tits and pussy in front of me anymore?" He laughed. "Not in the mood? Awww, what a shame! You're all outta time, and I'm all outta fucks to give."

He reached for his checkbook and tore out the check he'd been working on, then let it fall from his fingertips. It fluttered to the white fur, landing face up. She paused, her chest heaving and breathing harsh as she reached for it and read it. The paper shook in her hand. With shaky legs, she got to her feet.

A check showing:
1025
DATE Your dooms day
PAY TO THE ORDER OF **Bitch, you're busted.** $ 0.00
zero motherfucking dollars———— DOLLARS
MEMO **To a whore that tried to ruin my life** King Lazariet Zander - Remember my name!
⑆000000000⑆ ⑆000000000⑆ 1025

"Get out... Get out. GET OUT!"

He stood back up to his feet, elation filling him, and he was sure it showed. Shoving his hands in his pockets, he glared down at her.

"Now see, the old me would present all of this shit to the judge right now and have your ass thrown in jail before the sun set. But someone I love told me I should feel sorry for you, and not hate you. I'm not there yet... I'm not on Sky's level when it comes to this whole forgiveness bullshit, but let me tell you something." He dropped low and jammed his finger in her face. "If you so much as *think* about fuckin' me over, coming to the Fallen Angel which you are banned from, contacting my mother, my sister, or Sky again, I will be singing like a motherfuckin' bird, my ass down at the courthouse in person with goddamn bells on! You're lucky I don't hit women, Mimi." He seethed.

"Because my mind is tellin' me no... but this fist!" He balled it up and bared his teeth like an enraged lion. "This fist is tellin' me yeeeessss!"

He snatched himself up to his full height. "And for the record, guess what? I'm gettin' married. That sweet, little innocent woman you think I'm in love with is not as sweet and innocent as you think she is. She used to fuck up women like you. She and her little friends would beat the daylights outta people they felt did them wrong. Sky had a few assault charges from back in the day. Boy, is she scrappy! See, I do background checks now—I learned my lesson. Trust me, she's *definitely* my type. At one point in time, she didn't take shit lying down, either. She was angry, mad at the world... But now, she's matured. A guy like me though?" He grimaced as shook his head. "I'm still a card carrying petty ass motherfuck-er."

He grabbed his cane and twirled it some more, laughing and dancing his way on out the door...

LEO

CHAPTER TWENTY

Experience is the Father of Wisdom

D AD WAS SITTING at his cluttered desk in the busy social services office, the printer buzzing behind him as it spat out copies of God only knew what. It was a noisy place, full of chatter and crying babies.

He chewed on the end of his black Bic pen, his thin rimmed glasses sliding a bit down his narrow nose. Deep, dark flawless skin, with the exception of a scar he'd received as a boy playing stick ball, glowed under the office light. Pulling out a drawer with a hard tug, he removed his paper bag lunch, from which he retrieved a shiny red apple. He began to type again, only pausing to take a bite from it. Sky rolled her eyes, crossed her arms over her chest, and flopped back in her chair across from him.

"Dad, what are you doing?"

"What's it look like? I'm working."

"You invited us up to have lunch with you so you could finally meet Lazarist. He's down there waiting and you know it."

"He can wait for a minute. I have work to do… I'm a very busy man," he stated matter-of-factly, speaking around a mouthful of mushed apple.

This is a game to him… some passive aggressive mess. He always does this when he doesn't like what's going on!

"Just admit it. When I told you that Lazarist asked me to marry him and I said yes, you weren't happy."

"I said I was happy for ya, didn't I?" The man looked perturbed. Lips pursed, he looked her up and down, as if *she* were suddenly the problem. Hopping up from her seat, she gathered her coat and purse.

"I'm not doin' this with you today, Dad. I am going down to the cafeteria. We'll wait for you there. If you come you come. If you don't, you don't."

Dad said nothing, just sat there chewing his apple and looking at the computer screen as if she wasn't there speaking to him. Sky made her way towards the elevator. Minutes later, she found Lazarist sitting in the large, busy cafeteria, a tray before him with three bags of potato chips, three sodas, three saran wrapped sandwiches, three saran wrapped salads, three pre-packaged large cookies probably laden with preservatives, and a big, shit-eating grin on his face. She marched towards him and sat beside him, mad as hell.

"What's up?" He cracked open a can of Diet Coke

and handed it to her.

She grabbed the soda, then a straw off the tray. After plopping it inside of the container, she took a long drawl and swallowed hard.

"He's acting up. I can't stand this shit. He's such a big ass baby! Now he is stalling, inconveniencing people on purpose." At this, Lazarist chuckled. "It's not funny, Laz. You have no idea how irritating he is when he gets like this. It's his way of trying to keep control of everything. First, he cancelled on us twice when you tried to meet him. Now he is up there at his desk acting like he has a pressing matter to attend to. He processes Head Start applications and WIC benefits! He acts like he is up there doing mayoral duties!"

Lazarist laughed even louder this time and leaned in close, taking her hand.

"If he feels like he has to be in control, then let's just pretend like he is... at least at first."

His eyes narrowed on her. She didn't know what the hell Lazarist was talking about, and then, it suddenly sank in.

"I told you that he was strict when I was kid." Lazarist nodded as he reached for the chips, opened the packet, and began to eat. "When I got older, I was harder to control and he and I would butt heads. My father is very old fashioned, despite not being really that old. But, he loved me and took great care of me. I can never take that away from him. Like, for example, he never had a bunch of strange women in the house. He'd introduce me to various girlfriends over the years, but only after he'd dated them for quite some time. He was real careful about who was around me… said he didn't want any bad influences."

Bringing up that memory made her feel a bit less edgy, less angry at Dad. Laz squeezed her hand.

"And that's what he's doing now. Protecting you, or at least, that's what he believes. He knows marriage is supposed to be a lifelong commitment, Sky. He wants the best for you. He probably thinks I am not it, and that's fine. We're still getting married regardless, but give me some credit, now. I deal with hardnosed business negotiations from time to time. I am used to men like your father. I'm the king of bullshit, remember?"

She shoved him on the shoulder and burst into giggles. Just then, she saw her father in the distance.

"There he is…" she whispered, as if the guy approaching were some FBI agent. Laz looked over where she pointed.

"All right, let me handle this." He wiped his hands with a napkin and sat a bit taller, then stood to his full height. Sky instantly noticed people turning and looking at Laz. Yup. When he got up from the chair, he looked like a giant, especially now that he stood next to her father, who was 5'10 on his best day. Dad, however, didn't look the least bit moved or intimidated. He glared up at her man. Lazarist extended his hand. With a stern expression, Dad shook it.

"Hello, Mr. Jordan. It's a pleasure to finally meet you."

Dad smiled ever so slightly but didn't return the

compliment. Instead, he plopped down on the chair opposite them and placed his paper bag lunch onto the table. He removed a small container of soup, a silver spoon from home, and what looked to be leftover jerk chicken, rice, and fried plantains. Lazarist clasped his hands and smiled.

"Mr. Jordan, your daughter and I are getting married."

"I know. I don't like how I found out. I think this is pretty damn disrespectful. This isn't the way this shoulda gone, and I mean that." Dad shot her a harsh look.

"Oh, here we go…" Sky rolled her eyes and shook her head.

"I'm not certain I follow you, Mr. Jordan."

"Well then, let me draw you a map with words so you can follow along. Wouldn't want you getting lost," Dad barked, being as indignant as he wanted to be. "In my day, the man would ask the parents for permission to marry their daughter. I—"

"Dad you are a trip! I can't believe this… Well, actually I can. Your day has been over since Moses parted the Red Sea. You know what, this is ridiculous! We have better things to do than—"

Lazarist reached below the table and tapped her knee, stopping her in mid-sentence.

"Let him finish," Lazarist stated in almost a whisper.

"Thank you." Dad narrowed his eyes on Sky, then turned his venom back towards Lazarist. "Now, I'm going to be real with you. My parents were from Jamaica so I understand things are different here. My ex-wife,

Sky's mother, was African American. She knew nothing else but this place. I was born and raised here, too, but my parents were old school and I tried to follow in their footsteps—and that includes respecting their way of how men and women handle marriage. Another problem I have—and I will be honest though once again, it's not the most popular thought... I am not one of these liberals though and I believe in pride in oneself."

"Don't you dare start up with this Black love mess again!"

"I wanted Sky with someone like herself." Laz cocked his head to the side, but remained quiet. "She's my only child... my only daughter." He pointed at her. "And this isn't anything personal against you, but I don't understand that with *all* of the Black men in New York, my daughter had to bring the tallest White son of uh gun she could find to my door! Not only that, you've been married a gazillion times. Something isn't right here and I'm not going to pretend like it is!"

"You just had to do it, didn't you?" Sky jerked around in her seat, wishing to just leave and never look back. Lazarist, on the other hand, was smiling from ear to ear as he leaned into the table and clasped his hands.

"Mr. Jordan, I can sympathize with how you feel. I don't have any children, so I can't understand what it's like to be a father." He took Sky's hand in his as he continued to speak. "But, I imagine if and when I become one, I would honestly just want someone for my children who treats them right... someone who loves them and is committed to them, takes care of their needs, and is a good support system to them."

Dad visibly rolled his eyes and huffed, then crossed his legs.

"At the end of the day, we have to trust their judgment, even if we have concerns. You've raised her; that's over with now. I can more than take care of Sky, Mr. Jordan. I assure you of that."

"I don't care about your money, Lazarist." Dad readjusted his glasses. "I know most parents would probably lick your boots just to have you in their family because they know they'd be taken care of. That's not me!" Dad said, pointing at himself. "On top of it all, haven't you been married like, five or six times? With all due respect, Lazarist, what do you possibly know about commitment?"

"Well, now, that's the second time you've brought up my past marriages, so let's address that. The first thing we need to do, Mr. Jordan," Lazarist stated calmly, "is to try to keep things factual. You and I can't have a discussion if it's only based on emotional statements or manipulative tactics to try and illustrate someone's unworthiness. Oh, and before I forget, when I brought up taking care of Sky, I wasn't just talking about the financial aspects. That's where your mind immediately ventured to—not mine. Now, back to my gazillion marriages…" Laz leisurely cracked open a can of Pepsi and chugged some of it before continuing. "Marriage is an emotional thing, I get it, but it's also logical and so, if we look at things from that angle, we can navigate this better. If I need to draw you a map so that *you* now can follow along, just let me know."

Dad's eyes grew large, but thank goodness, he didn't say anything snappy. "So, let's look at the facts." Lazarist began to count off his fingers. "One, I have two ex-wives. Only two. One I married very young, just as you'd done with your ex-wife. We loved one another but as people mature, they change, and that's essentially what happened. That's why, in my opinion, looking back, people under twenty-five shouldn't get married because we're still getting to know ourselves. But that was a long time ago. She and I are on good terms and there are no hard feelings.

"My second marriage was a huge mistake. I will be the first to admit that. I got married for the wrong reasons. We were not in the same book, let alone on the same page or even chapter. That marriage ended and it didn't end well. I've made my mistakes, Mr. Jordan. I'm a man… and men make mistakes, regardless of our nationality, religion, and occupation. White, Black, Red or Blue, people are flawed. There is no perfect man out here to marry your daughter. A Black man is not guaranteed to treat your daughter any better than I can. Now sure, they'd have more in common culturally, but that within itself doesn't guarantee a solid, long lasting marriage.

"The divorce rate, for instance, between Black men and Black women is alarming, just like the divorce rate between White men and White women. Did you know, however, that the divorce rate between White men and Black women is the lowest out of all pairings? That's even more interesting when you consider the fact that these unions still make up a very small percentage of the population. If that's not beating the odds, I don't know what is. This isn't to say marriages like ours will always last; some couples obviously split up. But what it *does* say is that due to reactions like yours right now, and the world as a whole, we're already standing up for what we want and going against the grain. We're getting married despite parental disapproval. We're getting married despite the blatant racism in this country, and so on.

"That makes for stronger, more focused couples. You're divorced, Mr. Jordan. Sky told me your parents divorced when you were in your twenties, too. So, Black on Black love is not a guaranteed recipe for success. You're proof of that. I work hard at everything I do in life, and I promise you, that I will work hard at this marriage, too. This time, I have the maturity and the wisdom to know a good thing when I see it, and Sky definitely fits the bill. I love your daughter with all of my being, Mr. Jordan. I would never try to hurt her or do anything to cause her harm. I mean that. I promise you that, okay? You raised a very smart, sweet young lady. She can take care of herself. I'm just blessed she let me come along for the ride."

Dad looked at Lazarist long and hard, then peeled off the lid of the clear Tupperware container.

"All right... you're a good speaker, you know that? Very persuasive. Like Bill Clinton and Obama. That's a sure sign of a good liar, but I'll go with it for now," Dad said gruffly. "Sky said your birthday was in August... so was her mother's. Leos are very persuasive… manipulative. Clinton and Obama are Leos, too. Gotta watch them."

Sky bit down a laugh and shook her head.

My father is a real piece of work.

"Zander… isn't that a Jewish last name?"

"Oh Lord…" Sky huffed. Lazarist burst out laughing. "Dad, don't start!"

"Yes, it is."

"You're Jewish then… not White."

"Well, actually, that's not true. Had my mother been Jewish, I'd be considered such, Mr. Jordan. My mother is half Italian and half Irish. My father is the one who is Jewish, and he is in fact White because his ancestors came from Europe—Russia, to be exact. There are Jews all over the world, and though I do understand the argument that it's an ethnicity, that's not the case here."

"I consider you Jewish," Dad said dismissively as he jammed his fork into his chicken and took a few dedicated chews. "I like Jews."

Lazarist threw up his hands and shook his head.

"All right, well, if that makes you feel better, you can call me Jewish. It was very nice meeting you today, Mr. Jordan."

"Likewise," Dad said, keeping his nose in his food. "Sky, go on up to Connie over there in the chow line and get a couple of plates and forks. I want Lazarist to taste this…"

Sky grinned and slowly got to her feet. Before she left the two alone, she dipped low and whispered in his ear, "He's sharing his food with you. That means he likes you. Welcome to my insane family…"

LEO

…A few weeks later

FALLEN ANGEL WAS thumping, the music blaring as bodies swayed and bumped around to the beats of the guest DJ—DJ Destruction. Lazarist walked about, twirling his cane, the brown and white one with the ivory marble tip. He greeted his guests, shaking hands and feeling invigorated to see the crowd enjoying themselves, letting loose for the weekend. After a few minutes, Heathen approached him. That was strange…

Heathen rarely left his post, but here he was, tapping his shoulder.

"Boss, you gotta call downstairs," he yelled over the music. "They say it's important!" His heart thumped a bit harder.

"Who is it?"

"I don't know." Heathen shrugged. "I didn't answer the phone. Ted just told me to come get you."

"All right." He threw on a smile once again, greeted a couple others who came up to him as he was exiting, and quickly made his way out of the club and down the steps. He walked through the restaurant, where a patron yelled his name.

"Mr. Zander! Can I have a word with you please?"

Shit! Not now!

Still, he turned back around and approached the man. "Hello, how can I help you, sir?"

"I asked for my steak to be cooked medium rare, but it's medium… just medium. This is unacceptable. I come here at least a few times a year and I need for your—"

"Okay, sir, my apologies. In the future, if you have an issue with your meal or your experience here, that is something you tell your waitstaff, okay? Hold on." He held up his finger. "I will get this straightened out."

Can't believe this shit!

Lazarist stormed into the kitchen, the doors swinging behind him.

"Who is taking care of the guy at table 7?!"

"Rita!" someone yelled.

"Where is she? I didn't see her out on the floor! Never mind! Look, I have an emergency and don't have time for this shit right now. Someone needs to get out there, apologize to the guy, and redo his fucking steak. Offer his dinner for free, but only *after* he requests the check! Have I made myself clear?"

"Yes!" several people shouted as he walked out of there.

I'm not going to have him running up a tab if he knows in advance!

Lazarist stormed off, making a beeline towards his office. He took notice of the red light flashing on his phone, indicating that a call was waiting. As he approached, he paused. His heart was beating so fast and hard, it hurt. He slid his cellphone out of his pocket and noticed several missed calls.

Shit, I didn't hear my phone...

He approached his desk and took a deep breath before he answered.

"Hello."

"I've been trying to call you!"

"I know, Eliza, I'm sorry. I didn't hear or feel my phone. I was in the club and—"

"Dad is in the hospital in critical condition! He got a cut of some sort and it got infected. The infection got into his bloodstream." Eliza was beside herself, falling apart on the phone. He heard it beginning to rain outside.

"Okay... okay," He swallowed, his world becoming fuzzy and gray. "What hospital is he at?"

"Mount Sinai. I'm already here, but I can't see him yet... I'm waiting in the lobby. They're working on him now."

"Okay, stay put. I'm on my way!" Lazarist grabbed his coat and umbrella and headed out of the club.

As he approached his car, he kept telling himself to 'wake up.' He felt trapped in some wild, strange dream...

The man he both loved and hated was at death's door...

Guilt consumed him, tearing him apart. He threw himself behind the wheel and called Sky with a shaky hand.

"Hi, baby!" she stated with glee. She was having a girls' night with her friends over at Scarlet's house.

"Sky… Sky…" Tears began to fall from his eyes as he worked his car into drive and merged into traffic.

"Wait a minute, y'all! Hold up! It's too loud in here!" He could hear her practically running, then he heard a door close. "Okay, I can hear you better now, baby… Are you okay? You don't sound okay."

"Sky, my father is at Mount Sinai in critical condition."

"Oh my God! Honey, what happened?!"

"I'm not exactly sure, but he had some sort of infection and it got into his blood. I'm on my way there now."

"I'll meet you over there!"

"No… no. Please stay with your friends. I just…" His chest hurt so badly as the emotions built up and took him under. He felt as if he were drowning. "He tried to come over last week, Sky!" he cried out. "I told him to leave me the fuck alone, that I never wanted to see him again!" His throat burned as he screamed.

Regret…

Regret…

Regret…

"I turned my back on him and look what happened?! I coulda prevented this. I could have just—"

"Lazarist, stop it! Don't do this to yourself. This is not your fault! He was being verbally and emotionally abusive for years! You even let me hear a few of his voicemails to you and the words he said were some of the cruelest I'd ever heard! You put an end to it but that didn't mean you didn't love him! You tried *everything* in your power to help him. Don't you dare blame yourself!"

He dropped his head while the rain began to fall harder.

"I'm coming to the hospital."

"Please just… just stay where you are, okay, Sky? I'll keep you updated."

There was a long silence on the other end.

"Oh… okay. I love you, Lazarist. It's going to be all right, okay?"

"Yeah… okay. I love you, too."

He disconnected the call and hurried on his way, praying he'd make it in time to tell his father that he loved him, too, before it was too late…

LEO

SCARLET STOOD IN her blue denim overalls and gray bodysuit beneath it. Her bleach blonde short cropped hair was swooped to the side as she leaned against the bar counter in her apartment, barefoot and sipping on some Sangria. The music was now turned low and the ladies were sitting around, the zest sucked out of the room like a vacuum. Scarlet picked up her joint and took a long drag, then placed it back down into the ashtray. Blowing smoke out the side of her mouth, she glared at Sky. Sky turned away, twiddling her thumbs, feeling broken up inside… not certain what to do with herself.

"Sky, get ya coat on. I'm driving you over there."

"But he said—"

"I don't give a shit what he said. Look at you— you're a mess. And men say shit like that all the time." She slipped her feet into some nearby slides. "With what you told me about him and his father, he needs you there, trust me."

She took another swallow of her drink and set it down. "This man is your fiancé... the fucker you're about to marry. I'm the Maid of Honor, and as your best friend, it is my duty to tell you right from wrong and what to do with your life."

Sky smiled ever so slightly, appreciative of Scarlet's humor at such a somber time.

"Thankfully, I've only had one glass of wine so far, so I'm good. If he'd called two hours from now I woulda be fucked up." Toi and the others stood to their feet. "No, you all stay here. I'll be back." Scarlet waved at them. "I'm just gonna make sure Sky gets there okay, all right?" They all nodded and sat back down.

Minutes later, she was sitting in Scarlet's electric blue Toyota Camry while 'Erase Me' by Said the Sky played from the radio. The song was so relaxing, the beat mingling with the falling rain. The city was slick with lights and colors, rainbow oil from cars appearing in puddles along the way.

"I know you blame yourself, too."

Scarlet rolled down her window a bit and lit a ciga-rette. Drops of rain came in, sprinkling on her face, but she didn't seem to mind. "You encouraged him to cut that negativity loose."

Sky hung her head and cried. The truth hurt like hell!

"I was just tryna help! Scarlet, what if he dies? I'll never forgive myself. I gave him bad advice!"

"You didn't give him bad advice. Would you say you gave his ass bad advice if the Devil was knockin' at the door and you told him not to let him in, huh? Sometimes our own parents are the fuckin' worst! And you know I know all about that first hand!" Scarlet took a big long draw of her freshly lit cigarette, then tossed it out the open window and rolled it back up.

The soothing music filled the air, but she felt so scared inside.

"Let me tell you something, baby. I know that this is his father, and as God is my witness, I don't wish death on nobody. Mental illness is a real life mothafuckin' situation; It's nothing to play with. But, this man had a bunch of people tryna help him yet he didn't want it. He wanted to do shit on his own terms so because of that, here are the consequences. He has to deal with those now, too."

"You're right... I know... but..." She sniffed, got ready to protest, but stopped short. She had to try and pull it together.

"All of us, Sky, mentally unstable, emotionally abused, abandoned by parents, treated like shit by sisters and brothers, fucked up, drug addicts, alcoholics, people with daddy and mama issues, whatever the fuck we have going on—we still have to face the consequences for our actions. There comes a time in your life where you have to stop blaming everybody else for your fuck ups. When you know better, you have to lean on that truth. We're grown! Even crazy people sometimes know right from wrong. Please don't get it twisted. Some people use that shit as an excuse to get over... a crutch. They try and do shady shit and have people feel sorry for them. That's bullshit.

"My mother used to do that shit, Sky! Talk about how she got this and that goin' on, blame it on her illness instead of taking responsibility that she chose to have all of us kids and left us abandoned time after time! Even in the courtroom, she wanted to talk to the judge about her messed up childhood, how hard she had it— fuck the six of us that she left in that apartment wit' no damn heat! It was always all about *her*! Fuck when I told 'er all the shit that was happening. She knew it was wrong, but it was easier for her to say, 'I'm sick' and not do nothin' else, to run away from her responsibilities.

"She wasn't sick when she was bringing all those men around me and my brothers and sister. She wasn't actin' sick when she was sellin' drugs and counting everything up to perfection. She wasn't sick when the social workers came over and she had the house spic and span all of a sudden, when just an hour prior everything was all torn up and we was wearing the same clothes for several days in a row. I get sick of all of these damn excuses!"

Scarlet beat the steering wheel with a hard fist. "We've all been screwed over by life a time or two... we deal wit' it! We can't pick our parents. Lazarist didn't pick his, you didn't pick yours, and I didn't pick mine.

We got what we got. It's our job to make the most out of the mess. I don't know who my father is, and I had to just accept that and move on. Life happens. We still have to live it. I put my own ass through school! I'm a damn good beautician, own my own shop. I ain't sell my pussy to do it, either!

"You didn't have it easy, either. Drug addict absentee mother and all, you still made it big and now you've worked with J-Lo and all kinds of people! People know your name! Lazarist had it good, then had it bad, all within the blink of an eye, and his ass is now a self-made multi-millionaire. Fuck mental illness, Sky! It's a real mothafuckin' thing—but there's people that care and medication that can help. This ain't 1889 when assistance was limited and people were getting experimental lobotomies! Makes no goddamn sense and that man was a big time lawyer! He had health insurance, for God's sake."

Scarlet drew quiet from her rant for a spell, but Sky appreciated that her best friend knew she needed these words. This was the way she could get up and around from herself, be strong for her man.

"It's hard to not feel sorry though, Scarlet, for people with these sorts of conditions."

Scarlet rolled her eyes as she changed lanes, the rain finally slowing down.

"You think if some crazy mothafucka went outside and shot up a school full of kids, those parents would give two fucks about him bein' sick in the head? Nope! They'd want answers, like why in the hell wasn't he locked up somewhere?! Why didn't the school have more security? Shit like that. When the shit hits the fan, don't nobody care 'bout shoulda, woulda, coulda, Sky. Don't nobody care about what kinda childhood they had 'nd shit. The only people that care about that are the ones whose kids didn't get shot in the goddamn head! I ain't on that bullshit, and you know it.

"Lazarist is a strong man, but that father of his is his weakness. He told you that out of his own mouth. He's going to struggle with this, so you have to keep assuring him that he did the right thing, Sky, no matter what happens. After all of that shit with his ex-wife and now this, I know he is exhausted. It's a damn shame!" Scarlet reached over and grabbed her hand and squeezed it.

"Thank you, Scarlet. You're a good friend… I needed to hear that. I just finished telling him to not beat himself up and now here I am, doing it to myself. It was just shocking, I guess."

"Yeah? Well, shock yourself back into reality and pull it together. We're here… and he needs you." Sure enough, they'd arrived at the hospital. Scarlet pulled into the visitor area and Sky got out of the car. "You want me to come in with you, baby? I can park in the parking lot." She pointed in that direction.

"No, I'm good! You've helped enough!" Sky smiled sadly as she looked inside the car at her friend.

"All right, call me and let me know how things are going when you can, okay?"

"I will. I promise." Sky leaned back inside the car. "You're like… one of the best friends I could ever have!" Her voice trembled.

"Bitch, that's just the alcohol talkin'. Take yo' raggedy ass in that hospital and go give your man a blow job or somethin'. He needs it so he can relax his nerves."

Sky burst out laughing and slammed the door. She could hear Scarlet laughing before she pulled away from the curb. After Scarlet's car disappeared into the night, she let out a deep sigh and entered the hospital…

LEO

CHAPTER TWENTY-ONE

My vessel in Sickness and in Health

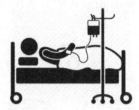

TIME CRAWLED BY like a sleepy spider resting at a corner, between two walls…

Lazarist pressed his head against the cold arm of the hospital chair, his eyelids heavy and burning with spent tears. Dad lay in the bed, his eyes closed, his complexion a deathly shade of blue. Tubes ran in all directions out of his nose and wrists.

Eliza was on the phone in the lobby giving others the news. Much to his surprise, Mom was on her way. He didn't believe she had any desire to see Dad, even though he was practically on his deathbed, but she said she was coming for him and Eliza, and that meant a hell of a lot. They'd finally allowed Lazarist back into the room after the first heavy dose of antibiotics started taking effect. Dad was now in stable condition, but the doctor explained things were still touch and go.

He heard a familiar voice in the hall.

"He's over here? Oh… yes, thank you. Okay, I appreciate it."

Lazarist looked over at the door and watched Sky enter. He'd never felt so relieved. Getting to his feet, he raced over to her, hugging her tight. Her love surrounded him like a shawl, her warmth his medicine. She layered his face with kisses and rocked him against her. Taking her hand, he led her over to the chair he'd just vacated and sat her down.

"He's stable," he whispered. "He had septicemia. He almost lost his life."

"So he's okay now?" she asked as she reached for his hands, hope shining in her big brown eyes.

"Well, we don't know. They have to keep him. He's better than when he arrived, that's for certain, and it didn't turn into sepsis. They are trying to ensure he doesn't have any permanent organ damage, but that could take days or even weeks to discover. My sister thought it was from a cut he'd had that was hard to heal, and that definitely didn't help because it lowered his immune system—but it was more likely a bladder and kidney infection that got the ball rolling. Right now, he's on oxygen and several rounds of antibiotics. He's being given fluids intravenously."

He pointed to one of the tubes jetting out of his father.

"Have you been here all by yourself?"

"No." He pulled up a chair next to her. "Eliza is talking to some people and letting them know what's going on, and my mother is on her way. Tobias was here for a bit a while ago, but I told him to go home. You didn't have to come, really, but thank you."

He reached for her and held her close.

"Baby, where else would I be? Your father could have lost his life. Of course I'd be here by your side."

They sat side by side, quietly holding hands. Only the machines buzzing and the light chatter of people talking out in the hallways could be heard. He disappeared inside of himself, his thoughts all over the place. An image of his father flashed in his mind, and he looked down at the floor, his body rocking, his heart shattering.

"You want some coffee or something to drink, Laz?" she whispered, caressing his arm.

"Yeah, that would be good, I guess."

She released him and walked off, leaving him there in the stillness of the room. He looked back over at his father and shook his head. Running his fingers through his hair, he leaned forward and grazed the old man's fingertips.

It can't end like this, Dad. It just can't...

LEO

...One week later

IT HAD BEEN a long, draining ordeal, but Mr. Zander, Lazarist's father, was now speaking and coherent.

Lazarist was splitting his days between the hospital and work, and even managed to meet her for dinner one evening for some much-needed R&R. Sky spent as much time as she could with him at the hospital until he all but threw her out, insisting that she go to her scheduled appointment with her friends to go look at and try on dresses.

As she stood in the luxury bridal salon on 5th Avenue, 'Bridal Reflections', it was hard to keep from smiling for so many things were going her way. All of her girls stood around slipping into various shimmery and swanky gowns—some they loved, others they hated—and then they argued about what cut was more flattering.

"Ladies, don't try to change the colors. That's permanent. I told you I would compromise on which ones were chosen, but the color of your gowns is plum. Period." She found herself having to be a bridezella at times, for they were snatching white, saucy red, and black dresses that barely covered their breasts, had three slits, and looked like something to wear at the damn club.

"I'm not wearin' this moo-moo, Sky! I'm tryna secure the damn bag!" Scarlet hooted. "I know all of Lazarist's rich ass friends will be there. I gotta play the damn part! You tryna fuck up my coins again!"

"Scarlet, don't you start." Sky rolled her eyes, then grabbed a tiny glass of white wine and downed it.

"You stole my man. The least you could do is let me wear a hoochie mama dress so I can get another chance at bat. Stingy ass… there's enough to go around." At this, everyone burst out laughing. "Anyway, try your shit on. We wanna see it and rate you from one to ten. The first two dresses sucked."

"Thank you… I know I can always count on you for encouragement." Sky smirked as she slipped out of the last gown, to her bare essentials.

"Don't get mad at me. Shit! The first one had you lookin' like a big ass gallon of milk. Made me want to dip some chocolate chip cookies in the crack of ya ass! The second one looked like a balled-up piece of paper… some shit found in a high school English class on the damn floor. Bitch, get it together!"

All the ladies sat down as she went into the dressing room for the third time. After a few minutes, she realized that, although the next gown was gorgeous, it was rather cumbersome to squeeze into.

I hope I can zip this dress up!

Two more minutes passed to no avail. Her brow was covered with sweat and her forefinger was red and angry from straining at the zipper and snaps for far too long.

"Scarlet, I need your help!" Seconds later, the tall, blonde woman with the deep bronze complexion was hovering over her, her lips twisted and her arms crossed.

"Why'd you have us waiting all this time?!" Scarlet jumped in to assist. Snatching the damn thing back half way down to her hips, she began to pull and tug at her white waist trainer and bra straps.

"You don't have to be so rough!"

"You don't have to be so damn ridiculous. In here

wrestlin' with yourself like it's WWE. Shoulda *been* calling me in here—you know we have a dinner reservation after this and you in here wasting time trying to get your Vienna sausage shaped body into this damn uncooked macaroni shaped dress!"

"Oh, so you're making fun of my body now?! I think I look good!" Sky popped out her hip in a sassy sort of way. "I should knock your head off and roll it down the road like the bowling ball that it is!"

They both giggled as they poked fun at one another.

"I know what the problem is. You're bloated… Lay off the salt," her friend warned until finally, she had the dress zipped up for her and everything in place.

"Everything okay, ladies?" one of the employees of the salon asked.

"Yes!" they both said in unison.

Sky pushed the dressing room doors open and stepped out. Her friends started to 'ohhh' and 'awww'. She spun around and checked herself out in the mirrors.

"That's the one!" someone yelled out. "Girl, you look like a damn snack!"

Toi began to cry as she got to her feet, jumping up and down in place. "Yes, Sky! You look beautiful, girl! Oh my God!"

"Don't make me cry, Toi! Stop it!" Sky warned, her eyes glossing up now, too.

She felt Scarlet's hand surround her shoulders.

"Sky, you're the most beautiful bride I've ever seen… and I'm serious about that." The woman turned her around to face her. Lifting her chin, she looked her in the eyes, seriousness in her expression. "All jokes and silliness aside, you deserve this, girl. I am so, so, so damn happy for you! I really like Lazarist, and I think he'll do you right. You were made for each other."

Scarlet drew her in for a big hug.

"When you secure the bag, you secure the money, honey," Scarlet whispered in her ear. "You secure peace of mind. Life is so hard but so beautiful, too. When you find your soulmate, you hold on tight to him. Because when I say, 'Secure the bag', I'm not just talkin' about a bankroll. I'm talkin' about you securing your placement in that man's heart. You did that, boo. Ain't nowhere to go but up!"

Tears traced a path down Sky's cheek.

"I love you so much, Scarlet. Things are so good right now!" Sky tossed up her hands. "After all of my struggles, things are finally falling into place. I got the bank loan so I get the new spot in Manhattan. Laz's dad is much better. My father actually told someone that his daughter was getting married, and he had a smile on his face when he said it. And I have the best damn friends, ever!"

All the ladies stood to their feet and surrounded her in a big, warm embrace. Scarlet wrapped her hands around her face, tears welling in her eyes.

"You've got us, baby, because you're a damn good person. This is sisterhood… this thing you and I got is special. Ain't nobody, and I mean *no*body, gonna come between us. You've been rockin' with me for over ten years, and I couldn't imagine life without you, Sky.

You're a ray of sunshine in a gray, miserable world. Real sisterhood is bein' happy for your girlfriends, even when you wish you had the same things they had, too. I want to see you rise up, succeed, be in love and be happy. I'm seein' it right now. I joke with you about taking my man, but you know I wanted this for you so bad! It couldn't have happened to a better person."

"I know you do, Scarlet! I know."

"We as Black women gotta stop tearin' each other down." Her friends nodded their heads in agreement. "We always feel the lowest out here, the ones being treated the worst, talked about, ignored… so what do we do? We scratch out tha eyes of people that look just like us. That don't help us see any better, we just all end up blind. Instead of being crabs in a barrel, we need to reach down and across the aisle and lend a helping hand, aiding one another to get over to the other side."

"So damn true." One of the other ladies shook her head.

"We should encourage each other more, we're all we got…" Toi gripped Scarlet's hand as more tears flowed.

"There's plenty room for everybody… all we want is to be happy." Scarlet's eyes sheened. "That's the common goal, right? To be respected and appreciated… to be *loved*. This isn't a competition, baby. It's not a race, either. It's a long journey to the land of love—self-love, too…nothin' more, nothin' less. We're tryna manage this thing called life, and if we support one another, we'll get much farther than we ever imagined. We've gotta be comfortable in our own skin! Okay being by ourselves first – just like Sky has done. We never heard her talking about needing no man. Not that she didn't feel that way, but her life didn't revolve around it, and look who she attracted. All of us are worthy of love!" Several heads nodded in agreement. "Black girl magic? What is it? It's not a mystery or something you pull out of a damn hat.

"It's in each and every one of us. Bein' a boss bitch isn't just about handlin' yours, being 'THAT' girl, is about handling your sister's heart with care, about bein' true blue and giving a damn, and telling the truth while you do it. I don't wear my heart on my sleeve, but I feel things so deep, only me, myself and I would ever understand. Black women, we have so much love to give, and always give it away to the wrong damn people." Tears streamed down Scarlet's face. Sky could count on one hand how many times she saw this woman cry, a rare occurrence indeed. "That's why I say, first, we have to start giving it ourselves first. You can't pour nothin' from an empty vessel, but a vessel that's full can nourish the whole damn world…"

LEO

♌

CHAPTER TWENTY-TWO

Having a Screw Loose, Off His Rocker, and a Total Basket Case

D AD SAT IN the large, plush, floral printed chair by the enormous window with the sun streaming through. His salt and pepper hair appeared clean and cut nicely. His face was clean shaven, which made him look at least ten years younger. He'd been admitted into the Department of Psychiatry of the NYU Langone Hospital Medical Center.

After five and a half weeks of treatment, his new medications began to take effect. Lazarist had never seen his father this lucid in years, but he couldn't get his hopes up just yet. Perhaps the past had been too traumatic, and though seeing was believing, he'd learned the hard way that good things in life sometimes were short-lived.

Lazarist sat down on a seat upholstered with a calm, floral print on a beige background. He rested his hat on his knee and kept his cane close to his person. He was a mere foot or so away from his father but this time, not in his kitchen at three in the morning.

His sister, Eliza, sat by his side, too. They'd joined their father in the small eating area of the facility. Dad pursed his lips and brought his cup of hot tea with lemon to his mouth. After taking a sip, he set it gingerly back down.

"Still a little hot," he mumbled. His blue, gray and black checkered robe covered a white shirt and loose jogging pants. On Dad's feet were thick white socks and beige rubber slippers. Everything clean, everything new, everything neat.

Dad offered a rather disturbing smile, then chuckled.

"Guess I gave everyone quite a scare!" He clapped his hands, as if his life were some Broadway show everyone was enjoying.

"Yeah, you did." Eliza huffed and crossed her legs.

Dad shifted his attention to her. For a moment, it seemed he didn't even recognize who she was, and then his face split in an all-knowing grin.

"What a beautiful woman you are, Eliza! I'm so lucky to have such uh nice lookin' kid. You look just like Evelyn. Hey." Dad looked around the place, even rising up out of his seat to glance over his shoulder for a spell. "Why isn't Evelyn here? Where's your mother?" He spoke with hope, with unrealistic optimism, the kind no one would want to trample over and squash with the cold hard truth, regardless of the hell he'd taken them through.

For a second, Lazarist wondered if Dad even recalled that he'd been divorced for over twenty years. At this point, there were still so many questions, some of which would probably never be answered.

"Now that you're okay, Dad, she chose, uh, to not come," Lazarist explained.

Dad's smile slowly melted. His father's tall frame bent like a tree branch with the weight of the world suddenly upon it. All went quiet for a spell. Lazarist cleared his throat, placed his cane on the arm of the chair, and gathered a packet of papers that was lying nearby.

"Dad, we have some things to discuss regarding your future care… Despite what happened, and as much as I love you…" He faltered. Eliza grabbed his hand and squeezed it. "I can't… I can't let what was happening continue. It's not healthy for you. It's not healthy for me."

"What was happening that you can't let continue?" Dad's voice and tone were calm as he reached for his tea and took another sip, then set the cup back down. Clasping his hands over his lap, the man waited, looking truly perplexed.

"For years, you've been coming to my home during various states of paranoia. Those episodes led to you behaving in a manner that was unacceptable more times than not. Now, it's not just about me anymore, Dad. I am getting married. My fiancée will be moving into my home. Therefore, it will be *our* home, not just mine anymore… and she needs to be able to feel safe, okay?

She *deserves* to feel safe."

Dad's facial expression never changed. In fact, he looked utterly bewildered.

"What unacceptable behavior?"

Lazarist sighed in frustration and briefly closed his eyes.

"Dad," Eliza jumped in. "Do you remember goin' over to Laz's house a couple times a month sometimes, bangin' on the door at three or four in the morning?" Eliza questioned.

Dad took a while to respond, but then nodded as if it had just come to mind.

"Yes, I remember."

"Do you remember what you'd do when you'd get there?" Eliza probed deeper.

"I, um, I would come in, ya know, after he'd turn off the alarm. I think then I would, uh, go shower, right?" Lazarist nodded. "I sometimes would use the phone... Lazarist had a lot of nice clothes for me!" Dad grinned from ear to ear, as if they were Hanukkah gifts he'd receive just for the hell of it. "I would put some on and then I'd eat... and he and I would talk... and then, uh, I'd leave, right?"

Eliza and Lazarist stared at him.

"Right?" he repeated.

"No, Dad. That's not what would happen." Lazarist leaned forward and clasped his hands. "More times than not, you were belligerent. You'd curse me out at the top of your lungs, ask about Mom and accuse her of being promiscuous and a bunch of other crap. You would go into a whole spiel about Eliza not being your daughter, too. Now, not all of this always happened, but each visit was unsettling, regardless. If you weren't talking out of your mind, then you were accusing me of things I hadn't done—the same with Mom and Eliza. One time you and I even got into a physical altercation and I had to call the police on you, but you were gone before they arrived.

"I have asked you over and over, Dad, to *please* allow me to check you into a psychiatric facility. We wouldn't shove you in Bellevue, which you were deeply afraid of due to their reputation. I promised we'd get you someplace else where you'd be comfortable and get the care you needed, but you refused. I attempted to have you committed, as well. I was the only family member you were speaking to after a while. Mom still had an active restraining order against you, but after consulting with an attorney, I realized that would be trickier to do than I thought, in part because it would be hard to prove that you were a threat to yourself or society. Right now, you are thinking clearly… You're lucid."

Dad crossed his arms real tight over his body, and his muscles seemed to stiffen and lock. His thick brows bunched and anxiety was written all over his face.

"That is due to the medication, this environment, the facility as a whole and the therapy sessions, which the staff has stated you're doing exceptionally well," Lazarist continued. "However, as soon as you get off the medication, stop taking it against doctor's orders as you have done time and time again, and you leave here, you will spiral back out of control if a plan is not put in place *before*hand. We can't go back to business as usual, and we're prepared to take action."

Dad's eyes sheened and he dropped his head.

"So… this is where we're at now…"

Dad huffed as he looked out the window, not making eye contact with either of them.

"Yes, this is where we're at. Something really bad is going to happen, Dad, and this time, you may not come back from it. You're lucky to even be alive right now. Had that infection gone on even a couple days longer, you would've been dead. It's dangerous on the streets. At the hospital, they gave you a physical. Your liver, despite you not being a big drinker, is in bad shape. You've had so many untreated infections, the doctor believes, that it has taken a toll on your body. These things happen and are exacerbated by you living on the streets."

The older man reached over with a trembling hand and took another sip of tea. When he faced them again, tears were streaming down his face. The sight broke Lazarist's heart. Dad wasn't a big crier; in fact, he wouldn't describe his father as emotional at all, even before the illness had taken him down.

"Dad, it's not your fault, okay? You didn't ask for this to happen to you, but it has," Eliza stated as she reached over and took Dad's hand. "However, using the resources available to ya *is* your responsibility."

"Eliza is right. You're in a great position right now. You have a family that loves you… not everyone can say that in these cases. All Eliza and I want is for you to be healthy and happy, in spite of your diagnosis and struggles."

"Do ya think I could, uh, get your mom back if I stuck to the program and kept on takin' my medication?"

"Dad," Lazarist began, trying to choose the right words, though he was so sick and fucking tired of the man wrapping his world around his mother, the same woman he'd practically destroyed. "Mom has moved on, okay? And even if she hadn't, even if you could some-how rekindle things with her, that's not how this works. You need to do this for *you*." He pointed at the man.

"You could have a happy life if you keep yourself healthy. Think of yourself as like, hell, I don't know…" Lazarist tossed up his hands. "A diabetic, I guess you could say. As long as you take your insulin, eat healthy and exercise, your life will not be drastically affected by the disease and you have your entire future ahead of you. But if you don't do what you're supposed to do, things could go downhill fast. At this point, it's life or death."

"Do either of you have a cigarette?" Dad asked as he flopped back in his seat, a look of irritation in his tone. His complexion had deepened, and his hand shook ever so slightly, but at least he wasn't hollering or cursing. That was a relief.

"I haven't smoked in years, Dad, and Eliza never did." The older man nodded in understanding. "So, I think—"

"Alright, Lazarist," the old man said, cutting him off. "So, I take it, it's safe to assume, based on what you're both sayin' to me, that you want me committed, right?

You want me to sign something?" Dad looked over at the packet.

"Well, yes. We want you to allow for—"

"I know where this is going, all right? I don't need to hear the lecture." The man's voice was slightly elevated. "You want me to have a babysitter basically, someone to make sure I don't go all looney tunes!" The man jetted out his tongue, crossed his eyes, and made a silly face like some deranged clown as he waved his hands about. "And if I get outta control, you want my permission ahead of time to toss my ass in a crazy bin so they can make me do what I'm supposed to. I get it. No need to try to muscle me around or play hardball. Fine. I'll do it."

Lazarist couldn't believe his ears. Though his father was obviously agitated, he was agreeing to such a thing. He had been prepared this time for reinforcement, but it appeared that was no longer needed.

"I want Eliza to be my power of attorney. Is that fine with you, 'Liza?"

"Uh." She shrugged. "Yeah… that's fine, Dad."

That was a surprise to them both, too. Lazarist had been the one doing most of the care due to Dad alienating himself from others and denying her paternity. How strange. Regardless, that news gave him a sense of relief.

Dad snatched the packet out of Lazarist's hands and ripped it open, dumping the papers all over the table beside him like he was handling a big bag of potato chips. A few minutes later, the guy had his reading glasses on and had scanned several of the documents. "I know that I've fucked up my life." He stared at the last page where his signature was required. "I know that I've fucked up your and Eliza's life, too. Ya don't have to tell me."

"You didn't fuck up our lives. You made them harder, *much* harder, but I never gave you that type of control over me. You don't have that sort of power."

Dad smirked at him, then looked back at the papers.

"Pompous son of uh bitch… always got somethin' smart to say," the old man mumbled, but Lazarist refused to allow the bastard to rile him up one last time for old time's sake. He simply chose to not respond to the curt response. "So, you're gettin' married, huh?" The guy snapped his fingers. "Somebody give me a fuckin' pen, please."

Eliza scrambled about in her purse, pulled one out, and handed it to him.

"Yes."

"When?"

"Two months from now. We've been planning it for a little while."

"What number marriage is this, Laz?" Dad scribbled his name on the bottom and dated it.

"Three."

"Three, huh? Three blind mice… three wise men… three, three, three…" The guy giggled, then flipped back to the first page and began to study the agreement packet all over again. "is she White?"

"Nope." Lazarist crossed his arms over his chest.

Here we go with this shit again. I was hoping the medicine would nip it in the bud.

"Didn't think so… Keep up with what you like, though; nothing wrong with that. You've always been consistent." Dad chuckled. "Nothin' wrong with that," he repeated. "I knew what was going on when your mother and I had that one Black girl watch you and 'Liza for a few months when I'd have to go to those business dinners a long time ago. We needed someone to watch you kids. Her name was Taylor, I believe."

Lazarist had forgotten all about Taylor. He couldn't help but smile. That girl must've been his very first crush…

"Taylor's mom was friends with Evelyn. The girl wanted to make a few extra bucks for college or some-thin' like that… her books, I think." The old man shrugged as he flipped to another page, looking it over now with a discerning eye even though he'd already signed it. "You followed the girl wherever she went… did whatever she said. All googly-eyed. It was hilarious. Your mother would tease you and Eliza liked her, too… said she played fun games."

Eliza laughed lightly. "Yeah, he's right!"

"I knew then that that was what you liked. Everyone has their preferences, I suppose. Gotta watch little boys, though." He waved his finger in their direction but kept his eye on the paperwork. "Little boys will tell you all about their future, if you pay close enough attention. See, Lazarist, you were pretty easy to read. You were a little hyper, a hothead, sensitive, and a know-it-all, too. But sometimes you could be really sweet." The old man smiled. "You always shared your toys with your little sister and you had a lot of friends. Everybody liked ya. You insisted on having two piggy banks in your room. One was to spend up and buy all those little cars you used to like to collect... ya had hundreds of 'em!"

"Hot Wheels."

"Yeah! Hot Wheels. The other piggy bank was for savings. I told you how important it was to save for a rainy day and how to make your money grow."

"You did. I will always remember that, and I'm grateful."

"And then you wanted your own bank account so at age six, that's what your mother and I did. We did the same for Eliza. You'd save up money for two or three months, and then we'd take it all down to the bank for you to deposit. You always found some hustle, too..."

He flipped another page. "Like sellin' some of the Hot Wheels you no longer wanted or that you had multiples of, or takin' some of your mother's brownies and sellin' them at lunchtime in school. You always found ways to make a little money, even as a little boy. You showed me who you were, Laz, when you were a little, fuckin' smart mouthed showoff, a survivor, a charismatic guy who loved Black and Hispanic broads... Jesus. I asked you about it one time when you were a teenager. You and I weren't on the best of terms then, and you basically told me to go fuck myself and refused to answer. I wasn't comin' to you in a bad way about it, though. I was just curious was all.

"Nothin' you've ever done or said has surprised me.

You both are made of damn good stock. I'm lucky, ya know? I'm fuckin' proud of both of you." The man shot them a pointed look, then shoved the papers in Eliza's lap and placed the pen gently atop the pile of documents. He turned towards Lazarist and leaned forward. "I love the hell out of you. You may not believe that, but I do. I always wanted what was best for you, Laz."

"Dad, please. Let's not do this, okay?" Lazarist's tolerance for the bullshit was extremely low. All he wanted was the papers signed and to be on his way, but Dad wouldn't allow it. He just kept right on talking.

"I knew you would do great things in life as long as you didn't get sidetracked, ya know? You used to get sidetracked a lot. You cared too much about what other people thought, too, and that used to upset me about ya. You pretended like you didn't care, but you did. It would really hurt ya when someone you liked and trusted did something to upset you. You had a problem with women, too. You fell in love at the drop of a fuckin' dime. It was insane! I knew it was going to be a prob- lem."

Lazarist lowered his head, prepared for his father to do what he always did—berate him. He reached for his coat to leave, but Dad leaned over and touched his arm.

"Dad, I'm leaving. We're not doing this, okay? I'm not going to listen to any more of this."

"Let me finish, all right? This is important."

Lazarist relaxed a bit, though it was a struggle.

"You got a lotta attention from women, and that made you feel good. I mean, let's face it. You're good lookin'. You know all the slick things to say to make people feel comfortable. You're book smart, arrogant, and that has pros and cons. Shit, I've been accused of bein' arrogant, too," The old man shrugged. "But Laz, the thing about you that's so amazing is that you know how to handle your business. Still, you always had to have a little somethin' goin' on the side that would mess up your focus... and more times than not, it was a woman. Everybody's got something that helps them forget the pain, right?"

Dad smiled sadly.

"The problem was me, though. If I had been consistent and got help as soon as I started havin' problems, I could have helped you navigate that better. Hormones kicked in, and you didn't have a fighting chance. What had been just an interest became a habit for you—relying on others to feel good about yourself. I could've stopped it before it became a problem. You were lookin' for distractions, Lazarist. Does that make sense or do ya just think I'm talkin' out my ass, tryna get under your skin? 'Cause I'm not, I promise you that."

The old man smirked and threw up his hands. After a couple of seconds, Lazarist nodded.

"No. You're right. I'm not in denial about that."

"Good. Because as the therapist explained it to me, and yeah, I've talked a lot about you two since I've been here, it boils down to the fact that you were lookin' for the relationship your mother and I had when you were a little boy, the one that went up in smoke. You kept tryna find love out here in the world that matches that, but you were going about it the wrong way. You wanted to be praised, doted on and complimented, because deep down—"

"I felt like shit." Lazarist gritted his teeth as his body heated with rage and sadness.

Dad threw him a curious look, then his expression turned to one of resignation.

"Yeah, you did. But you already had everything you needed right here, inside ya, son!" Dad tapped on his chest. "You were worthy, all right?! It was *I* who felt like shit! I was a piece of shit to you and your sister, because I… I wanted to save ya both, but I couldn't! I couldn't control myself anymore. I couldn't make money to take care of my family. My brain was doin' and saying things… stupid, crazy things! I couldn't even take care of my own wife and kids! How humiliating!"

Tears streamed fast down the old man's face.

"I saw so much potential in both of you and instead of takin' responsibility for my part in the way you were goin', I blamed you. Eliza, you've done pretty well despite everything. Laz, you still woulda been girl crazy whether I was in the picture or not… that was just your personality, but you woulda just liked it, ya know? You wouldn't have *needed* it, son. When you need something, it weakens ya, stops you from thinking clearly. Makes you do impulsive shit, and impulsive shit always has consequences. Then you cut off your feelings all together. You went from being sensitive and easily offended, to not givin' a flyin' shit, or at least you were better at pretending that you didn't. It scared me, I think it scared a lot of people. You became intimidating and malicious. At times I was afraid of my own son! I didn't want ya to know, but I was. I didn't want the good parts of you to die… it wasn't all bad that you cared so much, but then… you changed. You became cold. You no longer loved women, ya just used 'em. You didn't wanna get hurt again… I get it. Worst of all, I'm to blame for all of it. I'm sorry… I'm real fuckin' sorry."

Dad grabbed his mug, took a final swallow, then suddenly got to his feet. He leaned over and kissed Eliza on the top of the head while she sat there and cried her damn eyes out.

"Not that I deserve it, Laz, but I'd like to come to your wedding. Think about inviting me."

And with that, he headed down the hall, leaving his two children alone…

LEO

♌

CHAPTER TWENTY-THREE

A Match Made in Heaven

...Two months later

S KY HELD THE dark red, leather-bound photo album with shaky hands. Dressed in her wedding gown, her makeup professionally done, and her hair completely slayed by Scarlet, she stood in her father's small apartment—just the two of them, with only the sound of his old clock ticking and muted noise from the street below.

Papers lay scattered about in his cramped space, and the scent of cigarette smoke and Joop cologne hung in the air. These were the smells she associated with her father—ones of comfort.

"Your mother and I got married in Central Park. It was free to do so way back then."

She listened to her father but her thoughts drifted here and there, her wedding jittery nerves distracting her from following any line of thought.

The limousine was downstairs, waiting to take her to meet her soon-to-be new husband at the Brooklyn

Winery, which boasted of a bucolic feel, a lush garden, and glass ceiling that allowed plentiful natural light. How she wanted to step foot inside that beautiful venue and officially become Mrs. Zander.

"Go on, open it," Dad stated as he crushed his cigarette in the small, tin ashtray.

After a deep breath, she did as he requested and uncovered a worn photo of her mother, a beautiful woman with large, dark brown, doe eyes, mouth agape, and a reddish brown curly afro, holding a record.

Sky smiled at the photo. It warmed her heart and filled in one of thousands of missing pieces. Mama looked surprised in the photo, as if she'd be taken off guard. She'd loved music. Dad said she'd wanted that album and he'd surprised her and had bought it for her on her birthday. Funny, her birth date happened to be the day before Lazarist's...

Sky flipped to the next page and saw another photo of her mother. This time, the woman was in mid-laugh when the photo was taken, and she was sitting on the steps of a brownstone, one leg up, donning a pair of knee-high socks and super short light pink shorts. Her hair was slicked back in a ponytail.

"I've never seen this picture of Mom before, either," she stated quietly. "Why am I just now seeing these, Dad? These are incredible."

"I didn't have them until recently. I just got that album about, oh, a few weeks ago."

"Really? Who gave it to you?"

"Your grandmother called me and told me she'd found it in the storage area of her apartment. She seldom went through any of that old stuff. It was stored amongst some of our wedding things from way back then… I didn't go get it right away. But then," he said with a shrug, "I figured you'd want to have it. First though, I needed to finish grieving."

Dad's eyes watered. He snatched his glasses off and placed them on the table, amongst the envelopes and old magazines. "I never completely got over Veronica, Sky… It was a hard thing, you know?"

She nodded. With a sniff, she turned to another page. One after the other, she looked into the eyes of a woman that she favored so much. She'd seen several photos of her mother, but none like these…

These featured a happy young woman, full of life and exuberance.

"Why doesn't Mama's family ever come around, Dad?"

"Same answer as I've given you for years, Sky." He

jammed his hands into his suit jacket pockets and shook his head, a blank stare in his eyes. His expression broke her heart. "They'd written her off a long time ago. Luckily, she left many things with my mother instead of her own or I wouldn't have this to give you, either. Turn to the last page."

She did and covered her mouth with a shaky hand. There Mama and Dad stood on their wedding day at the reception, looking at each other, so in love...

Mama was dressed in her gorgeous white gown and veil as she danced with Dad. She'd seen only one wedding photo of them together, inside of a box along with mama's old wedding dress, all folded up and shoved under Dad's bed. Sky couldn't get over how they were looking at one another. Their love was almost tangible— two young people, head over heels for one another.

"I want you to know that I asked your mother to marry me twice, before you were conceived. We didn't get married because she was pregnant, Sky, contrary to anything you may have heard or believed. We got married because we were in love." Dad tapped his fingers nervously on the table. "She told me no the first two times I proposed. She did so because neither of us had a decent job at the time. I worked, but my income was inconsistent. I took what I could, you know? Your mother worked a couple temp jobs but they didn't pay much.

"We were just two very young people in love… living our lives. When I found out she was pregnant, I didn't come home that day until I found work. I begged a man inside a restaurant to let me wash the dishes and sweep the floors… told him I had a baby on the way. I then used that money to enroll in school and get an associate's degree.

"I went into social work and took some extra business courses, too… as you know, of course."

Sky looked up and cast her eyes towards the wall, where Dad's old, yellowed degree hung, still in the cheap plastic frame. He'd made everyone in his family so proud… and she was proud of him, too.

"Then, soon after you were born, I am not really sure what happened… but your mother was acting different. Could've been postpartum depression, I don't know, but her family wasn't really a support system. She relied on me and my family for everything. She started experimenting here and there, and then, the heroin abuse emerged… and the dope. It got so bad… It got so bad, Sky, I couldn't take it anymore.

"She was taking the little bit of money we had— money for your food, diapers, milk, and rent. I was afraid she was going to do something to you. She'd become neglectful… I'd be at work all day, come home, and you would be inside the apartment crying, alone. You'd have on a soiled diaper, you were hungry… your mother nowhere to be found. You deserved better.

"You were so young, I doubt you remember, but that was it. I knew she had to go. Off and on for the next couple of years after that, she'd get clean for a minute, then be right back into it. And then one day, she just stopped comin' around. I called the hospitals, her sister, her mother, everyone. No one had seen her. Days went on, and then I called the police. Your mother disappeared so often, so at first I wasn't alarmed. But she'd never been gone that long. Something was wrong, I could feel it. To the police, she was just another Black junkie off on some binge. They didn't care to find her. After some years had passed, I figured she was dead."

He nodded, as if finally accepting it for himself. "There'd been many bodies found around that time… Some were prostitutes, some junkies, mostly both. I'm not sure what happened to your mother, Sky, but I imagine she either got a hold of something that took her out, or she trusted the wrong person.

"Either way, I've never seen her again. I've never seen her again. I've… never… seen her again."

He lowered his head and started to sob uncontrollably. Sky stepped behind her father and wrapped her arms around him. She rested her forehead on his back and held him close, her hands clasped around his waist.

"Today is a special, wonderful day! My daughter's

getting married!" He broke free from her, a big, forced smile on his face. "I never want to ruin your day! My intentions, my dear, were to show you more wedding pictures of Victoria and me, happy times... and yet, here we are." He lowered his head, as if ashamed... as if he'd done her some grave disservice. "I apologize for ruining everything. I had no idea I'd react like this."

"Dad, no." She reached for his wrist and pulled him towards her. "This is the most beautiful wedding gift you could have ever given me! A piece of my mother... more of the truth. I've processed this, okay? Though I was so young when this all happened, anything I hear about her, good or bad, gives me peace!"

He wrapped his arms around her and squeezed, then kissed her cheek.

"Sometimes when I see you, Sky, it's like looking at a ghost... like right now... you look so much like her! You know, I believe she'd be very proud of you. Your mother liked to dance, too. She was a natural entertainer."

Sky laughed lightly. "I know, you told me."

"I mean, really dance. She could cut a rug... and though we've moved on," he said, his smile fading, "the heart wants what the heart wants. I've been seeing Brenda, as you know, for over ten years. She's my girlfriend and I love her very much... but, I told her, as I did my girlfriends before her, that I would never get married again. Your mother had that spot... and I guess, I'm not quite strong enough to ever give it away. That's her seat in my heart. Despite the drugs and the pain she caused us, this will never change the fact that she was my first love. She gave me my first and only child, she was my first everything. And I knew, had she not fallen prey to addiction, she would have been a good mother to you, Sky... a great mother."

Sky closed the photo album and placed it on the table.

"So, though I hated your mother at times and blamed myself for so many things that had gone wrong in our lives, she was, and *always* will be, my first love. She was my beautiful bride..." From a box, he pulled out a small pair of earrings and handed them to her. "These belonged to your mother. To ensure she didn't pawn them for drugs, I hid them from her. They were a gift I'd given her once I got my second check at that restaurant." He gave a sad chuckle. "She'd been eyeing them, wanted them."

"Oh my God..." Sky looked down at her hand, admiring the small diamond studs. She immediately removed her own earrings, and swapped them with the pair. "They're beautiful! Thank you, Dad!" She leapt into his arms and hugged him tight.

"Come on now, child. Your chariot awaits downstairs."

He grabbed his umbrella, took her hand, and turned off the lights. Together, they walked out of the apartment, hand in hand...

LEO

EIGHT GROOMSMEN STOOD to Lazarist's right, all dressed in tailored slate gray suits, white shirts, and plum ties. All of Sky's friends were on the other side, all their dresses in different styles but in the exact same shade of reddish-purple.

The Brooklyn Winery was a popular wedding venue, but it paled in comparison to the bride that graced the scene. Lazarist tried to stand a bit straighter, but his knees kept turning to damn jelly.

If you ever see a Queen walk down the aisle to meet her King, then you'll understand how I felt when I watched a vision of beauty, my soon-to-be wife, dressed in a stunning white dress, approach me with love in her eyes in a garden in Brooklyn...

"I've done this two other damn times. You'd think I'd be used to it by now. I'm a seasoned pro. I run these groomzilla streets!" he whispered, joking and teasing with Tobias who stood right next to him. The two laughed lightly as his nerves skyrocketed.

"She's beautiful..." Tobias whispered, resting his hand on his shoulder.

Sky practically floated down the aisle, holding a bouquet of mauve and sapphire flowers, her hand securely wrapped around her father's arm. Kane Brown crooned 'Heaven' as she drew closer. Everyone was on their feet looking at the queen of his heart gliding towards him.

When she finally arrived, the minister looked at her father and asked who was giving her away. With tears in his eyes, Sky's father shook Lazarist's hands.

"I do... I give my daughter away to this man, Lazarist Zander." His father-in-law directed a grave expression his way. "I trust you with my pride and joy. She means *every*thing to me."

Lazarist leaned in close to the man and drew him in a firm hug.

"I promise to treat your daughter like the queen that she is. You have my word."

The older man nodded, sniffed, and took his seat in the front row. At that moment, he took notice of his mother sitting next to Eliza, and directly behind them was his father. The man looked rather somber, dressed to kill in his tuxedo. He raised his hand and gave a little wave as they made eye contact. Lazarist nodded, acknowledging his presence and feeling happy to see him, then turned back towards his fiancée. Lifting her veil, he exposed her to their friends and family. He blinked several times, fighting the tears.

"You're beautiful." His voice cracked like a teenage boy's.

"Thank you," she mouthed with a sweet smile.

He wanted to drag her away, kiss her all over her body, ravish her, and do it all over again. He wished he could push a fast-forward button and have them already married and celebrating their two-week honeymoon in the Maldives. The minister shook him out of his deliberations as he began to walk them through their vows. They'd taken the traditional route, but he had his own words to share, too. Looking out towards the audience for a spell, he cleared his throat, his gaze back on Sky.

"I had, uh, originally written these things down and was going to stand here and recite them... but that didn't seem right. I spent a lot of time writing it all down, too. What I wanted to say to ya... to express how I feel... it's difficult to say. Most people in here know that we met at Fallen Angel, my club. You were there with your friends havin' a good time. I was doing my typical rounds, checking in on my customers, but I'd already seen you a bit earlier that evening on the camera. I have to admit, when I saw ya I thought, 'My God... she's beautiful.'"

Sky smiled at his words. He reached for her hands and held them.

"I said to myself, I gotta meet her. I have to introduce myself and say, 'hello.' What started as my typical hunt for a good time soon grew into me falling in love with one of the kindest and wisest women I've ever known. Your beauty is unmistakable, you're a go-getter and you don't want any handouts... just encouragement and devotion.

"When I realized that, uh... I was in love with ya, I was scared to death. It wasn't in the cards, it wasn't what I thought I wanted. But... it was exactly what I need-ed... To finally not be afraid to feel anymore. To not be terrified of how big my heart was and what that entailed. My father told me not too long ago that I had closed myself off, became cold because I'd been hurt. He was right. It was on purpose. It was how I was surviving. I was thinkin' that being the king of this concrete jungle meant I had to not give a damn about anyone... at least make a good show of it, but that's not true.

"Lions have heart... we're courageous. To be afraid to fall in love again was cowardly, and unless you're from the Wizard of Oz, no one likes a cowardly lion." There were pockets of light laughter at his words. "I was scared of what a love like this would do to me... being exposed, vulnerable, but you're the best thing that's ever happened to me, Sky. I thought I had it all before I met you... but I had no idea, absolutely no clue.

"This time, it's built to last. We respect one another, want what's best for each other. I have maturity, life lessons, and understanding on my side, and a lover and best friend like I've never known.

"I needed you *more* than you'll ever realize, Sky. I need you like all living things need air. I need you like the birds need wings. I need you like a castle needs a king and a queen... and you're mine. You rule my heart. It's all yours."

He placed his hand across his heart; the damn thing was beating so fast, it seemed unnatural.

"You consume my thoughts and every time I see your face, I smile. Every time I hear your name, I can't stop grinning. You danced into my life and I hooked you with my cane, bringing you close so that you couldn't get away." She smiled from ear to ear, her eyes gleaming. "Because I can't imagine life without you, baby, it's really as simple as that. Thank you for giving me the best shiny gift of all, the prettiest diamond in the world... that being *you*..."

He quieted and sniffed away tears, though he heard many people in the audience crying, filled with emotion. The minister went on to complete the vows then asked for the wedding bands to be exchanged. Sky slid a thick, platinum and diamond wedding band onto his finger. He never believed he'd wear such jewelry again, but there he was, and this time, it felt so right, so perfect.

"I now pronounce you husband and wife. You may kiss your bride."

He took her in his arms, holding her so close to claim her lips in a kiss. Applause erupted from the audience. The heat of her mouth sent waves through his body and dirty thoughts of ripping her clothing off later that night took over his brain like a hostage situation. Minutes later they were shaking hands and hugging their friends and family, thanking them for coming out to join them on their special day. Sky floated away for a spell and took many photos with her friends. The professional photographer had them pose in all sorts of ways. He watched the little group having fun until someone walked up to him and tapped him on the shoulder. When he saw who it was, he yelled in excitement.

"Giovanni!!! Oh my God, I didn't think you'd be able to make it! Where is Vanessa?" He looked about into the crowd before everyone dispersed to begin the reception festivities.

"She's here! She went to the restroom and will back

in a bit. Of course I'm here, man! I wouldn't miss your wedding for the world, Laz!"

"Awww man, this is great! I know you've been so busy and all with the work-out show and everything. That's great. So proud of ya, Gio."

"Yeah, yeah, things are goin' good. The wife's company is doing well, too. The kids are good. Congratulations, Laz. I'm so glad you're trying again, ya know? Bein' in love is a beautiful thing."

"Thank you… we gotta get Vanessa and Sky together, you know? I think they'd get along real well."

"Oh, for sure. Sorry about missin' your birthday party. I was out of town."

"No problem! We've all got lives."

"Yeah, but maybe we can go on a double date soon. I've only known ya for five years, but you feel like a brother to me. It's been good between us, ya know? I love ya, man. And your wife… wow! What a knockout!"

They both chuckled at that. Lazarist loved it when someone admired Sky's beauty and his great taste.

"You telling me that I'm like a brother… well damn, man. That means a lot comin' from you, Gio. You're good people." Just then, he saw another familiar face coming his way. "Dom!"

He grabbed the guy and gave him a big hug. He'd met Dom through Giovanni; the two were practically inseparable. Giovanni had been his personal trainer and Dom had some great marketing ideas for the Fallen Angel. The man was rough around the edges but very talented—he had a knack for such things and was a natural when it came to promotion and sales. "I told Gio to invite you but I didn't think you'd come! Last I checked, you were still in Jersey, right?"

"I'm back in New York City, man!" Dom threw up his hands. The tall, slender guy was smoother than butter rolling down a playground slide in the summertime. "Yeah, I'm not missin' any wedding reception, okay? 'Specially one from a high roller like you where I know the best liquor will be flowin' and the hos will be hoin'!"

Lazarist hated that he couldn't control himself, but he and Giovanni burst out laughing at the man's words. Dominic was a real card. Soon, Sky came back over and wrapped her arm possessively around his. As he was introducing her to the pair of guys, her friend Scarlet came over, too.

"I'm ready to get fucked up." She jetted her finger in his face. "Your wife has been a real pain in the ass today, Lazarist."

He cracked up, only to have Sky give him a perturbed expression, then elbow him in the side.

"Uh oh, lover's quarrel. I got my own damn problems." Giovanni cackled. "I'm gettin' outta here to go find Vanessa. I'll see ya on the dance floor."

The buff man, who was practically bursting out of his suit jacket, turned and walked off. Apparently still angry, Sky bopped him on the shoulder.

"What?!" He smiled. "I didn't say it. Scarlet did!"

"I sure as hell did. I said it and I meant it. Who gon-na check me? Record me. Take a picture, too. Make a note of it, jot it down like they're the winning numbers to the lotto! I don't give uh fuck! Don't get mad, Sky; you know you have been a total pain in the ass."

The woman arched an eyebrow. "Taking all of your anxieties on innocent bystanders today 'nd shit. Get on my goddamn nerves... I shoulda burned you with the hot comb when I was taking care of those edges and that kitchen on this frontal, getting it blended to perfection just so you can sweat it all out tonight when Lazarist bends you over like the Brooklyn Bridge fallin' down and makes you scream 'Daddy!' in five different languages. Ain't nobody got time for this shit! Anyway..." She thrust her arm out, her wrist limp. "Can someone *please* point me in the direction of the damn bar and a place that passes out Vicodin like candy? Sky hopped on my last nerve and rode that mothafucka into the ground. I'm ready to drink my ass off, dance until my feet catch on fire, stuff my face and put that shit on repeat."

"Damn! You're funny... sassy... pretty as fuck, too... I like that," Dom spoke up as he buttoned his blazer, holding his chin high. He then winked at the woman.

Scarlet smirked at the man, looking him up and down as she placed her hand on her hip.

"You like that, huh? Who the hell are you, may I ask?"

"My name is Sebastiano, but my friends and family call me by my middle name, Dominic."

"Well, Sebastiano, 'cause I'm not your friend or your family, where do you work? Do you have a good job because I'm tryna secure a motherfuckin' bag. You're cute and all but handsome don't pay the damn bills and we both know you're just tryna fuck. Meanwhile, I'm looking for something a bit more serious. I wanna settle down but also tryna get paid. I got my own shit but I want some of somebody else's too… that's just the way the damn cookie crumbles so, uh, let's just get down to the nitty gritty. Are you broke or what?"

"Scarlet!" Sky exclaimed. Everyone burst out laughing, including Dom—with the exception of Sky, who stood there looking mortified at her friend's behavior.

"Bridal Black Barbie bitch, please. I love ya, I'm happy as hell for you, but I am too old to play silly ass games and mince words. I am ready to get up outta these shoes, too!"

Scarlet rolled her eyes, ripped her heels off, and hung the straps over her finger and she sauntered off, leaving them all in the dust. The tall man that had been introduced as Dom ran his fingers through his hair and grinned like a sneaky son of a bitch, looking all turned on and horny.

"So, uh, Mrs. Zander, congratulations. Beautiful wedding." The sly looking bastard ran his hands together like a fly about to land on a pile of fresh shit. "I'll need you as backup tonight in case your friend Scarlet there doesn't want to give me her number. I'd like to get to know her better… by any means necessary."

"Uh, first of all, thank you for the congrats. That's nice of you, Dom, but I don't know you so unfortunately, I'm not giving you Scarlet's number. That would be an invasion of my friend's privacy. If she wants to give it to you though, I'm sure she will."

Sky leaned in and landed a kiss on Lazarist's face before laying her head against his shoulder.

"Oh, she will, I guarantee you that, but I *always* like to have a Plan B just in case."

With that, he turned on his heels and walked off, no doubt in hot pursuit. Sky and Lazarist looked at one another and burst out laughing.

"We have some *insane* friends, oh my God!" She giggled, then rose up on tiptoes for another kiss.

"We do... but hey, they make the world go 'round."

He leaned down to press his lips to hers, happy out of his mind, and began to sway with her as he closed his eyes, immersing himself into his new beautiful reality...

She's mine now... we've done it... it's magic. I'm going to make this work. No such thing as divorce with this woman. I'm all in, mind, body, and soul.

"You make me wanna be a better man." He cupped her face with both hands as a tear streamed down his face. "I'll never take you for granted. I'm going to love you like there's a hundred men tryna take my place... because if they knew what I had, there would be... and then a thousand more would follow..."

LEO

♌

CHAPTER TWENTY-FOUR

Castle in the Sky

One year later...

"**S**O THAT NEEDS to be completed by this time next week at the latest, okay? I mean, I'm not tryna be an ass, but we've got deadlines for uh reason, ya know?"

Lazarist stood from his office chair at Fallen Angel and grabbed his car keys.

"That's fine. I may have it finished sooner, Lazarist."

"Sounds like a plan, Howie. I'll chat with you later. Take it easy... but not too fuckin' easy."

Lazarist disconnected the phone and headed out the door in a huff, swinging his cane to and fro. He had a bunch of shit to do, but he always seemed to work best under pressure. He looked down at his Rolex, noting the time, then made a pitstop into the kitchen.

Let me take a look in here before I head out. It's about to get mad busy...

"Everything okay in here? The lunch crowd will be rolling out in a bit." He looked at his watch again then tapped his cane against the floor.

"Everything's great, boss!" Mateo called out, a big smile on his face.

"Hey, I was gonna head over to the pizzeria, but if it's good enough, I can just get something from here to go. Mateo, what are the specials today?"

The young man approached him sporting his white waiter jacket, looking dapper as hell.

"Today's soups are caramelized French Onion and New England Clam chowder. The lunch entrée specials are tuna tartare with mango and avocado sauce, Caesar salad with blackened chicken breast, bone-in aged dried NY strip with baked potato, and lobster and crab burger with lemon tartar sauce."

Lazarist smiled and weighed his choices.

"Get me one order of the Caesar salad with blackened chicken breast and a NY strip, rare, please. I want a side salad, too. I'm going to make some quick calls then pick it up. Chop, chop, baby."

"Got it! I'll tell chef right now!" Mateo disappeared from view, calling out the order. Lazarist made his way over to an empty booth and slid down on the seat. The kitchen staff were playing some easy listening tunes. The notes of 'Hey Nineteen' by Steely Dan filled the space with a welcome vibe. He could hear it over their chatter, the sear of the grill, and the pans knocking about.

It was always so quiet in the club during weekdays. He rather enjoyed these special moments of reprieve.

Sliding his phone out, he made a few business calls, checking up on various deliveries and ensuring that security would arrive on time come Saturday evening. The last thing he needed was a place full of drunk angry men brawling in the middle of the dancefloor.

"Boss! Food is up!" the head chef called out.

Before he could get to his feet, Mateo had it bagged up nice and neat.

"Got forks, napkins and shit?"

"Yes, it's all in there."

Lazarist accepted the boxes wrapped in black plastic bags, thanked the guy, and made his way to his car. The air was crisp, the sun bright. He stood there for a spell, inhaling the smoggy air he'd grown to love, but the strong, mouthwatering aroma of the food caused his stomach to growl in anticipation. He got in the car and drove over to Manhattan, enjoying a few moments of people-watching. People walked about, some smiling, many with their heads down, looking at their phone screens.

Look up motherfuckers, the world is passin' you by!

He leaned forward and turned on the radio. Deep Blue Something's 'Breakfast at Tiffany's' was on. He bobbed his head to the beat and thumped his hand against the steering wheel. Lazarist hadn't heard this song in a while, and he'd loved it for many years. It made him happy inside, colored his mood in shades of Sky. Moments later, he pulled up to a meter, slid some money in, and made a mad dash into the tall building on 36th Avenue.

"Now twist those waists! Again!" He opened the door and took note of his wife, turning her hips to and fro as she shimmied from right to left like some belly dancer. Wearing skin tight blue leggings and a white top that hugged her ample breasts, she turned him on. An erection threatened to come and invade the space...

What the fuck do you have on? Looks niiiice! I might have to bend her fuckin' ass over and drill her pussy for oil as soon as the damn room clears...

A few ladies dressed in black leotards danced behind her, keeping up well, if he said so himself. He smiled as Sky kept on with her flirty movements, the sounds of Nikki Minaj's 'Ganja Burns' playing through the speakers in high volume.

He stood there grinning with the plastic bags in his hands, leaning against the door, ankles crossed.

This sexy mothafucker is mine... all mine! That's my wife! Look at all that! Delicious...

His eyes narrowed on her, possessive as he was...

She moved like an ocean, her arms like waves, her gorgeous long legs following suit and her long, black hair swinging in all directions. She caught his image in the mirrored reflection; their gazes hooked and she winked. He swayed to the music, being silly and imitating her, and it was obvious she was fighting a laugh. Minutes later, she finally wrapped up the session.

"All right, ladies! You did great!"

Breathing heavy, the woman grabbed a black towel and patted the sweat off the side of her face. The women talked amongst themselves, grabbing their bags, letting out a few bursts of laughter here and there. He leisurely moved away from the door and made way for them to pass.

"Heeeey, baby…" she said real easy like, switching her hips and dancing toward him like a dream come true. He took her in his arms, forcing the bags of food to sway against her ass as he crushed her lips in a kiss. "What are you doing here?" She pulled away and looked him up and down. "Not that I'm complaining. Always nice to see you, baby."

She swiped away her lipstick from his mouth with the pad of her thumb. As she turned and walked away, he stalked her… his eyes on her ass.

"I thought we could have lunch together before we both have to get back to work."

Sitting down cross-legged on the floor, he removed the food and two bottles of ice cold water from the bag. She sat next to him, blessed him with a smile and another kiss, then reached for the container with the salad.

"Did you talk to your father today?" she asked as she poked her fork into the Romaine lettuce.

He opened his bottle of water, took a swallow, and nodded.

"Yeah… he's in his new apartment now. He still sounds really good. I asked him if he was stressed out or anything and he said not really. He was just happy to be out of the hospital. He is just scheduled to go to therapy two times a week. He also has a gym membership now, so that'll help."

"That's great. I'm glad that he transitioned okay! Does he, uh… does he know about your mother being engaged?" Her eyes grew large with concern. That was the white elephant in the room as of late.

"Yeah, Eliza broke the news to him and he seemed okay. He said he was surprised it took so long, actually." He reached for a packet of black pepper and tore it open. "Sooo… how are *you* doing today, huh? Any more sickness? I was careful to not get you anything that would make you any more nauseous… or at least, I hope."

He kissed her on her cheek then sprinkled the pepper on his potato.

"You did well! You know I love Caesar salad. Actually, I feel pretty good today! It's amazing that morning sickness doesn't just hit in the morning. Those damn baby books lied!" she joked, causing him to chuckle. "Can you believe it?" She took a small bite of her salad, chewed daintily, then swallowed. "We're going to be parents, Lazarist… What the hell?! I am still in shock that I'm pregnant!"

She giggled, her elation in no way greater than his own.

"Yeah… we were both shocked. But what a beautiful surprise, ya know? My mother and Eliza are so excited."

"So is my dad! I don't care if we have a boy or a girl, either. I just want a healthy child…"

They were quiet for a spell, preparing their food to their liking and eating it a bit at a time. His heart thumped as he looked down at her stomach, knowing life was growing inside of her... a life they'd created out of adoration and pure love for one another.

"I love you so much, Laz." She took his hand and squeezed it, her eyes watering. A lone tear fell down her cheek.

"Here we go with those pregnancy hormones! Turn off the waterworks, lady!"

He chuckled as he leaned over and kissed her nose, then gently wiped the tear away. Looking into her eyes, he tried his damnedest to keep it together. He placed his hand on her stomach, and then... it was too late. His eyes glazed over, but he blinked the emotion away before he showed evidence of his exploding heart.

She's the Beauty and I'm the Beast...

"I love you too, baby... you're the absolute best! If I created my perfect lady I couldn't have even imagined you the way you are... you're just that damn good. You're my queen, ya know that?"

"And you're my king." She smiled proudly.

"Yeah, that's right. I *am* the king. And you've humbled me, made me who I am today. We've built our castle in the sky, and there is nowhere else I'd rather be..."

~ THE END ~

LEO
♌

LEO
the lion

proud confident loyal
ambitious big-hearted

Leo – Mr. Boss

Did you enjoy this story? Then please leave a review! It's one of the coolest and most helpful things you can do.

Thank you so much!

Please join Tiana Laveen's newsletter to get the latest and greatest updates, contest details, and giveaways!

You can join her newsletter at:
www.tianalaveen.com/contact.html#newsletter

www.tianalaveen.com

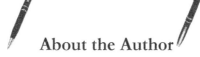

About the Author

Tiana Laveen is a USA Today Best Selling author. She was born in Cincinnati, Ohio though her soul resides in

New York.

Tiana Laveen is a uniquely creative and innovative author whose fiction novels are geared towards those who not only want to temporarily escape from the daily routines of life, but also become pleasantly caught up in the well-developed journeys of her unique characters. As the author of over 39 novels, Tiana creates a painting with words as she guides her reader into the lives of each and every main character. Her dedication to detail and staying true to her characters is evident in each novel that she writes.

Tiana Laveen lives inside her mind, but her heart is occupied with her family and twisted imagination. She enjoys a fulfilling and enriching life that includes writing books, public speaking, drawing, painting, listening to music, cooking, and spending time with loved ones.

If you wish to communicate with Tiana Laveen, please follow her on Instagram, Facebook and Pinterest.

www.tianalaveen.com

Made in United States
North Haven, CT
27 July 2024

55505320R00225